Matched

Matched

A NAVY SEALS OF LITTLE CREEK ROMANCE

PARIS WYNTERS

TULE
PUBLISHING

ACKNOWLEDGMENTS

First and foremost, thank you to my Heavenly Father for blessing me beyond all measure.

Thank you to my family for your support and encouragement. For picking up the slack and adjusting your lives so that I could get this manuscript done. Thank you for the laughs we shared about how I was writing a romance book, yet how you pushed me to finish it.

Thank you my amazing agent, Tricia Skinner, for believing in me. Thank you to Jane Porter and Meghan Farrell for believing in this book. Thank you to Sinclair Sawhney for pushing me with the edits and guidance to make this story the best it could possibly be.

A huge, HUGE, thank you to Liz Hess at Pearl Edits. I don't think I would have ever gotten the first draft of this book to where it needed to be without you. And thank you for all the lessons on blocking and for making me sketch out rooms. It was destined for me to find you.

Thank you to all my amazing CPs, my readers, and author friends who make me strive to become a better and more daring writer. And thank you to Raul, aka @latinlector on IG, for doing a beta read. I truly appreciate your help.

And lastly, THANK YOU with all my heart to those men and women, their families and friends, who voluntarily sacrifice their lives, well-being, and time to defend this great country we live in. Your sacrifices and memories will never be forgotten.

CHAPTER ONE

Tony

THE SUN IS out, the birds are singing, and I've had not just one bowl of cereal this morning, but two. It's a perfect day for a good, old-fashioned fist up the ass. Luckily, my commanding officer and his permanent scowl seem more than willing to accommodate me on that front.

I take a deep breath and grin as heat rains down my neck and back like the breath of hell. Thankfully, a breeze rolls in through the cracked window carrying the scent of summer rain just as new recruits jog past. Their voices ring out, rising in a familiar chant that seems to dip in unison with their every footfall.

"Is it crack?" Captain George Redding snaps. "Is that what you smoke? You smoke crack? Because it's the only thing that makes sense. There's no way in hell one of my men would be this idiotic."

The muscles in my back spasm from overuse and there's a hard ball of pressure against the arch of my foot. The chair stationed before Redding's desk calls my name, but I ignore it. He's already pissed, and he'd probably keel over if I sit without permission while he's busy tearing me a third asshole.

Unfortunately, my team leader and good friend, Jim Stephens, beat him to the construction of the second one as soon as he found out what I'd done. Even my best friend and teammate, Lucas Craiger, gave me a hard time. The only one who isn't currently riding my ass about the exciting new change to my relationship status is my other teammate, Bear, since he's off with his wife picking up their eldest daughter, Hayden, from college. After she went to Italy for a study-abroad program last summer, Bear wasn't taking any chances of his daughter finding another reason to spend the summer away from home.

"Anthony!"

Shit.

He's calling me by my first name. If the number of ass whoopings I received from my *abuela* after she called out my full first name when I was a kid was anything to go by, that means I'm currently at DEFCON 1. Time to lay on the charm.

I straighten to my full height and stare straight ahead. If standing at attention were an Olympic sport, they'd owe me a fucking gold medal. "No, sir! I'm not on crack, sir."

With a groan that seems to embody every one of his fifty-two years, my commanding officer lowers himself into his seat and massages his temples. "What's going on with you, Martinez? You've been back for eight hours and already I want to strangle you." Redding shakes his head, his lips pressing into a thin line, his expression full of disapproval. "Do you have any idea the position you've put me in?"

My throat constricts. Signing up for the Issued Partner Program wasn't some drunken mistake. We'd been outside the wire and got ambushed. Pinned down for hours. It'd been one of the worst firefights I'd been in. When we got back to the Forward Operating Base, I'd been exhausted and . . . overwhelmed. Then I'd seen my teammates talking to their families and it was as if a horse kicked me directly in the chest because I didn't have anyone to call.

I swallow past the knot in my throat, ghosts of the emotions from that day clawing their way into my conscience. Not exactly sure how I'd arrived at the conclusion later that night that allowing the military to issue me a wife would solve my problems by alleviating my loneliness while giving me a leg up on Officer Candidate School, but I had, and here I am now. No way am I explaining what really happened. If there's one trait most likely to kill my chances of getting accepted to OCS, it's my impulsivity. "To be honest, sir, when I signed up for the Issued Partner Program, you weren't exactly the first thought on my mind."

Redding's face flushes red and his gaze darkens. "Well, maybe I should have been."

The twinge of guilt is unexpected and unwelcome. It isn't as if I don't understand Redding's position. The program is still new. Still being tested. Which means anyone who signs up must have also have a recommendation from their CO. The problem is that while I technically meet all the qualifications, I'm no one's Golden Boy, least of all George Redding's. That honor is reserved exclusively for Jim, which means I have to work twice as hard for the same amount of praise. For me, there's no room for mistakes. But that didn't seem to stop me from screwing this up.

Redding's fingers lace together. He takes a deep breath and the tension in his shoulders eases. "This isn't something you'll be able to bullshit your way through, Martinez. If I find out you're screwing around—no, if I even hear a single whisper that you're not busting your ass to make this marriage work before the entire three hundred and sixty-five days are up—I'll make sure you aren't accepted into OCS. Hell, I may even discharge your ass."

A muscle in my jaw ticks. Three hundred and sixty-five days, holy hell. When he lays the minimum timeline out like that, it sounds like an eternity. Still, I'd gotten myself into this. Now I had to suck it up. One year before I can request an annulment. I could do this. I had to because the alternative is unacceptable. I stand a little straighter. "Sir, I take the program and my inclusion in it *very* seriously."

I love the military, but I didn't enlist because of an overwhelming sense of patriotism, like Jim, a need to protect, like Bear, or for a sense of direction, like Craiger. I signed up because I was running away. But that doesn't negate the fact that I'm a goddamn warrior and would make one hell of an officer—even if I'm the only one who sees it right now. I'm resilient as hell, and quitting isn't a part of my vocabulary. I'm a leader. Always have been. Shit, ever since *Mamá* died,

I'd had to be.

Shaking my head, I force away the past and bring my focus back to the here and now. This isn't the time or place. My job is on the line. Especially since I have to convince Redding I'm not some fuckup deserving of a dishonorable discharge.

He still looks doubtful and I scramble for something else to say, anything to convince him that I'm sincere. Scanning the room, my eyes land on a picture of Redding's grandson on a bookcase near the window and I puff my chest out. "Scout's honor."

Redding studies me for an interminable amount of time before reaching into his desk and pulling out a manila envelope. To be the key to my future, it doesn't look like much. Plain. Not very thick. Boring.

"For your sake, Martinez, I hope you make a better husband than you did a Scout."

Since I've never been a Boy Scout, that should be a piece of cake. I accept the envelope and escape while I still can. The paper wrinkles in my fist as I stride out the door, and I take a deep breath and relax my hand before I step outside.

The fresh air is a welcome respite from the stale atmosphere of Redding's office. Hell, I can practically smell the Ugg boots and vanilla chai latte. The scent of America. The scent of *true* freedom. The scent of horny girls on summer break. An impish smile spreads across my face. God, it's good to be back in the States. The slight clink of metal on metal as the rings inside collide catches my attention and my smile dies a limp-dicked death. I'm only halfway across base and already I've forgotten that I'm about to be married.

I roll my shoulders and a surge of excitement bubbles in my gut. Rings aside, I'm eager to find out who I'm hitched to. I mean, how bad can it be? I get all the perks of a wife with an option for a way out after a year. Jim lucked out with Taya. If that grim bastard can pull a ten, there's no way in hell I can do any worse. For a moment I lose myself in the daydream of what married life must be like. Lots of fucking, obviously. And home-cooked meals, if I'm lucky enough to get someone who can cook, unlike Jim, whose wife manages to burn microwavable pancakes.

I chuckle and shake my head. "Shit, I don't need a cook. I'm a Latino Gordon-fucking-Ramsey."

A passing recruit shoots me a look and I bare my teeth in reply. He hurries away and I know that in the future, he'll try a little harder to mind his own goddamn business. This is America, for fuck's sake. A man should be allowed to talk to himself in public without people getting all judgmental. Unable to contain myself, I slide into my car, open the envelope, and pull out the paperwork so I can get a look at my new bride.

Nah. This can't be right. I glance out the window from side to side before popping open the glove compartment. Inside is a pair of reading glasses. Last week, I told Jim he was so old, he probably shits dust. I stand behind the statement, of course, but my credibility for further smack talking goes out the window the second any of my teammates find out I'm packing CVS non-prescription-rack reading glasses.

I peer through the lenses, frowning like a disapproving *abuela* as I scan the words again. "Oh, shit."

This is karma. It has to be. God saw all the times I looked at Taya's ass when Jim wasn't paying attention and now has decided to match me to Inara Ramirez, Taya's best friend. The woman I once flirted with in Taya's hospital room. Then again at the vending machine in the hallway. Her head was bent, body slumped with exhaustion and worry, and where her shirt lay crooked over one shoulder, I could just make out the edge of what had to be a tattoo. And, of course, I said the dumbest thing I could've managed to say.

"What's a sexy senorita like yourself doing in a place like this?"

I groan and lean forward until the steering wheel digs into my forehead. I meant the comment to come across as charming, cute even, but the look she shot me chilled the blood in my veins. There couldn't have been a worse time for me to flirt. Not after Taya was attacked by some hitman and each of us were worried and angry, struggling to cope with the knowledge that some New York crime boss had put a hit out on her.

Flirting should have been the last thing on my mind, but the knee-jerk reaction to form a connection, a bond, something Inara could remember me by took over. It wasn't my finest moment, but it wasn't my worst either, so maybe there's still hope we can make this marriage thing last for the year. Long enough for my application into OCS to be accepted.

Unable to help myself, I take a second look at the photo of Inara. She's smiling brightly, brown eyes twinkling, and interest raises its dark head. Just like the first time I saw her at Shaken and Stirred, a restaurant down by the pier where Taya works. It had been my birthday, and though I'd already had company on my arm, I'd been momentarily distracted by the pretty little hostess who showed us to our table. At the time, she reminded me of the dolls my sisters used to play with growing up. Small and perfect, with ink-black curls traveling down the length of her back, and large, dark brown eyes that took a chunk out of my soul every time she glanced my way. The classic lines of her face and that plump mouth would have been distracting enough, but then she smiled and it had been like a one-two punch to the gut.

I shrug and toss the files onto the passenger's seat, then crank the car, ignoring the strident groan the engine makes before it comes to life once more. So we got off to a bad start. That doesn't make my new wife any less hot, or the two of us any less stuck together. Might as well make the most of it.

Still, I can't help but grin, thinking about the expression on Inara's face when she gets the news, probably any minute now. If only I could be a fly on the wall when she reads my name.

CHAPTER TWO

Inara

ANTHONY. FUCKING. MARTINEZ.

The mere thought of his name makes me grit my teeth. That's the husband the United States military's spouse-matching program assigned to me. Of all the fucking luck, of all the men in the world, why *him*? How had the Issued Partner Program figured that oversexed jackass was the best match for me?

I drive my elbow into the unsuspecting box of Cheerios sitting on the kitchen counter next to the microwave and imagine the smug little bee on the front wearing Tony Martinez's face. It's not nearly good enough, but at least it's something.

"Inara?"

I freeze as Taya's voice trickles into the kitchen from the living room, the dented box of cereal and bumblebee-Tony seconds away from a pile driver.

"Coming." I take a final look at the box and shove it over onto its back just to be petty, then I grab the popcorn out of the microwave, bypass the island cart in the cozy kitchen space, and head back into the living room where my best friend is perched cross-legged on the edge of the overstuffed couch. Like most of the furnishings in my apartment, I picked the L-shaped couch for its mix of comfort and style. With the midafternoon sun streaming through the windows, the soft creamy color really brightens the modest-sized room. I sigh. Too bad it can't do the same for my mood.

Tony Martinez. I'm marrying Tony-fucking-Martinez. What terrible wrong had I committed in another life to earn myself this fate? Here I'd tried so hard to avoid my mom's relationship mistakes by taking a scientific approach to matrimony—only to have the whole thing blow up in my face.

Taya's eyes narrow and her lips purse when she tilts her head slightly. "What took you so long?"

I hesitate, consider coming up with a lie, but it's too much work. Why the hell am I trying to pretend as if I'm fine with the news when I'm not? Some of my anger fades, leaving behind a tightness in my chest. The program was supposed to be my saving grace, a way to find a man who wants to be married and have a family. The psychologists and committee are supposed to succeed at a task that, based on my pitiful relationship history and my mom's stormy track record, I have no confidence I can conquer on my own—find the ideal partner for me. Instead, the assholes paired me with the one man I know for a fact will never settle down.

After setting the popcorn on the coffee table, I flop onto

the couch next to Taya. My weight brings her swaying in my direction, but she doesn't shift away. Instead, we sit arm to arm, the popcorn between us, and the volume of the flat screen turned low.

So much for binging on chick flicks and comedies. I tuck a loose curl behind my ear. "So, Jim's ready for kids?"

She flicks the back of my hand and I move over so she can get at the popcorn while we stare at the actors on the screen, our feet messily strewn across the footrest in front of us. It's a movie we've both seen before, so at least we aren't missing out on anything. Besides, the light creeping in from the floor-to-ceiling windows on the west side of the apartment is reflecting off the screen and blinding me. I huff. The acting isn't all that good anyway, but it would be nice for *something* to go my way today.

"Don't change the subject." Taya shoves her hand back into the bag for more.

"I'm not changing anything. We were talking about how you and lover boy are going to start popping out mini-lover boys pretty soon." I freeze, hand halfway to my mouth. My mind fills with an image of an infant with Jim's scary-ass head attached to its body and I shudder. He's attractive in a Brawny man sort of way, but not my type.

"No, you were talking about Jim and I having kids when you know I'm scared to death of the subject because you want to avoid discussing the contents of the envelope sitting on the floor in the corner."

After opening the manila envelope two days ago, I'd

launched it across the room where it still lies dejectedly at the base of a potted fern. My pet tortoise, Simon, wandered over while I was in the kitchen. He sniffs the envelope and then his little mouth clamps onto the edge and tugs.

Taya frowns. "What's he doing?"

"Simon has a lot of pent-up hostility. Hashtag 'Red-Footed Tortoise Problems,' am I right?"

Not that Simon is angsty. He's just a naturally grumpy bastard. A lot like Jim actually. Maybe that's why we get along so well. Jim isn't my idea of a romantic anything, but after Taya got out of the hospital, the big guy and I became quick friends. He's no-nonsense and likes to get straight to the point, and I respect the hell out of him.

Which is more than I can say for my soon-to-be husband. I scowl and my chest tightens even more.

"Personally, I don't think you have anything to worry about." I hand over the popcorn so I can pull my leg up on the couch and wrap my arms around it. Lying my cheek against my knee, I give up on the television and focus my full attention on Taya. "You'll make a great mom."

Taya pales and sets the bag on the coffee table before turning to face me. "First off, you're deflecting. Second, motherhood is scary, yeah, but Jim and I are really happy." Some of the color returns to her face as her lips turn up into a big grin. "I'm not afraid of having kids with the man I love, I'm afraid that . . ." She swallows hard and I reach out to grip her hand where it lies clenched in her lap.

"What?"

"Santoro."

The crime boss's name is a dropped bomb between the two of us and the silence grows heavy.

"His trial's coming up." It isn't a question, but she nods anyway. I grip her hand as she begins to shake and squeeze it gently. "He's going to get what he deserves, Taya, and you won't ever have to think about him again."

Taya laughs, but the tone is flat, forced, and without humor. "My brain tells me he can't hurt me." She shakes her head and her eyes glisten with newly formed tears. "But my heart? Inara, it's saying something entirely different. I can't help but think that once I let my guard down, someone else is going to swoop in and destroy everything Jim and I have built. And to bring a baby into the mix . . ."

I'd love nothing more than to march into the prison holding Santoro and beat him senseless for everything he did to Taya and all the ways he still affects her life. She doesn't deserve to go through any of it. No matter how much I want to fix it for her, to make it all go away, I'm practical enough to know that there's only so much I can do.

Silence falls between the two of us again and I glance at Taya to find her chewing her bottom lip. Time to change the subject before she starts sobbing. I bump her with my shoulder and chuckle. "Just think, this time last year, you and Jim were trying not to kill each other and now you're thinking about babies. Who knows? Maybe if I stop bitching for five seconds, I, too, can achieve marital bliss."

Taya bursts into a loud, harsh cackle of laughter. "I can't

even picture the two of you surviving the night, let alone having kids. I've already started planning how to hide his body."

"You and me both." I blow out a puff of air to chase away a strand of hair from my eyes. All those trainings Taya and I did with the cadaver dogs on our search and rescue team may actually come in use. I snort and shake my head. Guess the dark sense of humor from the K-9 handlers is rubbing off a little too much on me. I turn back to my best friend and flick an upturned hand in the air. "On the bright side, I guess I won't have to worry about how to pay for my rent increase once Tony moves in."

My landlord died a month after I'd been accepted into the program and his son had taken over, springing the little surprise on me and the tenant upstairs that he'd be increasing our rent. Doubling it, in fact. For the past three months, I've had to take extra shifts at work and still can barely cover my bills. In fact, last month I had to borrow money from *Mami*. I love my place and I hate the idea of moving. And two days ago, when I came home to the envelope in my mailbox, I'd taken it as an auspicious sign that I'd found a solution to my problem.

Ha! That's what I get for being optimistic.

Taya arches a brow. "Pretty drastic step for finding a roommate."

I sigh, too embarrassed to vocalize my main reason for signing up with the Issued Partner Program because it sounds so stupid right now, given that I've been matched with Tony. "You think? You know he hit on me back at the hospital."

Taya snorts. "Hello, I might have been on pain meds, but I do remember that whole STD line."

My palm strikes my forehead and I groan. "That's only half of it. So, check this out, Tony follows me out to the vending machines, right? I'm minding my business, trying to get a coffee when this *hijo de las mil putas* struts over and continues to drop cheesy pick-up lines for another five minutes and then asks me what shampoo I used because— and I quote—'I want to make sure I have a bottle waiting in my shower for you come morning.' I shot his ass down, of course. But then tell me why the next time I see this fool, he's spitting the same game to the nurse at the counter?"

Taya's eyes grow wide and she presses a hand over her mouth. Granted, Tony isn't the reason I signed up for the program. That honor belongs to the guy I'd met shortly after, a financial advisor. He'd been respectful, considerate, and even attended Taya's wedding as my plus-one. And then the shit hit the fan. Waiting for us in the parking lot of the reception was the idiot's wife.

My jaw clenches at the memory, at the embarrassment. And, of course, my soon-to-be husband was the only one of the group to bear witness to the catastrophe, making sure I got into my car safely. None of the group knows exactly what happened to my former boyfriend, not even Taya. I'm too ashamed to tell her and Tony's kept his mouth shut on the subject so far. A fact I appreciate. Then, two days later I signed up for the Issued Partner Program because my own instincts on men can't be trusted.

The doorbell rings, interrupting my thoughts and making my entire body go rigid. The only company I'm expecting is the marriage officiant, and Jim and Tony, and neither option is especially welcome. I sigh. Not like I have a choice in whether or not to answer the door.

"Here goes nothing." I rise to my feet and meander around the coffee table, stopping at the window to peek through the blinds. The first thing that catches my eye is a black Durango with tinted windows sitting in my driveway. In the street is Jim's pickup, so I'm pretty certain I can guess the Durango's owner. As I'm taking the last few steps to the door, the doorbell rings three more times in rapid succession.

I curse under my breath. If I wasn't one-hundred-percent sure of whose Durango it was before, I am now. I yank open the front door, my lips pressed into a tight line. "Tony."

"Wifey!" Tony grins, his bald head practically glowing beneath the sun, but he doesn't seem to mind. He grabs me around the waist, lifting me off my feet so he can wrap me in his enormous arms.

Before I can quell it, a thrill works itself through my middle. Tony is physically mouthwatering. He's six foot and made of pure muscle. His features are chiseled and his thick, black brows only draw attention to those sultry brown of his eyes. His lashes are longer than mine and, coupled with his easy smile and penchant for troublemaking, he always looks as if he's about to get into mischief. Maybe, if he can keep his mouth shut and just let me look at him, we might be successful in the program. But that happening is about as likely as pigs flying.

The thrill fizzles, leaving behind a growing determination. Guess I'd better work on finding some pig-sized wings and teaching the bigmouth when to zip it because damned if I'm going to let this marriage fail.

"You looking to get tased?" Over Tony's shoulder, Jim hovers in the doorway and hefts a cardboard box a little higher in his arms. "Because snatching a woman out of her house while screaming 'wifey' is how you get tased."

Tony leans back far enough to put down at me and then winks. "Ignore him. He's just cranky because he hasn't gotten laid today."

I arch an eyebrow. "And you have?"

Tony opens his mouth, only to shut it abruptly. He brushes my shoulders and adjusts the hem of my T-shirt until I slap his hands away while heat rises to my cheeks. Between his muscled body and Jim's, the foyer is suddenly unbearably warm and cramped, so I edge away until my legs hit the back of the couch.

"Where do you want this?" Jim interrupts and makes his way over to the kitchen island.

I frown as I finally focus on the box in his hands. "What are you talking about? What is that?"

Jim glances between Tony and me and then closes his eyes while he takes a slow, deep breath, as if searching for patience. "You didn't call to tell her you were moving in today."

Tony shrugs. "Didn't think about it actually."

While my mouth gapes open, Tony breezes past me to the other side of the couch to say hello to Taya. I cross my arms over my chest and turn my attention to Jim.

"Don't glare at me." He strides forward and I grumble beneath my breath as I move out of his way and bump my hip on the counter I previously used as a karate block. "I told him he should call first. *Wifey.*"

I hit Jim's arm as he passes and he chuckles. The two of us step into the living room as Tony grabs the bag of popcorn and plops onto the love seat sitting perpendicular to the couch. Jim drops the box in the corner of the room and Taya, Tony, and I all wince as something inside shatters.

"Dude, not cool. What if it was something important?" Tony eats the popcorn one buttery puff at a time, which strikes me as odd. He's so obnoxious I would have expected him to shovel it in by the handful.

Taya glares at her husband and turns back to Tony. "What was it?"

"No clue." He grins and puts his feet up on the coffee table. *My* coffee table. The wooden square that I'd picked out myself and would rather remained boot-free.

Jim runs a hand through his hair and his jaw ticks. "What's 'not cool' is the fact I took the day off to help your ass move at the last minute, and you won't even help carry the boxes."

The doorbell rings again, snapping everyone's attention

to the storm door where an older man in a dark-gray suit stands. His black hair is neatly cut and sprinkled with gray, and rectangular, wire-framed glasses perch on his nose. In his hands, he holds a manila folder.

The officiant is here.

My heart beats erratically, nervousness replacing my ire. I'm about to get married to Tony. I swallow as I glance at my soon-to-be husband, then back to the officiant. Taya joined the IPP program because she'd been desperate to escape New York. But for me, well . . . I'm thirty-one years old and haven't been in a relationship for longer than a few weeks. Something always goes wrong, like with the married jackass I took to Taya's wedding. One time, after a nasty breakup with husband number three, *Mami* had a little too much to drink and told me the women in our family were cursed when it came to love. I scoffed back then, but as time marched on, well, part of me started to worry that she had a point. Which especially sucks given the way my biological clock ticks double time whenever I'm around Bear and his family or listen to Taya talk about Jim, making the lonely ache in my chest burrow a little deeper.

The officiant clears his throat.

"Inara?" Taya says gently.

I blink and look over my shoulder to find everyone is staring at me. Waiting for me to invite the man in, since it's my house.

I steal a sidelong glance at Tony and gulp. At least, it *was* my house, until today. Now I guess it's *our* house, technically speaking. Which is exactly what I wanted, right? A husband and someone to help me keep this place now that the landlord raised the rent.

I take a deep breath, straighten my spine, and head over to the door to let the officiant in. "Let's get this show on the road."

The officiant heads into the living room where Taya and Jim are seated. After saying a perfunctory hello to the two, he places his briefcase on the coffee table, then pulls the papers from the manila envelope in his hand. While he thumbs through them, the tension builds. To keep myself from hyperventilating, I mentally retrace the steps that led me here.

During the final interview, the member of the committee assigned to me explained how the military hopes the program will reduce the divorce rates among Spec Ops personnel by pairing them with compatible spouses. Up to that point, I'd been wavering a little, but that knowledge had sealed the deal for me. I didn't want five husbands. I didn't even want two. I wanted a partner I could count on to stick around. Since choosing her own partners hadn't worked out for my mother, I figured maybe the solution was in letting experts pick for me.

Except . . . now I'm stuck with Tony. The man standing right next to me, shooting me wicked grins that I'm trying my best to ignore. God only knows why he signed up for the program. No one seems to know, and Tony is keeping his lips sealed. I'm hoping the big guy upstairs has the answers as to why the committee figured Tony and I would be a good match because our interactions have proven anything but.

I lift my chin. I can only hope Tony will take the program seriously because I am not getting married again. This is my one shot and, as much as Tony grates my nerves, I will make our union work because, when it comes to marriage, I refuse to follow in my mother's footsteps.

I suck in a deep breath and try to calm myself down. I'm not the only one who signed up for the program. Tony did too. No one forced him into this, which means he'll have his own reasons to make this mismatch work. Right?

The sound of the manila folder smacking the coffee table jerks my attention back to the officiant. He stands up straight and smiles at Tony and me. He explains to us he is here to both witness our consent and to validate the marriage for legal purposes.

This is it, then. No going back after this. I lace my hands together to hide their trembling as we recite the vows, Tony's deep baritone voice a bit too loud in the enclosed space. When we finish, the officiant flips to a page marked with a Post-it. "I need both of you to look over the marriage license. Make sure your information is accurate and then sign it. Once that is complete, I'll have your witnesses sign it."

I take it and glance over my information. Everything is perfect. I grab a pen from the table and swallow past the lump in my throat as I scribble my signature on the empty line. Then I hand the license over to Tony. When he is done, he hands it back to the officiant.

Once the man completes his section of the license and Taya and Jim sign off, we all walk the man out. My shoulders sag as I sigh, not sure if I am relieved or sad. Either way, this is my life now.

The four of us make short work of moving the rest of the boxes out of the bed of Jim's truck after the officiant drives off. Not that carrying in ten boxes would take anyone very long. Plus, what little Tony has isn't all that heavy. Everything he owns fits in the entryway in three neat stacks.

I stare and my chest tightens. I'm not sure what bothers me more—the fact that Tony's entire life could probably fit into my closet, or the fact that he will have a toothbrush in my bathroom. Panic tries to dig its claws into me, but I shove it away.

I glance outside. Jim is heading to his truck, scanning the middle-class neighborhood I've called home for the last five years. His shoulders are tense, hands ready at his sides, searching for signs of a threat. I turn away, unwilling to draw Taya's attention to him and remind her about Santoro.

I extend my arms out and around Taya, hugging her goodbye. "Now go be with your man, and let me deal with this moron who I'm now married to."

She makes a strange choking sound that ends in a laugh and pulls away. "If you need someone with a shovel, just give me a call. I'm sure we have an extra tarp in the garage somewhere too."

Once she's in the truck with Jim, I close the door and lean against the wood frame, some of my bravado leaving with my best friend. What am I supposed to do now with that man parked on my couch who's expecting God knows what today from this ludicrous arrangement? *Mierda*. Surely he doesn't think we're going to jump straight into bed? My pulse pounds in my ears, my heart racing from a dizzying mix of anxiety and some other emotion I'd rather not examine too closely.

After straightening to my full height and pulling my shoulders back, I head into the living room. Tony is scrolling through Netflix but when he stops and looks up at me I'm struck, yet again, by how handsome he is, how imposing, even while sitting. It's almost impossible to catch a breath when in the same room as a man who takes up so much damn space.

Then—as if by design—he ruins my silent appreciation by opening his damn mouth. "Where do I sleep, by the way? Is there like a guest room, or do you have bunk beds in the master bedroom? Not that I would mind sharing, but I *really* like bunk beds."

Bunk beds.

I'm nervous about, oh, potentially being trapped with the wrong person for the rest of my life, and Tony's talking about *bunk beds.* I grind my molars. Are my hands too small to wrap all the way around his stupid neck? On the plus side, my nerves have all but disappeared. Now I'm just irritated.

I huff and stomp down the hall to the linen closet where I grab a blanket and pillow. I return and chuck them at his lap with no small amount of satisfaction and then lean down and pat him on the cheek. "Oh honey, I have the next best thing. It's called a couch."

The disappointed slump of his shoulders gives me both a sense of satisfaction and sympathy as I spin and strut down the hall for the comfort of my own room for the rest of the evening. The man has been deployed and I'm asking him to sleep on the couch. But then again, this is Anthony Martinez and sharing my bedroom right away will give him the wrong impression. A marriage isn't built on sex.

So for now, the couch will have to do.

CHAPTER THREE

Tony

O NCE INARA FLOUNCES off and her bedroom door slams shut, I flip my feet up onto the couch, fold my hands under my head, and scan my surroundings. Her place isn't bad. Not in as much as I don't have a room. That part's bad, but at least the sofa isn't the most uncomfortable piece of furniture I've ever slept on, with its cozy, chenille-like fabric and plump cushions. Definitely better than the barracks, even with my feet dangling off the end. And her entire place is decorated in bright colors and filled with a floral scent. Like something inherently Inara.

I close my eyes and drift off as the television plays in the background, only to be awakened at some godforsaken hour by a hideous screeching noise and a crick in my back.

What the hell? Where am I?

As I rub my eyes, reality returns. Shit, that's right. I'm at Inara's. I'm married.

And that god-awful noise is my sweet wife stomping through my sleeping area and whistling like a horn-blowing reveille player before the sun even pokes over the horizon.

I growl and hoist myself off the couch. "For God's sake, woman! There isn't a flag that needs raising."

This must be payback for me acting like a jackass and hitting on her back when Taya was in the hospital. If that's the case, I'd better apologize sooner versus later if I plan to ever get a good night's sleep.

Since this is my home now, I don't bother putting on a pair of pants and walk into the kitchen in my boxers. Perfectly respectable boxers. Boxer briefs in an attractive shade of hunter green to be exact. Unfortunately, she's bending over to take a pan of cinnamon rolls out of the oven and, being I just woke up, I might as well be part lumberjack for all the wood I have. My wife has an ass I could stare at all day, hang on to all night, and appreciate in memory when we're apart.

Because I don't want to startle her into burning herself, I wait until she closes the oven door and twists the knob to the off position before I dare make a sound. She turns when I clear my throat—as much fair warning as a guy who hasn't taken his morning piss can give—and looks me up and down, stopping when she gets to my waistline and gapes like she's seen a ghost. "Jesus, Tony. You don't own pants?"

Relief floods me when I look down and find I'm still covered. For a second there, I'd thought maybe I'd flashed her somehow. "At eight in the morning, I don't know that I own anything."

She continues to look over her shoulder at me. Her skin is the shade of a ripe tomato and her eyes are wide. "We need boners."

Now it's my turn to gape. "Excuse me?"

The red shade on her face turns fifty shades darker. "I mean, rules. About boners."

"Rules about boners?" My lips twitch. Now this is a conversation I am more than willing to take part in.

"You aren't allowed to have boners." She shakes her head again and rolls her eyes. "I mean in the kitchen. Or in the house at all."

"So, I should confine my boner to the front yard? Won't the neighbors complain?" I should take pity on her and stop, but I can't help myself. Seeing her flustered is refreshing. Breathtaking. Hot as fuck. "Besides, I can't help what you do to me. In the kitchen. Or anywhere else, for that matter."

"My mom could come over." She's looking everywhere but at me. Still cute. "She'll see your—" She shakes her head and sputters, then points. "That."

To my credit—for which, I should get big kudos—I don't point out that history and her birth prove her mother knows her way around a boner. Instead, I walk closer and reach around her for an apple sitting on the counter in a powder-blue fruit bowl that matches the wall color, the coffee maker and a stand mixer I can't wait to show her I know how to use. Chicks love guys who can cook. It's helped me score on more than one occasion. But while I'm ready to score with my new wife whenever she says the word, a part of me is just as eager to prove to her I'm good for more than terrible pick-up lines.

She gives a little gasp as my fingers brush against hers, and I shiver. Yeah, no. Getting to know my wife in the biblical sense definitely edges out proving my usefulness on the scale of things I'd like to accomplish today.

I could cover up. Could even take a piss and get rid of the problem, but this is more fun than I've had in a couple of days. More like months. And I'm not itching to hurry it away. "So, is this breakfast you've baked for me?"

Her eyes go dark, what could be classified as deadly, and she smiles slow, devious, a smirk of proportions so epic, I've never seen another like it. "Cold day in hell, *mi esposo*. And before you even think to open that stupid mouth of yours once more, for the indefinite future, your *situations* are your problem." She wax-on/wax-offs her hands in front of her. "This is off-limits until further notice."

She's pretty confident for a woman who hasn't benefitted from the full effects of said situations. I cross my arms, stare directly at her, and wiggle my eyebrows playfully. "I think we're gonna need to check the contract on that."

She cackles and I'm reminded of a children's movie. Wicked witch and all. "I checked already. As soon as I saw your name. And guess what? You're on your own, big boy. No boner clause is in the contract."

I cock my head. She's taking a bit too much delight for my liking. "Pretty sure of yourself, huh? Think you can resist"—I mimic her wax-on/wax-off move—"all of this?" I add a little hip thrust for good measure.

She goes rigid at first and narrows her eyes. Then her

smirk becomes wider and brighter. "Without breaking a sweat."

"Oh, baby, don't you know?" I drop my voice low and move in close enough to whisper in her ear. "The sweating comes later."

She coughs as if choking while I set my apple on the counter and wink. "I need a shower. Wanna join me?" I take a pause, a practiced pause, to let the words sink in and to give her time to form the image in her head.

Her beautiful face broadcasts a whole arsenal of feelings, but she's cool and seemingly unaffected when she finally responds. "Bathroom's down the hall. Towels are in the linen closet."

Her rejection doesn't faze me. I've got an entire year to win her over. Really, it's only a matter of time before she's unable to resist her bad-ass, love-machine hubby. For now though, I need a shower, shave, and toothbrush.

I whistle while I walk down the short hall to the bathroom, which is so small I can barely manage a full about-face. The bathtub is white, the wall is orange, and there's some abstract painting that looks suspiciously like a Georgia O'Keeffe hanging on the wall. The towels are soft and plush, emanating the scent of fabric softener. And I'm standing in the bathroom, still hard, thinking of using one of these towels to wipe droplets of water from every one of Inara's luscious curves. Not helpful when one of my main objectives is not pissing on the ceiling.

But standing so close to her in the kitchen, inhaling the

scent of her—that same perfume that's lingering in the house and a blessedly fruity shampoo—while her face changed color, touching that silky skin, and no more can I claim the boner as morning wood. Part of me longed to keep baiting her until we ended up rolling around the countertop.

I groan at that image. So not helpful.

Instead of thinking more about her, I consider my options. Inara's going to be a tougher nut to crack than the usual airheads I go for. She doesn't fall for my lines, doesn't think my jokes are cute. And the way she looked at me—like I'm nothing but an annoyance—after our interlude in the kitchen, lessens my odds to somewhere around one in fifty of scoring anytime soon.

My fingers grip the ceramic of the sink as I take in more of my surroundings, hoping to uncover something that will help me figure out the quickest way to loosen Inara up. There are drawers in the vanity, a stack of shelves with accoutrements and baskets of hair essentials, and a cabinet. Because I've never really investigated a woman's bathroom before, I take a peek in the cabinet hanging over the toilet.

Jesus Christ.

How many tubes of mascara does one woman need? And why does she have four boxes of Band-Aids? I rub my hand over my head and groan when my gaze falls on the colorful box of tampons. This is so pointless. No, I'm not scared of tampons. I grew up with four sisters, so I know all about periods. Hell, they used to send me into the drugstore to buy them. And my sisters love me. But Inara. Forget love—she doesn't even like me. The woman is uncomfortable anytime I'm within a twenty-foot radius. Which is what led me to this pathetic situation of searching for clues among her feminine products on how to get her to relax.

I huff and slam the cabinet door shut. At least now my boner is deflated, and I can finally piss without becoming a water-wiggle. I would happily tackle shaving as well, except stupid me left my razor kit in one of the boxes still in the entryway. Along with my toothbrush. Fortunately, Inara left one in here. A quick rifle through the vanity drawer produces toothpaste and I'm a teeth-cleaning machine.

When I reappear after a quick shower, clad in a towel knotted at my waist because my clothes are also still in the boxes, she slips in the bathroom and shuts the door, keeping her gaze studiously off my naked chest. Spoilsport.

I'm elbow deep in one of the boxes when the door flings open. She walks toward me with murder in her eyes and the toothbrush she'd left for me in her fist like a weapon. "Did you use my toothbrush?"

"Your toothbrush?" Oops. Swapping spit while making out is one thing but her toothbrush? That crosses a line I can't uncross. "I didn't know."

"So, you just find a toothbrush in someone else's bathroom and shove it into that germ factory you call a mouth?" She's indignant and rightfully so, but also a little over the top. It's not like I used the damn thing to clean the toilet. Although I don't mention it because I'm not giving her the ammunition to compare my mouth to that.

Also, damn. Why does she have to look so hot when she's pissed off, with those flushed-pink cheeks and blazing eyes? I'd like to make her eyes blaze for an entirely different reason.

I pull my mind out of the gutter and shrug. I've already been shot down once in the past half hour. No need to sign up for round two quite so soon. Also, now my own face goes hot as my mistake sinks in, but I'm not about to let her figure out I'm embarrassed. "Figured you left a toothbrush for me, like a good wife." The idea gathers momentum and races out of my mouth like it was built by a NASCAR pit crew. This is at least partly her fault. She should've known I wouldn't have unpacked. And I would happily continue that line of thinking, but she's advancing like a tiger stalking her prey. I back up and the tall stack of boxes topples behind me, knocking over a book of word searches that skitters toward her feet.

Her glare is hot enough to make a heat-seeking missile find a new target as she kicks the book off to the side. "Like a good wife? Did you really just say *like a good wife*?" Her voice is high-pitched enough to shatter windows.

I put a finger in my ear and give it a good wiggle for show. I've seen the rocket's red glare and the bombs bursting in air up close and personal. But something about this little spitfire is more intimidating, and yet I will not be deterred. "I just came back from deployment and was in a rush to pack up. Thought maybe you made sure I'd have the basic necessities, like a toothbrush." I puff out my chest and cross my arms and stare at her, a look that has melted men twice her size to their knees in fear.

Not Inara. If she'd been red a while ago, she was positively maroon now. And she isn't quite done with her rant. "And it never occurred to you to bring your own damned toothbrush? You arrogant, disgusting pig."

Her spunk is adorable and I can't hide my grin. I have an urge to keep pushing her buttons even when it means I might become the first-ever toothbrush homicide. I step forward with my arms open to embrace her and she jabs me with the business end of the toothbrush. Rubbing my chest, I quirk an eyebrow at her. "I'm trying to end the fight here. A little cooperation on your part would go a long way."

I'm not prepared for the strength behind the shove she gives me. Had I been, I wouldn't be on my ass right now, with my towel gaping open and a diminutive woman who must be no taller than five feet peering at us through the storm door. My hands fly to cover my exposed dick before the woman lays eyes on my goods. "Uh . . . hi there."

"I heard yelling," the woman says as she enters the home.

Inara shake her head. "It was nothing, *Mami*. Just a discussion."

"Sounded like something. Anyway, I just stopped by to drop off some flan." She lifts a glass baking dish in one hand.

Mami. Ah, shit. I rub my hand over my scalp and suck in a deep breath. "Not the way I intended to meet my new mother-in-law. Please forgive me."

Inara goes rigid, her nostrils flaring. Before I figure out

what I did wrong now, she chucks one of my boxes at me, and the edge of the thing catches me right in the dick. I growl when it hits. Okay, holler is more like it. I scream like a baby. Pain explodes in my groin and black spots flash in front of my eyes. I try to curl into the fetal position, but I can't because there's a fucking box on me. Plus, I can't breathe. Or think. Or do more than lie there and gasp like I've run a marathon while my dick throbs in agony. Then, after she grabs her purse off the small console table, she stalks past me and steps around her mother, heading out the door.

"*Mija*, where are you going? You need to explain yourself."

"To the drugstore. I need to buy a new toothbrush. And yeah, I got married." Her words come to an end just as a car door slams, the engine revving a couple of seconds later. Tires rub against concrete before screeching to a halt. "Don't interrogate my new husband either. Or bother guilt-tripping me later. It's not like you ever informed me any of the five times you got married."

The tires squeal as she peels out of the driveway. I swallow hard. What the hell kind of family did I marry into? Five times?

I shrug at her mother, who has a renewed interest in my predicament. Before I can say a word, Inara's mom steps around me and heads into the kitchen, her black hair streaked with gray in a braid that hangs over one shoulder. After she sets the flan on the kitchen counter she returns, snorting in a way that reminds me of her daughter. "Well, it's nice to meet you . . ."

"Tony." I still sound like a kid whose voice hasn't changed yet, but the sense I might die is subsiding. Incrementally.

"I must get going. I've got an appointment with my divorce attorney." She makes her way to the door, stopping before she exits. She turns and looks at me over her shoulder. "Be kind to my daughter."

With that, she leaves.

I set the box on top of my lap aside and roll onto my knees, the pain subsiding to a seven on a scale of ten. Though I'm not sure what bothers me more—that Inara physically hurt me, that she took off and left me with her mother whom I'd never met, or the fact I came off like a giant asshat. Why do people bother getting married? If I had remained single, I highly doubt a situation like this would've ever occurred.

After picking through the boxes and finding a pair of pants, I make my way over to the couch. Not long after, Inara returns with her little white drugstore bag and two of the big-brand coffee-shop cups in her hand.

I prepare to be scolded for debris from the toppling boxes still on the floor. But Inara just steps over the mess and turns to hand me one of the cups. "A peace offering."

"Thank you." I sip the hot caffeine and sigh before setting the cup on the coffee table and squatting to stuff my belongings back into a box. When I'm finished, I hoist the box and stand. "Where can I take this so it's out of your way?"

A quick widening of her eyes is the only sign that I've caught her off guard. "The storage area in the garage would be great, thanks." She points the way and I make quick work of it, hauling the boxes away until her living area is once again tidy.

"Thank you." She fidgets with the cardboard sleeve on her cup. "And, I'm sorry I don't have a place for your clothes yet. I'll try to work on that within the next few days."

"No problem." She flashes me a genuine smile, which I meet with a slow grin of my own. And then I blow any newfound amnesty. "Could always move my stuff to the bedroom?"

Her smile fades, her eyes widening briefly before she spins on her heel and stalks away, muttering something about a shirt and duct tape.

The man who marries her next will be one lucky bastard. I pick up my cup and suck down a long swallow, my chest constricting at the thought of Inara with another man. But this union is temporary, something I must see through to make sure I get into OCS. Staying long-term, having a family even, is not for me.

CHAPTER FOUR

Inara

INSUFFERABLE. RIDICULOUS. *TIRÓN insoportable.* I sit at the kitchen table, grab a catalogue that came in the mail, and slap the counter with it. But instead of the images on the pages, all I can see is Tony. Tony with his towel slipping. Tony doing a sexy little stripper move without a shirt. All of Tony. I had no idea I liked broad shoulders and defined pecs so much. I mean, I've admired before, but never gawked. And there'd been gawking. Ogling. Maybe even a gape.

And damn it. I don't want to gawk or ogle or gape. I don't want to notice the flecks of gold in his brown eyes or the way the towel hadn't hidden much, before the main event where the towel gave up all hope. Not yet anyway. My mom had started at least two of her marriages based on sexual attraction alone . . . and look how far that had taken her. No, I want this union to last, so I plan to take things slowly. Mutual respect and affection first.

Unfortunately, my hormones are not on board. My skin is probably somewhere near the hundred-and-twenty-degree range, but damn. The man has a body, and I'm so flustered at the moment that I can't decide if duct tape for his mouth would make things better or worse.

He walks past the table straight to the fridge, and I force myself not to notice the cut of his jeans. Or how they seem to have been sewed just for him. How the pockets ride low in the back. How round and firm his ass looks. I grunt and turn back to the counter, but my mind is stuck on how his jeans hug his body in just the right way, emphasizing his incredible form.

I shake my head in short bursts. No. No, no, no. A serious relationship will never work based on lust. We must build some sort of emotional connection first. I refuse to doom our marriage to failure by giving in to baser needs.

And what if we do have sex and then Tony goes to the committee to say he can't stay with me any longer? My throat tightens. I'll lose my home.

Mierda.

Rent is due soon, which means it's time to talk to my new husband about splitting the financial responsibilities.

The refrigerator door opens and the distinct sound of the milk carton sliding out of its spot doesn't precede the sound of the cabinet opening or milk pouring into a glass. Nope. It precedes several glugs and I whip my head around because if he's put his mouth on my milk carton . . . and there he is . . . carton tipped up, head thrown back, carton to face.

"What the hell are you doing?" My fingernails bite into the palms of my hands. Finally, his unbelievable gall does the trick and helps simmer my hormones the hell down. Even if he does look like a walking Got Milk? ad.

Tony sets the carton down on the island and looks at it and then at me. His grin is back, topped by a slim white mustache, and he puffs out his chest. "Does my body good."

I waste two seconds of my life glaring at him from across the kitchen before rolling my eyes and burying myself in the catalogue to find that it's women's lingerie. Fine. Whatever. Anything is better than dealing with my Neanderthal husband at this point. Even half-naked women in . . . I tilt my head. A bra studded with so many Swarovski crystals that it reminds me of a chandelier. Huh, maybe it comes with a hidden switch somewhere that will make the model's boobs light up.

Before I can close the pages, Tony's standing over me. He chugs the last of the milk, then places the empty carton down on the table. "You trying to avoid talking to me? Or are you genuinely interested in this nonsense?"

I drum my fingernails against the tabletop and press my lips tightly together, because killing him will get me locked up, and I'm not one who can handle being confined to a small space. I'll have to figure out how to deal with this jerk eventually, if I want our marriage to work. What I won't do is sit in my kitchen while he desiccates my milk carton and finds me lacking in the comparison to page twenty-three. I don't know why I'm so mad, because this is exactly the type of behavior I was afraid of, from the first second I read his name on the matching-program paperwork. Maybe I'm just upset he's proving me right.

"Since you're here anyway, leering at my catalogue, now's as good of a time as any to tell you that I expect you to pay half of the rent every month." Having someone to split the surprise increase in rent with me hadn't been the reason for signing up for IPP. I'd been prepared to seek out a roommate. But when the committee called and notified me of a match, I'd been relieved. My new landlord can kiss my ass.

"Not a problem. If you read through the contract, there's a financial section. No freeloading allowed by members of the military. We're required to take care of our dependents. And I'm more than happy to go in on all the bills, groceries, the works."

I blink at him. I hadn't bothered to read through the entire contract. Maybe I should go through it and see what else is stuck in there.

"I'll get you a debit card tomorrow since we are also sharing my bank account. But I draw the line on you using my money for crystal bras." He jerks his head toward the page and studies the picture again, then trails his gaze over me, lingering on my chest. He taps his chin while that wicked grin slides across his face. "On second thought . . ."

I shove back my chair and stomp past him to my bedroom, flinging the door shut because sometimes, I just need the echo of a slamming door to fill the room. It soothes some of the rage boiling beneath my skin. This entire thing is ridiculous. What I need to do—instead of sitting on my bed muttering to myself—is call someone, let them know there's a flaw in the program and they've made a mistake. A big one. The epic kind, with ramifications that could destroy the program's integrity and kill the success rate. Maybe put funding in jeopardy if word got out how badly they'd messed up this match. Especially if I, say, end up in jail for shoving Tony in a locked closet for the next year with his mouth taped shut. Or worse.

But before I can hunt down my cell, he knocks and pushes my bedroom door open. It's wrong for my body to immediately react to the sight of his handsome face and the way his form perfectly fills the doorway, or to remind me of how I was hoping for more than a sparring partner to spend the next year with. It's wrong, but my body buzzes with anticipation anyway.

I exhale as my shoulders slump forward. "What do you want?"

Instead of answering, he walks farther into the room and runs his finger along the edge of my dresser, stopping to test the texture of a doily my *abuela* made. He picks up my perfume, removes the cap, and sniffs. An involuntary twitch pulls his lips upward at the corners as he puts the bottle back and moves toward the window. "This suits you."

"It's a place to sleep." Though it's actually my sanctuary. The place I go to when I don't want to be around anyone, and he's ruined that for me, because I will forever picture him standing inside my room, touching my things, investigating my life. I'm uncomfortably aware of the way my shoes are visibly jumbled within my open closet and how the thin layer of dust on my dresser and night table showcases I'm not a perfectly tidy person. Then I snort and lift my chin. Whatever. As if a guy who uses someone else's toothbrush without permission and drinks straight from the milk carton has room to judge.

He moves to sit on the side of the bed opposite mine. There is a stack of books next to him, ignored and ready to teeter to the floor that he straightens and then investigates. One of the classics, a few romance novels and a well-thumbed search and rescue training manual. He picks up one of the romance novels, a historical, and flips to the middle.

After a minute of reading, he looks up. "Love rod?"

I snort and quirk a brow. That one had thrown me too. "Euphemism."

He pokes his nose back into the book, reads some more, and then flips the page and turns to lie across the bed so that his head is near my hip. "'Her breasts heave in anticipation. If only he would touch her.'"

Mierda. In his voice, the words come to life and I imagine myself in a turn-of-the-century gown with my hair piled on top of my head and Tony, with his pirate pants unbuttoned, shirt open at the throat. Heat pulses under my skin. I snatch the book because if he reads another word aloud, I can't be held responsible for my actions. "It helps me sleep to read before bed."

"You know what else helps?"

He has that look in his eyes—the mischievous, teasing

one. But I can give as well as I can take. So, I lower my voice to something in the neighborhood between sultry and breathy. Tracing his ear with my finger probably isn't fair since I have no intention of backing any of it up, but he'd played with my fire one time too many. "Why don't you tell me?"

He gulps and the sound is as satisfying as it is loud.

"Warm milk." His voice comes out raspy and deep, like he's choking on a ball of sand.

For the first time since he entered my home, I'm not all off-balance from his presence. I have the upper hand for a change, and it's damn good. I trail my finger to his throat and scrape my nail lightly down to his collarbone. "You drank all the milk." My husky, semi-pouty voice has managed to make the pulse point in his neck kick into gear and I'm proud. I could be a vixen as much as the next girl. It's only fair, after he paraded around my house half-naked.

He clears his throat and in the blink of an eye, he's found his control again. The grin that stretches lazily across his face makes my traitorous pulse skip. I try to pull my hand away, but he's faster and grabs it to press a soft kiss against the pad of my index finger. Talk about heartbeats and shooting into the unknown.

"I have some other ideas we could explore." He moves on to kiss each of my fingertips. My, oh my, his lips are soft. And the way they brush so sweetly against my skin? Delicious.

When he's almost done, I snap out of the haze and yank

my hand back. "If we keep having this conversation and I have to keep shooting you down, I'm afraid your self-confidence will suffer. Then it's all shrink visits and psychotropic medication."

I stand because one more inhale of his cologne and I'm going to lose my shit . . . and by lose my shit, I mean melt into a puddle at his overconfident, annoying feet. Which is absurd. The day I can't resist a player like Tony is the day the world ends. No, this is less about him and more about me, and my sex drive reminding me that it's been too long. That must be what's happening here. My new husband might be hot, but he's far too obvious and immature for my taste.

I glance down into his smoldering brown eyes, and a bolt of electricity runs along my spine right to my aching sex. Who am I trying to kid? My body has other ideas. Which, when I think about it, is great! Because it's not like I have to resist him forever. No, I just need to keep my hands off him long enough for us to form some kind of bond that's not rooted in sexy times. He's making that a challenge though, because now not only do I have a mental picture of him in my room, but also one of him sprawled on my bed wearing his come-get-me grin, and it's an image complete with smell-o-vision. Maybe *Mami* knows a cleaning ritual or a special prayer I can say to clear my head of the clutter. And yeah. My new plan is to think of him as brain clutter for the foreseeable future.

"Get out." I wave my arm in a sweep toward the open

doorway. "I have to . . ." I can't think of a lie quick enough and he smirks, like he's filling in my silence with the dirtiest conclusion ever. Insufferable. Ridiculous. Jerk. How am I supposed to form a nonphysical connection with this idiot? "I have to get ready for work."

Because of my new *marriage*, I've been given the week off, and if I show up at the restaurant, the rumor mill will wind itself into God only knows what. But it'll involve me and I'm not into being the talk of the town. I don't even like being the talk of the house. But neither do I want to fall straight into bed with Tony and risk ruining any chance of making our union work for the long haul.

I push him out and slam the door before he can say another word. I walk over to my bed and fall onto the mattress where the scent of him—spice and citrus—mingles with the linen scent of my blanket to form the most intoxicating aroma. I want to bury my face in the material and inhale until it's all gone, and as I turn my head into the comforter, the door pops open and I jerk my head to find Tony and his smug smirk pointed at me. "I'm going out for milk. You need anything?"

God, yes. I need some common sense, a few unencumbered-by-Anthony-Martinez brain cells, and a big dose of whatever they sold that would form an impenetrable resistance to him. "I'm good. Thanks."

He winks again and shuts the door, whistling the first few bars of "I'm in the Mood for Love"—an oldie from way, way back I would have never guessed he'd ever heard. And a few minutes later while I shower, I belt out the first verse and the chorus before I realize what I'm doing and switch to an old Bon Jovi tune that seems to sum up the current state of my life. If anyone's living on a prayer, it's me.

The shower, with its multi-head spray jets that pulse and massage, eases the tension in my back and shoulders, but the rest of me is coiled like the spring in a jack-in-the-box. Tony being only be a few feet down the hallway from now on is going to be more temptation than I'd imagined.

If only the jackass didn't speak, maybe we'd get somewhere. Maybe I could get one of those no-bark collars for dogs modified into a no-talk collar.

I grab the towel and wrap it around my body before stepping onto the bathmat. After towel drying my hair a bit, I step into my room and dance like no one's watching while heading to the closet.

Tony always looks like he just stepped out of GQ magazine and by God, I won't be outdone by designer jeans and a Ralph Lauren button down. I know how to turn heads, how to dress for my body, how to accentuate my J.Lo-esque ass and Victoria's Secret cleavage. A little toss of my hair, one final look in the mirror, and I'm following my nose to the kitchen.

The kitchen is small, a U-shaped bank of cabinets interrupted by a dishwasher at the sink, and a refrigerator across from the stove. But at least when I'm standing at the sink hand-washing dishes, I can look out the window to the backyard and the garden of flowers my mom planted when I moved in. Except right now, Tony stands there with his big hands plunged deep into a bowl of peeled tomatoes.

Red juice squirts onto his shirt as he kneads and massages the fruit. My gaze fixates on the capable, rhythmic motion of his fingers. My legs wobble. *Mierda*. When did cooking become so erotic? This is unacceptable. I place one hand on my hip and drum the fingernails of the other against the countertop. "Tony, what are you doing?"

He grins and continues squeezing the tomatoes as his gaze wanders from my painted toes up my bare legs to the shorts of my romper, then to my halter top and the soft curls in my hair. "Making sauce for lasagna. Women like guys who can cook."

"Women do, huh?" To be honest, I'm not offended he's lumped us all into one category. To him, we probably are all one group of adoring fans. Conquests and notches on his bedpost.

Before I can ask about the ingredients scattered across the counter, he leans closer and sniffs the air. "You smell good too."

My cheeks heat and I twirl a strand of hair around my finger. "Thanks. I'm, um, going to the auto parts store to pick up some . . . uh . . ." I can't think of a single thing we need. "Motor oil." Oh, sweet Lord. But I can't stop now. I'm in too deep. "I need to change . . . uh . . ."

He bites his bottom lip as if to keep from laughing. "Your oil?"

Ugh. Of course I'd have to set myself up for one of his

lines. And I don't generally shop at the auto store in three-inch heels and a romper that costs a week's pay. Plus, I'd just changed the oil in my Wrangler last week. But I'm all in now. "Yep."

"Don't you have work?"

"You know, darnedest thing. I forgot I'm off this week. The newlywed-bonus week." I grimace. Why did I say that?

He looks up at me for a moment, then continues kneading. "Well, don't be too late. Dinner should be ready in about an hour and a half, tops."

I shoot the bowl of tomatoes one last suspicious glance. "Sure. Will do. I'll try to be back by then. Okay. I'm leaving now."

But instead of heading out the door, I'm standing in my kitchen as my husband washes his hands like he's performing some complicated surgery, and I'm mesmerized by how thorough he is, by the grace of his long fingers, by the muscles stretching his shirt tighter with each move of his shoulders.

This is bonkers. I shake myself as if clearing cobwebs from my skin and practically flee for my car. It's a chickenshit escape, but I need some air that isn't tainted by Tony Martinez and his cologne and his presence. Some space that isn't crowded by his bulging biceps and smirk.

Outside, the air is hot and humid. Another normal June day, and I breathe it in. Deep. Centering. Calming. There. Now I'm more like myself.

Maybe his cologne has magic powers. If so, that'll be the

second thing added to my ban list. Right after kitchen boners.

As I back the car out of the driveway, I start to laugh. One thing is for sure. Being paired with Tony is the opposite of boring.

After I cruise around for a while, flitting through a boutique, and yes, stopping by the auto supply store for motor oil that I don't need, I finally head back home after an hour and twenty minutes has passed by. My stomach is growling, so I hope Tony didn't strike out with dinner.

The second I open the door and inhale the delicious aroma of melting cheese, sweet tomato sauce and spicy sausage, my worry dissipates. When I enter the kitchen, Tony's wielding a metal spatula over a rectangular glass dish that sits on the stove. I head toward him to help, but he shoos me away. "Go sit down at the table. I've got this."

I don't need to be told twice. I take a seat while Tony dishes up hearty servings of steaming lasagna onto two plates and carries them over to the table. Two goblets full of ice water already sit across from each other, along with two place settings. He sets a plate in front of me with a flourish and then settles opposite me. He lifts his water glass toward me, so I mimic the motion.

"Cheers," he says, when our glasses clink together.

"Thank you. This looks delicious."

He takes a sip of water, then places the glass down on the table. "You don't have to sound so startled. I had three younger sisters growing up, so I did a lot of cooking since my older sister was away at college."

I nod and use my fork to dig in. The first bite I take is more like a nibble, but even that . . . whoa. So good. I quickly scoop up another bite and this time, close my eyes as the flavors practically explode in my mouth. The ricotta and sauce and mozzarella ratios are perfect, and the flavor is an amazing blend of spicy and sweet.

"You like?" Tony's nonchalant tone is belied by the way he's taking in my every little reaction.

Okay. I have to admit, it's kind of cute, the way he's so worried if I like his meal or not. "I love. This is absolutely delicious. Thank you for cooking for me. That was really sweet."

He freezes with his fork halfway to his mouth. "Sure. No problem."

We sit in companionable silence for the next few seconds while I take another bite. Maybe I'd judged him too harshly.

Then, that familiar cocky grin spreads across his face and he ruins it all by opening his mouth again. "You know, any time you want to get cooking in the bedroom, too, you just let me know."

I set my fork down after I forcefully swallow the contents in my mouth. "You just had to go there, didn't you? Wait— don't answer!" I hold up my hand. "How about we eat the rest in silence so I can focus on how appreciative I am of your delicious dinner versus how close I am to slapping a piece of duct tape over your mouth? And before you say it— no, not in a kinky way."

His shoulders slump at that last bit but, surprisingly, he does as I ask. Even more—he collects the dirty dishes and silverware when I finish before I have a chance to stand up, rinses them, and puts them in the dishwasher.

Never in a million years would I have guessed Tony Martinez was damned good at domestic activities. Maybe, just maybe, he's more capable of being a good husband than I first thought.

CHAPTER FIVE

Tony

I WAKE AND stretch and snuggle deeper into the blankets on Inara's bed. It took the whole week to unpack all of ten boxes thanks to work, and my shit is scattered throughout the apartment, since I still don't have an official room. Not that I really need one. Most of my belongings are back at home in California, and I'm not really into material things. Even after I moved to Virginia Beach, I never found the need to buy anything outside of clothes, especially with living on base and being gone so much for work.

While I'm starting to get used to my new home, I'm still bunking on the couch, though I've started sneaking into Inara's room when she's at work so I can have a few hours in an actual bed again. The sofa isn't even a pullout, and I don't give two shits about how stylish it is, when it's so small my calves hang over the edge, unless I condense myself into the fetal position for the hours it takes for Inara to wake up and leave.

I don't get it. We've been making progress. Like that afternoon when I made lasagna. And all the other nights I've cooked dinner since. We are getting closer and I figured my position on the couch would be a distant memory by now. Yet, here I am. Still contorted into unnatural positions while trying to sleep. Sucks. I mean, she signed up for the Issued Partner Program, too, right? Why sign up to get married if you don't want to reap all the benefits?

On the one hand, I'm frustrated, but on the other, I get it. I mean, it's probably smart for Inara to be cautious. Especially when, if things go as planned, I'll be heading for OCS in Rhode Island in less than a year. But still. That doesn't mean we shouldn't make the most of things while we're together. And by most I mean, enjoying all the benefits of long-term monogamy without having to do all of the wining and dining that typically precedes it. Not that I mind cooking for Inara. In fact, I enjoy it. Who knows? Maybe if things were different, courting her would have been a fun time. But we are already hitched. So I think it's only right that, with or without her, I've decided to engage in a close personal relationship with her sheets. A man needs at least a few hours a day of shut-eye where his limbs don't threaten to fall off in protest.

And it doesn't hurt that the sheets smell like her.

Oranges and cloves. I waste a moment promising myself I'm not going to do it, but in the end, I can't help but press my nose to the soft cotton and inhale the scent. I fill my lungs with her and my cock tents the lilac watercolor design on the blanket. With a curse, I roll out of the bed and scowl.

I head into the bathroom and take a cold shower, hoping

the chill will be enough to knock the starch from my cock. It doesn't, but I'm more clearheaded than a few minutes ago. From the clues I've gathered over the last few days, Inara's mom has no idea the Issued Partner Program is even a thing, and I haven't even talked to my wife about her mother's history of divorce.

I'm slipping on my shirt and simultaneously trying to ignore and get a closer peek at the strappy little red dress in the bedroom closet when the doorbell rings.

Fuck, I almost forgot they were coming over.

I take a few seconds to put the bed back the way I'd found it before hurrying down the hall to the main entrance where I find my teammate and best friend, Lucas Craiger, along with his son, Mason, on the front stoop.

"Uncle Tony!"

I brighten and after exchanging a fist bump with Craiger, I crouch down until I'm eye to eye with the little munchkin. He throws himself into my arms with such enthusiasm, it nearly knocks me backward and I push back on my heels to keep from falling onto my ass. Like his dad, Mason is all golden good looks and bright-blue eyes.

"Jesus, you're getting big." I groan, pretending to struggle as I rise to my feet. Mason leans back to look at me as I transfer him from my chest to one bicep, the expression on his face showing he knows I'm full of shit, even if he doesn't have the vernacular to call me out on it. In truth, he's a small kid—takes after his mother on that front—and he's already starting to complain about being picked on by the other kids in his school for being the shortest one in class.

I lead Craiger past the front door and into the living room. We haven't hung out with one another since getting back to the States and I could use a dose of the familiar after a little over a week of nonmarital bliss.

Craiger glances around the house, his gaze landing on my beer-stein collection prominently displayed on floating shelves on both sides of the television. Inara had some books she loved on the shelves—classics that were now stuffed in a box in the closet. Giving up the space was one of the first things she did. I'd expected there to be a problem, but surprisingly, she didn't appear to mind at all.

"You've got an Xbox?" Mason squirms to get down and investigate the extensive game collection and console on display on the entertainment center. Another of my contributions to the décor. Inara didn't mind that one either, since she could now access Netflix and Hulu on something other than her phone or laptop. I toss him on the couch and he giggles as he plops face-first into the pillows with all the grace of a stone sinking into the ocean.

"We got a tortoise too." I point out the angry little weirdo that's been stalking me for the last several days and Mason is faced with the crippling moral dilemma of which cool thing to play with first.

"That's gonna stump him for a while." Craiger grins and I nod, pleased with myself.

"Beer?"

He snorts. "Such a gracious host you're turning out to

be. The new missus must be a good influence on you."

Pissed at his comment, I stomp to the kitchen. I've always been a gracious host—it was one of the things my mom instilled in me. For anyone to think otherwise is a blow to the chest because disappointing *Mamá* or her memory is the last thing I ever want to do.

Something strikes me in the face and I blink, shaking my head to clear my mind before glaring at Craiger and Mason, heads bent together and whispering. Another pillow hits the center of my chest and flops onto the ground. Mason's high-pitched giggle and Craiger innocently eyeballing the ceiling are enough to inspire a full-fledged war. I stare down at the pillows. When was the last time I've been so unaware of my own surroundings? If we were out in the field, my inattention would have gotten me killed.

Shit.

What if something happens to me before the year is up? What if Inara begins to fret about my well-being and decides spending hours distressed is not the way she wants to live?

She can't leave before the year follow-up if I want any shot at becoming an officer. Redding will just take her request for departure as evidence I didn't give the program my all, that I don't deserve to be an officer. That I'm not as worthy as Jim.

My lips tighten and rather than allow the thoughts free rein, I bend and toss the pillow at Craiger, like a Frisbee. It connects with his face with enough force to push his head back. Mason falls over on the couch, laughing his narrow little ass off before he lets loose a war cry that would have put Braveheart to shame.

We spend the next few minutes play fighting and whooping like warriors. My weapon of choice—a delicate, white, frilly throw pillow perfect for smacking toddlers upside the head—goes wide, and there's a sudden hush of silence as it sails into a flower vase. The glass hits the floor with a loud crash and we gather around the remains. Mason's eyes are wide and his mouth is hanging open. But my guts are on fire.

Inara is going to strangle me.

"Oooh." Mason takes several steps back as if putting distance between himself and the scene of the crime. Smart kid. Not his mess. Mine.

"All right. WE can do this." I bend and pick up the pieces. "First step is to get rid of the evidence. No evidence, no crime."

The glass not only looks expensive but has a weight the cheap stuff doesn't. But maybe, if there's any luck in the world whatsoever, Inara won't notice it's gone. Not for three hundred and fifty or so more days.

Craiger shakes his head. "Can you not teach my son the best way to commit a crime?"

I snort. "Someone's high and mighty today. Sorry, *Dad*."

Craiger picks up Mason and shifts him back to the couch so he isn't in the way while we clean up the tiny shards of the glass. "Is it dad-like to say that you shouldn't have been having a pillow fight inside of the house?"

Dad-like. Hell, yeah. Definitely something a dad would say. Especially my own father. "Absolutely. It's also crazy talk. Where the hell else are you going to have a pillow fight? There are bound to be casualties sooner or later. And what the hell do you mean, 'you'? I didn't throw that first pillow at myself."

Craiger grins, strides into the kitchen, and comes back with a damp paper towel. "Sorry, I'm not taking the fall for this one. I've got a kid to think about."

"How 'Bear' of you." I ignore his laughter as he bends to wipe the hardwood to catch the slivers of glass I hadn't been able to grab. Once all evidence of the vase has been wiped from existence, we make lunch and settle on the couch to watch the game. The Sox are playing the Yankees at Fenway and it's a double-header. Unfortunately, before the first pitch, it becomes abundantly clear Mason has missed his nap. He's cranky and grouching about everything from his too-tight shoes to the lack of cheese puffs in the house. So, we end up watching Pixar and Disney for almost two hours. I enjoy animated movies as much as the next guy, but if I have to sing along with one more princess, I'm going to chuck the remote at the flat screen. Thank God, Mason finally curls into my side and falls asleep right about the time the ice queen is letting it go, and we can flip the channel to catch the last few innings of the game.

An unconscious Mason is a nice respite and I'm unwilling to jeopardize our temporary peace. Craiger moves in increments to grab the remote from the coffee table. We're men who've spent the afternoon drinking our beer to singing fish and a dancing snowman. We need to fuel our testosterone with swinging bats and balls hit deep to right center. But he bypasses ESPN for Bravo.

"This is my shit," I murmur in approval, nodding as the geniuses from *Queer Eye* teach some loser about the importance of accessorizing.

Craiger settles back on the couch and takes a swig of his beer. "Don't know if I like the reboot as much as the original."

We sit in silence for a while and I'm on the verge of nodding off myself when Craiger's voice drags me back to full consciousness. "What do you think of Graves?"

My jaw clenches. Trevor Graves is the newest member of our unit. He's also a glaring reminder of the man we'd lost during our last deployment. "Too quiet. Takes Jim's shit too much. Needs to give it back. Otherwise, he does his job, so I can't really complain."

Knox, Jim, Craiger, Bear, and I were brothers. Knox dying was hard on all of us, but Jim took it the worst. The two had grown up together. Not to mention after a falling out with Jim, Knox had volunteered to extend his deployment while the rest of us went home. Jim still blames himself and deflects onto Graves. All I could do was try to keep the team running smoothly. All of us promised Taya we would get Jim back home to her, and so long as his attitude didn't make me a liar, he was welcome to it.

Craiger swirls the remaining beer in his bottle, staring as

the liquid inside sloshes from side to side. "Speaking of awkward partnerships . . ."

I stare at the television screen with laser focus. Unfortunately, my action isn't very effective anymore thanks to the abrupt presence of commercials. One can only look interested in animated bears wiping their asses badly for so long. So, I slump, my chin touching my chest, and exhale long and hard. "Not sure I can make it through."

Craiger reaches across the couch and squeezes my shoulder, his smile fading around the edges. "Don't really have much of a choice. Besides, I'd rather have your ugly mug watching my back any day of the week, and I don't think Jim's blood pressure can handle another new face."

I rub a hand over my scalp. "Maybe if there's a mission and we are gone long, I could do it. But I'm out of my element. I don't do long-term and I think that may be what Inara wants. Not to mention all the added complications with her being tied to our group. Why couldn't it have been some stranger?"

Craiger quirks an eyebrow. "In other words, you care for her and don't want to hurt her."

I frown. Of course I do. She's one of us. If only Jim or Taya had mentioned Inara was considering the program, things might have been different. Maybe that would've been enough to stop me from signing up.

I glance down at Mason and brush his hair back from his forehead. He started snoring a few minutes ago, and now he's drooling on my forearm. "How do you and Lisa do it?

You two get along so well for being divorced."

"We have a common goal, for one." Craiger nods in Mason's direction. He finishes off his beer and leans forward to place the empty bottle on the coffee table. "Bit of advice? Stop breaking her shit."

The sound of a lock turning and the front door opening reaches my ears and I look over my shoulder as Inara walks inside. She smiles and waves at Craiger, who with careful exaggeration points to Mason and puts his finger against his lips.

Her eyes widen and she comes into the living room instead of heading back to her bedroom. When she circles the couch and finds Mason curled up between us, her expression softens. Holy shit. That look. Those eyes. I've never seen Inara so disarmed. The last time I'd caught even a hint of vulnerability had been at the hospital with Taya.

The way Inara focuses on Mason, the way the stern lines around her mouth disappear, giving way to a new and unexplored softness around her lips, hits me low and hard in the gut. It isn't lust, but something softer. Kinder. An affection that rises from the seeds of witnessing someone I care for unfurling in front of me. The image of Inara and I standing together, gazing down in that same adoring way at our little boy tucked into bed flashes in my mind, and my heart turns to mush.

I freeze, my face dampening with sweat.

Hold up. *Our* little boy? What the hell is wrong with me? I can't be picturing children with Inara. At the end of the year, when the program committee asks if I want an annulment, I'm out. No strings. No complications. No bringing kids into this world who will grow up full of anxiety I won't come home one day. Or suffer when they bury me because of a mission gone wrong. I won't be responsible for fathering a child only to have them suffer the way I did when my mom died.

I swipe the moisture off my forehead. No, definitely no kids. After the year is up, I plan to walk away as free of responsibilities as I was when I signed up. That's the best thing for both of us.

"Are you guys watching the Oprah Network?" Inara snorts slightly and to my surprise, squeezes onto the couch beside me. She could have taken the loveseat or sat next to Craiger. Hell, she could've ignored all of us and continued to her room. And while I put up my shields against the warmth of her skin against mine, there's no shield, no defense whatsoever, that blocks the scent of her.

"It's crazy how much he looks like you." Her voice is soft and alluring. As angelic as I've ever heard her.

The glow from the television casts her face in gentle lines and my fingers extend as images of brushing a loose curl back from her cheek fill my mind. I swallow hard and glance away. Shit. I've missed most of the conversation.

Craiger shakes his head. "Looks more like Lisa. Acts more like her too. Took my time dating her, figuring we'd last. Probably should've followed Martinez's lead."

I straighten, and Inara's head cocks to one side.

"What do you mean?" Her eyes narrow and she's staring at him hard. Suspicious.

Which is the same way I'm looking at him right now. Alarm bells sound off in my brain and my muscles clench. I never told any of the guys what led me to join the program in the first place, mostly because I'm not proud that I let what was essentially a woe-is-me, sleep-deprived panic attack propel me into the impulsive choice to sign up for a wife. But of course, the guys being the guys, well, they've come up with their own theories. None of which are going to please said wife. I flick my gaze to Inara's tense expression and swallow. Mason groans in his sleep and lists more completely into my lap. With no avenue of escape, all I can do is shoot Craiger a look, my face violently contorting in a silent order to shut his fucking mouth.

But it's too late.

"Oh, crap, no one told you." Craiger laughs, shifting on the couch so he's facing us. Poor, dumb bastard doesn't even understand the danger he's putting himself in. "Tony's been uncharacteristically tight-lipped about why he joined the program, but I'm pretty sure I know why."

And I'm pretty sure he doesn't, which means I'm gonna kill him, because the last thing I need is more tension with Inara. It's only fair that he knows what's coming, so I growl low in my throat that's only part desperation, but to Craiger it must have sounded like encouragement because he keeps going. He's like Chatty-fucking-Cathy as soon as he gets a few beers in him.

"The way I see it is, this moron must've lost a bet playing cards with the paratroopers—like he always does—and ended up signing up for the program. Always gotta prove how tough he is. Probably didn't think he'd get accepted." He chuckles uncomfortably, his gaze flittering from Inara to me and back again.

Her lips part slowly and a soft scoff escapes from her mouth. Her hand comes to rest on the back of mine, and horror-movie, doomed-teenager slow, I turn my head to meet her eyes in the flickering glow of the television. My balls clench, determined to crawl up into my body.

"Bedroom. Now." She grits out the words, and I wince at the venom in her tone.

I take my time carefully extracting myself from beneath Mason's limp body before pushing to my feet. "Thanks so much for that great story. You really know how to help a newlywed out. I owe you one." I glare at my former best friend before following my wife out of the room, my stomach plummeting with each step.

CHAPTER SIX

Inara

I RAKE MY fingers through my hair and pace, trying not to hyperventilate. I've never had a panic attack before, but I think I could start. Right here. Right now. Because I just found out that the man I'd been matched with as a life partner had joined the program after losing a round of poker. This is my life we're talking about. My life that this idiot treated like it was some kind of fucking reality show game. Just when I was starting to think we'd actually have a chance together after the past week of sharing meals and discovering that beneath that flippant exterior, Tony is a thoughtful man in a lot of ways I'd never imagined possible, like cooking, and cleaning. I'd even caught him weeding the flower bed one morning.

"Will you at least hear me out?" Tony is standing against the door, voice low, tone pleading.

"What's there to *hear out*? Was Craiger lying? Please tell me that's the case." A tiny, naïve hope flares in my chest. Maybe this is just an epic misunderstanding. Surely not even Tony would be foolish enough to sign up for a military program over a silly bet.

That hope dies a swift death when Tony shuffles his feet and his head drops so his gaze is focused on the floor, brows furrowed as if trying to come up with an answer. "I mean, I wasn't drunk. And there wasn't a bet or anything. So technically speaking, Craiger is out ten bucks."

"ARGH!" I pick up a stiletto out of my closet and chuck it at the floor. "Technically speaking? What does that even mean?" I shake my head and try to think. "So, you weren't drunk, and there wasn't a bet? But that means . . . you did sign up on a whim."

He clears his throat. "I, uh . . . sort of, I guess."

"You guess. Are you saying you don't even know why you signed up?"

Tony licks his lips and opens his mouth as if he's going to say something, then huffs and closes his mouth, giving a helpless shrug instead.

I groan. "Who does that? Signs up to get married as a lark? I can't believe this is happening. Except, wait, I can. Because this is you we're talking about. Master of juvenile behavior."

He winces at my harsh words, but I don't care. I bury my face in my hands. Who am I kidding? This is my fault. I should never have expected a guy like him to take marriage seriously.

Every morning when I sneak into the living room to find him ass up, face squished against a pillow, and drool pooling beneath one cheek, my guard comes down. With his fan of dark lashes and no devilish smirk to distract from his looks, he reminds me of a little boy. Or at least a more innocent, darker, and more handsome version of Mr. Clean. And that, combined with the cooking, suckered me into believing this whole thing could work out.

I'm so stupid. So naïve. At this rate I really will end up like . . .

I flinch. Nope. Not going there.

Anger flares again. I welcome the hot flame in my chest by picking up another shoe from the floor of the walk-in closet and launching it as hard as I can into the carpet. The wedge bounces and skitters across the floor until it smacks the wall.

Tony sidesteps and holds up both hands. "I know this sounds bad?"

"You think?" Damn him. Damn. Him.

And damn me. I toss my head, blowing a loose curl out of my face at the same time. Time for him to take some responsibility. Time to make the admission. I close my eyes and count to five while inhaling deeply, until I'm sure I can communicate without massacring my own shoes. "What do you think makes it sound bad?"

"Does that deep breathing stuff really work?" He straightens to his full height when he asks the question. I mirror the motion and growl a curse, and he has the good grace to flush. He toys with a bottle of perfume on my dresser, ducking his head and glancing up at me through his lashes. "Look. I'm an idiot. We both know it because I don't hide it. Hell, even Mason knows it, and he can't even wipe his own ass without someone around for quality control."

I hesitate, the image of Mason and Tony curled up together on the couch whittling away at my anger because I've never seen that side of him before. With Mason, he's a caregiver, a family man, a man capable of giving a shit, and that tempting little fantasy draws me in. I'm a fish on his hook. I want a family, kids, the whole shebang. Not even just one kid, but multiple. Growing up as an only child was lonely as hell. I want to give my kids built-in playmates. That way, if anything ever goes wrong, they'd at least have each other. I thought the program was my chance to get moving on that goal, but now I'm right back at ground zero. It's almost cruel, the way Tony leads me into believing we have a real shot at a future together one moment, and then yanks the illusion away the next.

My arms tighten around myself, a subconscious search for comfort. "You're an ass. Half the battle is admitting the problem. But how am I supposed to make this work when I know you signed up as a joke?" The words make my stomach hurt. And then a horrifying thought enters my head. "Oh my God, did you even answer the questions correctly?" Because if not . . . that would explain *sooo* much.

And would also mean we were completely fucked as a couple, because the program would have matched us based on false information.

Tony gives an emphatic shake of his head. "No! I promise. I answered everything as honestly as I could."

His admission is not much, but I'll take what I can get at this point. A tiny portion of the cramp in my lungs eases. Okay, he'd signed up as a whim. But it's a done deal now. And maybe, if the committee matched us up, we still had a shot at making this work. However minuscule that shot might be.

While I'm processing this new information, Tony edges toward me until we're both inside of the closet. He's eating up all the space, and I inhale the spicy scent of his cologne. He moves in as if he can drive his sincerity home with proximity alone. "Trust me, I need this situation to succeed. If we call it quits before the final meeting with the review board, I could lose my job. And I'd definitely be kissing my chances at Officer Candidate School goodbye."

I'd been staring sightless in the general vicinity of his chest, but after he speaks, my head whips back so I can look him in the eye, because I damned sure didn't read that in the contract. "Is this another joke? Because if so, I can't be responsible for my actions."

He throws his hands up. "No joke, I promise. Believe me, I wish it was." He glances aside and his jaw clenches in an uncharacteristic way.

This is another side of Tony I've never met. Brooding. Contemplative. Dare I say, thoughtful? Until today, I wasn't sure he was capable of many modes beyond goofy and annoying. Part of me wants to reach out and lay a hand against the tense line of his shoulder, but I curl my fingers into my fist instead. He doesn't deserve my comfort yet. He still has some explaining to do.

Tony meets my gaze once more, his brown gaze blazing with determination. "Redding doesn't believe I'll be dedicated enough to make it as an officer candidate. And this is the yardstick he's measuring my dedication against. So if I fuck this up, I'm out. I've been busting my ass to get this commendation. I *need* us to work. For a year. Then we can go our separate ways."

My pulse slows while my mind grasps for the significance of his revelation. Holy shit. His job is on the line if this marriage implodes? That's too much pressure. On him. On me. On us. And then the second part sinks in. A year. He's planning on asking for the annulment. Indignant anger burns my throat. Okay, so yeah, ever since I'd seen Tony's name displayed as my matched partner on the official papers, I'd been questioning how I could possibly make this arrangement last. But that didn't mean I couldn't take his lack of commitment to me personally.

Tears gather at the corners of my eyes. "What if I want to stay together for longer than a year?"

Tony's Adam's apple bobs when he swallows. "We both know that will never happen but sure, if things are going great, we can figure it out then, okay?" His voice softens. "Look, I'm sorry to unload everything on you like this, but it's gonna be okay. We'll work it out."

He takes my hand tenderly in his, and this surprisingly sweet side of him does a number on my senses. The knot in my throat eases up. Meanwhile, his touch causes every nerve to dance along the length of my arm. "I promise, I'm taking this all seriously, even when it seems like I'm not. The team is my family. If I'm discharged, I don't just lose everything I've been working for over the last few years, I lose them too."

I open my mouth to tell him he should have more faith in people he claims to consider family, that the others wouldn't shun him just because he was no longer a SEAL, but their reaction really isn't the point. Tony's sense of self is tied to being a team's guy. Without it, I'm not sure if he would even know how to belong with the others anymore, regardless of how understanding they may be. On top of that, being dishonorably discharged, especially after having such a prolific career, would follow him the rest of his life.

Mierda.

That's a lot, right there. And there's nothing like being weighted down under the additional pressure of his expectations. But I'm going to try my best not to let that show. Because right now, Tony knows who he is and what he wants. I don't want to be the person who inadvertently threatens to make him lose that identity. Not when I willingly signed up for this program on my own. "Okay, fine. You need to make this work. I want to make this work. So looks like the two of us need to start trying to make that happen. Hey, what a novel idea! Putting some effort into making a marriage successful. Just know I'm not doing this just for you. I have some pride, and I refuse to be known from here on out as that pathetic woman who ended up with an annulment in under a month."

No, I'm not being completely candid with him, but why would I bare my soul right now when he just told me he planned on bailing when a year was up? I have my work cut out for me, on multiple fronts, but I have my ways. And an entire year to get Tony to change his mind. Good thing I'm stubborn.

In the meantime, the last thing I want is for him to think I'll jump to do his bidding any time he tells me a sob story. And now that I have some leverage over him to act his age, damn right I'm going to use it to my advantage because I want a real husband. "I know for a fact Jim will kill you before Redding can. And neither of us wants to deal with the guilt of what will happen to Taya emotionally if her husband gets locked up for your murder. But you need to meet me halfway, which means you need to take our arrangement seriously. Agreed?"

His eyes narrow as a shit-eating grin splits his face. "What are you—?"

Oh God. I'm so screwed.

I inhale a slow breath and close my eyes for a second, then exhale and straighten my spine as I meet my husband's gaze. "We need rules. Real rules. Not boner rules, although, okay, maybe there's some overlap. Like, first of all, I want monogamy from the very start."

"Agreed." He nods and then winks. "Especially since that implies there'll be boners in your future. My boners."

I raise my eyes to the ceiling and glare. How? How did I

get matched with him? "Second, I expect my husband to act like he's married around the opposite sex. So nothing like what happened with that nurse." I'm trying not to snap at him as my mind drifts back to that day in the hospital. "You know, the one you were spitting game at two minutes after you hit on me."

He stares at me and I spot the exact moment realization hits him like a smack in the face. His eyes grow comically wide and his mouth gapes. "That wasn't—I wasn't—"

"I saw you." If nothing else—aside from a glare that would have put a weaker man on the ground—my tone dares him to deny it again. "You used the same lines, Tony."

"Okay, so no flirting with anyone besides you."

He waggles his eyebrows and my fists clench, but I don't know if I'm mad at him for still playing the part of the jokester . . . or at myself for allowing his warm brown eyes to suck me in. Just to be safe, I rip my gaze away from his. Before he can draw me any further under his spell.

He crosses his arms and broadens his stance. "What else?"

I clear my throat, consider telling him not to flirt with me either, and somehow, in the process, find my gaze drawn back to him. I look him up and down, slowly assessing the muscles hidden beneath his clothes. His eyes darken with flash of hunger. I lick my bottom lip, an unconscious invitation, and he sucks in a deep breath and looks away.

I blink rapidly. What the hell? I'm practically going green light and he's riding the brake. Not that I'm going to let things go further than that yet, but still. A girl has her pride. I take a step back, my arms folding across my chest, and swallow past the lump in my throat. If I'm going to persuade him he wants a real wife, I need him fully in the game. "I want a better ring."

Every muscle in my body goes rigid. I've never been materialistic, don't even care about the plain gold ring the military gave us. But Tony needs something *to do* rather than something *not to do*.

My husband takes a step back, eyes wide. "What?"

I hold up my hand to make sure the gold band around my finger is visible. "This generic bullshit isn't going to cut it. I'll email you the link to the one I want." This is all coming right out of my ass because I'd never even looked at rings before. But I keep going like the Energizer Bunny of confessors.

"When I imagined getting married, I . . ." My throat tightens and, out of nowhere, my eyes grow moist. When I imagined getting married, I visualized something entirely different from the situation I find myself in now. I promised myself I wouldn't end up like my mother, in a revolving door of marriages, but here I am, barely married a couple of weeks and already terrified that this partnership will end in a divorce. And after discovering the reasons Tony signed up, I'm even more frightened of letting my guard down with him. I've seen my mother's hurt and disappointment over the years. I don't want that for myself.

I swallow past the lump in my throat. There were no

guarantees when I signed up for this. I rolled the dice as surely as if I'd been gambling in a Vegas casino. I'd just been praying that the house odds would work in my favor. But despite his shortcomings, Tony didn't force my hand here. I joined the game all on my own. We both did. Now I owe it to both of us to see this relationship through. And maybe as time goes on, he'll dismiss the idea of an annulment.

But I'm scared he won't and that I'll never find someone to love me the way Bear loves Marge or Jim loves Taya. If this experiment with Tony crashes and burns, I'll have to lick my wounds and decide if marriage is even for me. I don't want to be a sixty-year-old woman still falling in love at the drop of a hat and turning my life upside down on the off chance that the next "I love you" would be the one to stick.

I wince at the thought of my mother and what she'd say about an annulment. Not because she'd get to throw that stone, but because she dreams of a family for me. I've seen her eyes light up when she talks about grandbabies. I swallow a mouthful of bile and close my eyes.

Tony walks closer to me and brushes his fingers against my cheek. I flinch and start to pull away, but the wall brings me up short, and his fingers delve beneath the heavy weight of my hair to curl along the back of my neck. He urges me closer, and his warmth seeps into me, along with his delicious scent. I forget about my worries for a moment, instead focusing on the butterflies flapping in my gut like they're trying to work their way out through my skin. And my hands are trembling. It's been too long since I've been with a man and longer still since I've known this kind of anticipation. That's probably why I'm acting like some timid virgin, leaning into his touch and parting my lips with a sigh. Okay. Maybe some of my body's reaction has to do with Tony himself. There's no denying that my husband is hot, especially now that he's given me hints that there's more to him beneath that cocky grin and obnoxious mouth.

"Maybe we should get to work on making this marriage work right now?" he says huskily.

A strange warmth suffuses my chest at his words, but I refuse to give in. Then his brown eyes lock with mine, studying every inch of my face and hesitating on my mouth, making it hard to breathe. His grip on my nape tightens along with something low in my belly. I exhale shakily and reach up to grip his wrist.

Hormones. Must be hormones.

Right?

I slip out of his grip, under his arm, and back into the bedroom to fill my lungs with air. Already, I want to go back to him, to bask in the heat of his body. The intensity of the need scares the shit out of me, and I stuff my shaky hands in my jean pockets.

This is bad.

Hormones or not, I can't afford to get attached. Not so soon. Tony might have a lot to lose, but as he already told me, our union has an expiration date. I need to go into this next year with my eyes wide open. I'm not my mom. I can't deal with recurrent heartbreaks. I suffered enough from hers over the years as it is.

"Inara? Any more rules?"

I swallow. "We treat each other with respect. Clean up after ourselves, help the other person out when we can, and communicate if there's a problem. Like a real marriage."

"Okay," he agrees, but the way he licks his lips and his gaze travels down my body tells me he's just as distracted as I am.

This won't do. I need space.

"I'm hungry." My voice is too bright, too cheery, and my smile is so fake, I probably look like a painted clown.

He's standing in the doorway of the closet, his hands gripping the top of the door frame above his head. The muscles in his forearms bulge and the edge of his *Walking Dead* T-shirt rises to expose the smooth bit of skin hidden between his navel and the top of his low-hanging sweatpants. Holy shit. That is a lot of man.

My gaze homes in on the deep V disappearing beneath the band of his boxers, and suddenly I'm not sure if I was talking about burgers and fries. I glance up at Tony, whose small smile adds to the overall effect, and I grit my teeth against the burst of desire. Oh no. I'm not ready to go down that path right now. Even if the path in question is sexy as hell.

I lick suddenly dry lips and then curse myself. I need to get my mind out of the gutter.

A faint noise comes from the other room, interrupting me with the distraction I need. Craiger! Mason! I'd almost forgotten they were here. Thank God.

"I'm hungry . . . for food," I clarify quickly, though not quickly enough, if the self-satisfied way he folds his arms across his chest and flexes his biceps is anything to go by.

"Oh yeah?" There's nothing casual in his tone or that gaze swiping up and down my body, leaving me hot and flushed and needy and breathless.

I nod toward the door. "But first, I need to take a shower. I also want to get out of my work clothes and find something more comfortable." I scoff when his eyes go wide. "Not like that. I mean sweats. Or shorts."

He grunts and has that look. Like he's undressing me mentally. And it's hot as fuck. I'm one short second from throwing him onto my bed and ripping his clothes off. Like I said, it's been a while. In desperation, I shove him toward the door. If we stay in this room any longer, I can't promise I won't do something I'll regret. Company or not.

"What about food?"

"Check the fridge, give Lucas and his son some options, and I'll make dinner as soon as I'm showered."

Jesus, how much time does it take a man with legs that long to leave a room? Finally, he shuts the door behind him and I can breathe. In. Out. Over and over. Eventually, my hormones quiet down to a manageable level. My shower is quick and a bit cooler than usual. I still have visions of naked Tony in my head, but I can pull it together.

When I step into the living room, Lucas and Mason are sitting on the couch. "Where's Tony?"

Lucas points toward the kitchen and for the first time I notice the scent of roasting garlic wafting through the house. Eyes narrowed, I follow my nose to find him standing at the stove, a panful of herbs already sizzling over one of the burners. "What are you doing?"

He shrugs without turning to look at me, pulls a knife and cutting board out, and sets it on the counter next to the sink. "You've been on your feet all day. Figured you could use some help."

My heart melts, just a little. The guy can do a one-eighty from being a jerk to a thoughtful partner so fast, that it makes my head spin. He places several strips of raw chicken on the cutting board and when his deft fingers go to work, slicing, chopping, holding the knife like he belongs on an episode of *Top Chef*, a soft whimper escapes my lips. Then I fake a cough to cover. "I don't mind cooking."

"Then we can do it together."

When I don't respond right away, he glances up. His expression is blank, neutral. We're together, at least for now. For better or for worse. Companionship is a good start. In time, maybe that can grow into respect. Affection. Eventually, a little midnight magic. I can make this work and show him that this marriage can survive longer, that having a partner like me is worth it. I roll the sleeves of my baggy sweatshirt up to my elbows and hip bump him out of the way. "Move over. You're doing it wrong."

"First of all, there's no 'wrong way' to cut chicken." Tony shoots me a look but moves over just enough to give me access to the other half of the cutting board. "Second, I'm pretty sure I know what I'm doing."

"Oh, really?" I pull a knife from the rack on the counter and begin to dice.

"I am a fabulous cook." He finishes with his half of the chicken and uses the point of the knife to steal back some of the pile I'm working on. "Probably better than you. You *can* cook, can't you?"

My mouth drops open and I turn to look up at him. "You're a cocky son of a bitch."

He winks. "Admit it, wifey, you love it."

My laughter is breathless because there's a part of me that does, in fact, love his confidence, his refusal to find even a single fuck to give because he's too busy doing and saying exactly what he wants, when he wants. It's the part of his personality that I envy.

We're standing almost as close as we'd been in the closet. I swallow hard but don't turn away from those big brown eyes. Instead, for a sweet, blissful moment, my doubts take a back seat while I play one of the most harmful mental games in existence.

What if . . . Tony isn't only in this to keep his job?

What if . . . we'd met under different, kinder circumstances?

What if . . . this really is the beginning of a real-life happily ever after?

"I'm hungry, Uncle Tony, how long before dinner?" Mason's voice is a bucket of cold water.

"Give us about thirty minutes, bud." Tony nudges me with his shoulder.

I snap back to reality and take a step back, camouflaging the motion by pretending to check the garlic and green onions sizzling on the stove. *Mami* is right, damn her. I'm a romantic at heart, just like her, and if I'm not careful, Anthony Martinez is gonna end up one heartbreak in a long line of many.

CHAPTER SEVEN

Tony

IS IT JUST my imagination or is the couch getting more comfortable? Almost as soon as the question occurs to me, my leg cramps and I roll off the edge of the torture device and onto the floor with a curse. The setback does nothing to diminish my good mood, and I bound to my feet without once insulting the couch's mother or intelligence.

And who's getting credit for my good mood? Inara. My beautiful, multifaceted wife.

All night, I dreamed of touching her, kissing her, hearing those little whimpers at the back of her throat as I explore every curve and plane of her body. I expected to spend another night struggling to turn my mind off, but sleep had come quickly and the dreams were a bonus.

And while I'm tempted to stick around and make a nuisance of myself, since Inara doesn't have to work today, I need some time away before I do something stupid, like get down on my hands and knees and beg for the kiss—or more—she's been denying me. I head toward the bathroom just as Inara is coming down the hall and we stop short, momentarily blocking one another.

"Morning." She's fresh-faced, in shorts and a tank top, as if she's going for a run.

One side step and she brushes past me. I twist to glance over my shoulder and it's a sight that's going to make the shower ten degrees cooler than I planned. That woman has a walk that could make a priest sigh, and there's a little purple butterfly tattoo on her left shoulder that I'm dying to kiss.

Twenty minutes later, I have yet another cold shower under my belt, have folded the blankets and put them away, and I'm now ready for a few hours at the gym. Sweats, a T-shirt, and gym shoes. My mini-break from training has been nice, but I can't afford to fall out of shape, unless I want my ass handed to me during combat exercises. And I most definitely don't want to be the weakest link.

I'm almost to the front door when my mother-in-law, wearing a yellow sundress and a full face of makeup, calls my name while simultaneously knocking. I open the door to find her standing on the porch, cradling two square aluminum baking dishes to her chest. They're both covered in foil, but the scent wafting my way is still heavenly.

I bend down and kiss the woman's cheek, catching the newly risen sun peeking from behind a cloud. "Let me carry those for you." I reach out to take the containers, which she gratefully pushes toward me. "Inara is in her, um, our room. Do you want to come in?"

"*Gracias*. I'm in a rush but wanted to drop these off. One of them is for you, but save some for Inara. I know how hungry you men can get for your sweets." She shakes a finger in my direction. "The other is for Bennett, and he'll tell me if they come up short."

I bite back a chuckle. Maybe Inara will be just as feisty thirty years from now. The grin melts right off my face a second later. No need to get carried away and envision Inara in thirty years because I won't be around for that.

I need a distraction from the weird pang in my chest. "Who's Bennett?"

Mrs. Ramirez cocks her head and frowns. "Inara's father. Her stepfather anyway. She hasn't told you about him?"

I grunt and shake my head, wishing my wife and I were as close as her mother assumed. "I wouldn't have pegged you as the type to bake flan for a man you're in the middle of divorcing."

She laughs again, a more full-bodied sound of amusement. "No, Bennett is number three. We've been divorced for years. He's the only one of the lot I would bake for. He and Inara have always been thick as thieves." Her brows furrow when her gaze lands on Inara's tactical boots. "You know, it's smart the two of you skipped the big expensive wedding and just went for the civil service. My daughter has to be good with her money since she only works at the restaurant so she could run around in the woods."

The note of disapproval in Inara's mom's voice makes me bristle. "You mean search and rescue? The program where Inara risks her own safety to help people who are lost and potentially in danger? I think that's a pretty worthwhile reason for giving up some extra salary, don't you?"

She sighs. "*Sí,* of course. It's just . . . I worry. It's hard surviving on your own these days." Mrs. Ramirez rests her hand on my forearm. "But now she has you, so at least she's not alone."

My throat tightens. It's not my place to mention the program to her mother, or the fact that Inara and I will only be married for a year. Especially when I haven't told my own family. When my gaze lands on my mother-in-law, my stomach flips once more. Four husbands, four failed marriages. And I would bet Inara was the one picking up the pieces after vacating her ringside seat to the failures. I can't imagine what it must have been like for her—practical, passionate, Inara—to go through all of that as a kid.

"Bennett and his church group are rebuilding houses for the some of the families who lost their homes during the last tornado. Whenever Inara gets free time, like today, she likes to head over to the worksite to help out." She nods to the pan I'm holding. "I like to assist where I can, every now and again. Speaking of, if you're not busy, why don't you swing by for a few hours? I'm sure Inara would appreciate the support."

Not a bad idea. And it's not like I have other Sunday plans outside of going to the gym.

Mrs. Ramirez waves goodbye and drives off only minutes before Inara comes into the hallway. She glances from the pans to me. "Where'd those come from?"

"Your mom," I say, then head into the kitchen to place

one of the trays into the refrigerator. "She was in a rush, but she told me you were going to help your stepfather today."

"Oh." Inara ducks her head and busies herself putting on her boots.

Grabbing the second tray of flan, I slide my feet into my own shoes and grab my keys. When Inara looks up, I shoot her a beaming grin. "I'm going with you. I want to help."

I could inform her about my background in construction, assure her I probably know more about building houses than a licensed contractor, thanks to the work I did both before and after I joined the military, but instead, I follow Inara to her car and slide into the passenger seat placing the pan of dessert on my lap. She doesn't try to get rid of me and simply backs the car out of the driveway and heads toward the worksite.

Thirty minutes later, we are in a neighborhood where trees line the road and rise behind the newly built and skeletal remains of the houses like silent sentries keeping guard over the middle-class families that had laid claim to this place. There's a school bus stop sign at the end of the road next to a terminal made from an old school bus, complete with bench and rain guards. The tornado must've shredded pieces of the shell as a bright-yellow panel stabbed through a wall across the street. A house two away from the bus stop hadn't been touched, and a woman is watering a grouping of plants as we drive past.

Such random devastation.

A team of volunteers is already hard at work when Inara

pulls onto the street where the church group is working. A red dumpster the size of a semi-trailer is stationed in the driveway of one house and two men are hauling a piece of furniture to tip over the top. A woman carries a window over and drops it in while I survey the debris field. There are pieces of the roof, both collapsed inside the house and on the lawn. Shingles lie beside a tree that looks about a hundred years old, and a group of workers is sawing away at it with a couple of chainsaws and some smaller handsaws. And still another group is busy assembling a pile of what I presume is salvaged goods from the house next door.

Inara and I pick our way through the debris of the house with the dumpster to the gaping hole in the wall where the front door should have been. Stud framing and blocking have been blown to smithereens in the center of the wall. Lumber lies everywhere, and the two-by-sixes on the sides that appeared to be spaced at sixteen inches on center are folded in on themselves like dominoes. Thank God the front wall wasn't load bearing; otherwise, there wouldn't be a second floor right now. I'm relieved that this can be repaired—even just a little bit. The inside is more organized than the outside, but 10d nails stick out at every which angle, and I adjust my posture and stance so I don't get poked. All the furniture and personal belongings have been cleared away and volunteers are working to tear out non-load-bearing walls. Above us, another group works on the roof.

I'm not sure what I expected Bennett to be like, but the

nerd Inara introduces me to isn't it. He's painfully thin, with thick bifocals and a shock of bright-red hair sticking out, as though he hasn't yet been introduced to brush or barber. He reminds me of what the love child of Chucky and a mad scientist would look like. And try as I might—which I do—I can't picture him with my mother-in-law, not until I shake his hand and see the sharp intelligence shining from behind those glasses, hear the easy calm in his voice, and watch the confident way he directs the members of his church. Then things start to make a lot more sense.

"I didn't know you were getting married." There's no censure in his voice, but Inara looks away, pained and stammering.

"It . . . I . . . I mean, we . . ." She glances at me and I nod, slinging my arm over her shoulder and tucking her in close to my body.

I straighten and meet the man's gaze. "It's my fault, sir. I didn't want to take the chance she'd change her mind. Plus, with my trainings and deployments, it's hard to make any concrete plans." She shoots me a grateful smile for covering for her and lays her hand over my heart. This, I could get used to.

Bennett chuckles and nods. "I remember feeling like that. The second I met Dana, I knew she was the one. I just wish it could have stuck."

Inara tries to slide away, but I'm a lean, mean, clinging machine. After talking to her mom, all I want to do is reassure her. Which is silly, since I don't plan on "sticking" around long-term, as Bennett phrased it. Still, I can show her that I'm here for now. I tighten my arm around her and stroke my thumb over her arm until she calms, then I lift the dessert pan Mrs. Ramirez gave me. "Flan?"

Bennett grins and takes the container before putting Inara and me to work on clearing the backyard. When the storm moved through, the heavy rains flooded this part of town and spawned a tornado that left a path of destruction. There are downed trees, broken fences, and debris in every conceivable corner and cranny. A bike is hanging upside down from a now-dead power line.

Inara takes a deep breath, absorbs the chaos for a heartbeat, and then dives in. Armed with gloves and plastic bags, we spend the first few hours gathering trash and dragging random shit to the dumpster. The sun climbs steadily and I'm sweaty enough to wring my shirt out. I strip it off and hang it over the porch railing, then glance up and meet Inara's gaze. Her arms are laden with pots and pans that had been blown from the kitchen into the vegetable garden. I'm about to ask her if she needs some help carrying them to the front, but she isn't looking at me.

Not in the eye anyway.

Instead, she's studying my body, gaze dragging over my shoulders and across my chest. Dipping lower with such propriety that it's like a physical touch. Blood surges straight to my cock and my stomach tightens with hunger. I stand still for several agonizing seconds, then she glances up at me from beneath her lashes and drags her teeth across her bottom lip.

Then she winks.

And strolls the fuck away.

Desire swims through my veins, but it isn't enough. More than once, Inara's gaze runs over me, each time bringing about another wave of heat.

Since I suck at focusing on my current task, I throw back on my shirt and search for Bennett to find out if there is something else I can focus on. Luckily, the house next door isn't as damaged and when asked if I'd be willing to help retile the upstairs bathroom I jump at the opportunity. The work is backbreaking but familiar, and soon my mind goes blank as muscle memory guides my hands.

"Where'd you learn to do all that?"

A part of me has been waiting for her to come find me, the same part that recognized her light tread as she came up the now-bare wood stairs, and the sound of her voice when she sighed on the top landing. I look over my shoulder to find her covered in a fine layer of dust. I clench my fingers to resist the urge aching inside me. I want to touch her, to lay claim to all those unexplored crevices her tank top and jeans aren't quite hiding. Despite the dust, the clean scent of her shampoo lingers in the air and my mind wanders, and I turn away before she notices the desire in my eyes.

"My dad." I'm so intent on bringing myself back under control that I don't consider the words.

She kneels next to me and hands me a tile. "Tell me about him?"

When I don't respond right away, she nudges me with her shoulder. She holds another ceramic square while I measure and spread the grout. We fall into an instinctive rhythm, as if we've been working together our whole lives. "Come on. You know about my dad."

"Bennett?"

"Well, technically, all of my stepdads helped raise me, but I've always been closest to Bennett. So, tell me something about your dad. You've met both of my parents. The least you can do is give me the intel on yours."

The request isn't outrageous, so why the hell am I ready to run for the mountains? Hell, I've faced enemies armed with rocket launchers. Surely I can handle a little heart-to-heart about my family. I focus on the task at hand as if placing the ceramic squares just right will somehow make the words easier to speak. "My father was a contractor. He owned his own company for a while, and I worked with him after school and during the weekends."

"The heir to the family business."

The disappointing heir. "Basically."

"So, how'd you end up in Special Forces?"

I shrug and it's awkward and jerky. "The company was always his thing, not mine." There aren't enough mental pep talks in the world to get me to elaborate, so I don't. "Two of my sisters took over the company."

Inara laughs and then pulls a face. "*Mami* would have killed me if I ever told her I was interested in 'men's work' when I was growing up. Hell, she practically had a panic attack when she found out about search and rescue." Her eyes are sparkling though, so it doesn't seem like her mom's disapproval left any lasting scars.

My heart lurches, the pain sudden and fierce. I don't talk about my mom. Ever. I suck in a greedy lungful of breath and hope I'm not swaying from lack of oxygen to my brain.

"Tony?"

Her tone is soft and I latch on to it, forcing my mind to turn away from the shadows lingering at the edge, and smile. "What do you want to do for dinner?"

"I'm sorry?" Inara blinks and shakes her head as if I've just asked her what to name our firstborn. Erm, *her* firstborn. Who will definitely be sired by a man who isn't me.

At the thought of what that would entail, a low growl rumbles up my throat. I give my head a quick shake. What the fuck is wrong with me? Must be too much sun.

"Dinner." Talking about food is safe ground, though admittedly anything would have been preferable to discussing my relationship with my parents. Or thinking about her making a baby with some random guy. "I'm too tired to cook. Maybe we could go out tonight?"

"Like a date?" She gushes in an exaggerated Southern drawl and an eye-rolling flutter of her lashes.

One side of my mouth hikes up in a lopsided smile. "Yup."

I don't undermine the request with a joke or cheapen it with a pick-up line or some bit of inferred innuendo. Instead, I study her with the same intensity she had outside.

Her gaze skirts around the room, and she tucks a curl behind one ear. If I didn't know better, I would say Mrs. Martinez is a bit bashful at the idea of dating her husband.

If I didn't know better.

But I do.

"Yeah, okay."

Her answer lifts a weight off my chest and I'm ready to give her whatever she wants. Hell, far as I'm concerned, we could head to a McDonald's drive-thru as long as she's in the car beside me. "Anywhere you want. You pick."

I stop working and sit back on my heels, my complete focus on my wife. And she's beautiful, even covered in dust. A curl flops back over her forehead and I'm itching to brush it back, but I sit and stare, mesmerized until she tilts her head and smiles. "I wanna sing."

Somehow that little curl has ended up like silk between my fingertips. I study it in silence for what may have been an eternity while Inara holds her breath. Something as sweet as it is dangerous has taken up some pretty valuable real estate in the center of my chest and I don't dare examine it because there's a part of me that already knows what I'll see.

"Well, all right." I tuck the curl behind her ear, fingers brushing the delicate curve where a small silver stud sits before I pull away. "I know just the place."

CHAPTER EIGHT

Inara

I TRY NOT to glare at the small redhead standing on stage, but it takes a lot more strength than I expect not to shoot her the evil eye. Marge had to be the first of the group to volunteer to get on stage, and she's launched into a rousing rendition of an old Spice Girls tune that has the entire bar on its feet, clapping their hands and singing along.

My fingers clench into small fists as my gaze falls on my darling husband.

Nine people isn't a date. It's a posse.

What was the sweet and attentive guy who was tiling the bathroom floor with me this afternoon thinking when he asked me out? I hoped it was a sign we might go the distance as a couple, that he was changing his stance. Instead, he invited all his friends on our *date*.

I huff and glance around The Rift. The place isn't nearly as nice as Shaken & Stirred, but the sketch factor is part of its charm. It's dark, and even though nobody smokes anymore, there's a haze lingering in the air. The bar is long and made of reclaimed wood and old bar tin, and the booths

MATCHED

and tables are some sort of glossy wood with postcards glazed into the tops and there's a lot of dark leather. It's the kind of place bachelor parties go after the strip club. Not couples who want to be alone.

Maybe that's the problem. Maybe it's not a couple who wants to be alone—just me.

Although, in Tony's defense, it's my own fault we're here. *I want to sing.* I should have been honest and told him what I really wanted: some honest-to-God alone time on a date with him so we could try to get to know each other better. But I didn't and now we're in the one place a girl can get her Sunday night sing on while sipping alcoholic beverages from tin cans.

Craiger and his date, a skinny brunette named Alexus, who seems nice enough, but I fear has more boobs than brain mass, are all too happy to play along and are already on their third canned vodka. I'm not sure why the guy dates the women he does. Nor do I want to know what Mason's mom must be like.

We're sitting in a padded booth, a suspicious amount of cans littering our table in addition to the songbook and several glasses of water. The bar is packed for a Sunday night, but The Rift is one of the few bars in town with themed nights. It doesn't have the kind of view patrons enjoy at S&S, and the food is shit, so the owners adapted in order to keep people coming back. As a result of this winning formula, the small indoor and outdoor space is teeming with karaoke enthusiasts, and the conversations around us consist

95

largely of song suggestions and random, quiet performance critiques.

"This is the dumbest shit I've ever seen."

I glance at the man beside me and wince. Jim's miserable, but Taya is having a ball. He's glowering. She's giggling. Poor guy. I pat his knee and lean in so he can hear me over the sound of Marge's soulful crooning. "Ten bucks if you can convince Bear to get on stage."

Jim's eyes narrow. "What song?"

"Something that'll make him feel like a woman."

He looks from me to Bear and back to me, his eyes bright with challenge, and nods. He pushes his big body away from our table and strides to where Bear stands at the edge of the stage, waiting for Marge to wrap up.

"What was that about?"

I settle back beside Tony and smile. "Nothing much. I just found a way to make this suck a little bit less for him."

Tony shrugs and takes a sip of his drink. "I'm surprised he even agreed to come."

I shake my head. "Why'd you invite them in the first place?"

He looks at me, eyes wide, but he isn't getting out of this one. I want an answer and I'll wait for it.

"Figured you'd be more comfortable with everyone here." His voice is low, and if I didn't know better, I might be convinced he's embarrassed.

"I was kind of looking forward to it being just us." The words slip out before I can recall them, and my cheeks flame.

Damn the sun. This must be heat stroke. Or an overtired brain. Or maybe just being around Tony all day.

His eyes widen before he drops his gaze to his drink and fiddles with his glass. "Sorry." He pauses to clear his throat. "You said you wanted to sing, so I wanted to make that happen. Figured it'd be easier on both of us with friendly faces around."

"I understand." Except I don't. Not at all. Is this his kind way of giving me a warning not to get too attached? To keep things nice and easy? Or am I reading too much into his casual words?

At the end of the day, I did say I wanted to sing. And it was nice of him to accommodate my wishes. As I study him, my fingers tighten around my own glass. This is the problem, right here. Tony Martinez is turning out to be way more decent than I ever imagined was possible. This man takes out the trash so I don't have to, mows the lawn without being asked, does laundry like a boss, and even folds and puts the clothes neatly away. And he cooks. Cleans like a neurotic housekeeper. Cuddles his friends' children while they sleep. I didn't give him enough credit before and now that I am, he's growing on me.

A lot.

"What?" he asks as I continue to study him.

I shrug. "You're not what I expected, that's all."

His brows lift. "Oh yeah? What were you expecting? Maybe this?" Then he pulls the most obnoxious face I've ever seen.

"Yes. Exactly that."

He laughs and tugs me back toward him, closer than before. It registers in the back of my mind that Jim somehow managed to get Bear on stage and they're singing an old Britney song while the place roars, but not even that's enough to make me turn away from the heat crackling to life between Tony and me.

His gaze sears my skin, lighting up every cell in my body.

I lick my lips. Or maybe I do know what I want. I simply need to decide to take that first step.

"I was joking," he says. "This is the part where you laugh."

As if they have a life of their own, my fingers trail from his hand to his forearm and to the edge of his sleeve to slip under. His muscle twitches, but I couldn't pull away if the whole place caught on fire. "I don't feel like laughing."

"What are you in the mood for?"

Heat surges just below my belly. I open my mouth to respond only to pause when Trevor Graves clears his throat awkwardly from the wall end of the booth. I glare at him. "Kind of having a moment here, pal."

He winces and nods. "Yeah, sorry, but uh, I need a bathroom?"

I sigh and swallow my mounting frustration. It's not Trevor's fault that my hormones picked a terrible moment to go into overdrive. Tony mutters under his breath, but I shove him out of the booth to make way for Graves. The newest member of the team doesn't make eye contact with either of us, but passes quickly.

Before I can turn back to Tony, though, Jim and Bear come striding back toward the table. I clench my hands together to hide my disappointment. Bear throws an arm over Marge's dainty shoulders while she hugs his middle. Envy settles in my chest, digging its way into my heart.

Jim drops into the seat, his unblinking eyes focused on Trevor. "Who invited him anyway?"

Tony grabs his drink and chugs it without stopping. Enough conversations have been had that I've figured out Jim isn't fond of the newest team member, so I follow my husband's lead in evasion and turn to Bear. "Mardi Gras beads?"

Marge laughs, jangling the set sitting around her husband's thick neck until he gently pushes her hands away. "The crowd started throwing them about halfway through the chorus."

Jim's glare isn't singularly aimed at one of us, but at us all. "You said tonight would be fun. So far I've lost five bucks, I've been publicly humiliated, and on top of that I have to deal with…*Graves*." He says the man's name like a curse, and his expression darkens. But when Taya lays a hand on his arm, the anger melts away, and he smiles.

"Five bucks?" I mouth to Marge, and she snorts and motions toward the stage.

"Bear wanted a cut if he was going to be *performing*."

I glance at the always good-natured Bear. No way would he miss the chance to drag Jim up on stage. Five bucks or not. And someday, hopefully soon, we'll all do this again, but tonight, my objective has shifted.

My gaze travels over the tantalizing shapes of my husband's shoulders and chest, and that familiar flame rekindles somewhere below my belly button. I'm horny. And I'm married. That is a perfect recipe for dragging—hopefully, it doesn't take much—my husband to bed. I want him. I want to feel him inside me. But more than that, I want to know if he can walk the walk.

And I'm ready. Really fucking ready. Because one thing that isn't going to make either of us get along better is forced celibacy for another three-hundred-plus days.

Jim, Tony, and Bear have formed their own little circle to gripe about Trevor, but I don't care. Tony has somewhere else to be and something—*someone*—else to do. I tuck myself under my husband's arm and raise my voice just enough to be heard over their bickering. "You guys should try a little harder with Graves." I ignore Jim's narrow-eyed glare. I'm not a terrorist, so I'm in no danger. "He's one of you now. All for one, one for all."

"That's *The Three Musketeers*." Tony smiles down at me and winks. "But she's right. He's one of us. And like the Musketeers took in D'Artagnan, who proved to be quite loyal, by the way, maybe we should give the kid a chance." When we all stare at him, he flushes and shrugs. "Can I help it if the chick in that one scene had amazing tits? I might've watched it a few times."

Marge groans and Taya rolls her eyes. Normally, this

would be the moment where I write Tony off, but tonight I don't. He shifts and I continue to stare. Our friends might be surprised when he exhibits a thought deeper than a puddle in a parking lot, but I've seen him sit and read, a book which I now suspect might be a copy of Dumas's musketeer tale. His intellectual shortfalls are an act. A good one, but still as pretend as unicorns and rainbow faeries. My husband works hard at keeping up his act of class clown.

I spot Trevor making his way back from the bathroom and the nervous glance he shoots all of us standing clustered together. As if he can tell he's the topic of discussion. It's as much for his benefit as mine that I start leading Tony toward the stage. He starts to give a token protest and then his eyes go wide.

"I can't sing." He hisses the words in a low, desperate whisper.

I shrug but don't slow. "Then don't. I'll do all the singing for both of us." I glance at him over my shoulder and smile. "I'm a former choir girl. Now, I belt out the oldies to blow off steam. Come sing with me."

His shoulders relax when he exhales. "My little sister likes to sing too." He's quiet for a moment. "You'd like her."

I laugh and pull him up the steps onto the stage. "Well, *mi esposo*, you'll just have to introduce us, then." I put my hand on his chest and walk him backward to the stool where performers usually sit for the slow ones. Leaning in, I press my lips against the shell of his ear. "This one's for you, babe."

I chat with the DJ tucked away in the shadows, so as not to draw attention to himself. I give him my song choice and he nods. By the time the opening bars of Amy Winehouse's "You Know That I'm No Good" start to roll through the bar, Tony is staring, brown eyes dark with what I hope is hunger for me.

I turn my back on him, gripping the mic and belting out the über-sultry opening lines to the crowd. I don't care about the people in the audience. Just the one to my right because I want him to want me as much as I want him and if this doesn't work, nothing will.

And I've got his total attention.

My heart swells and excitement stirs in my blood. And fair is fair. I walk backward and position myself between his knees, then sway us back and forth, like the couples on the dance floor. The words don't even matter anymore. His arms wrapped around my waist, his breath on my throat, the thumb stroking my belly . . . those things matter.

The music carries me away, and I turn into his body to trail my fingertips across his shoulders, down to his heart, press my breasts into his chest. "I told you I was trouble."

He shudders and grips my hips, pulling me in closer, until only clothes separate us, and his growl sends my pulse over the edge. I gasp, too distracted by the rigid curve of his cock against my hip to pay attention to the cheering crowd. We're both breathing hard and I lean back enough so that my voice doesn't get drowned out by the applause. "We should grab an Uber and go home."

"Yeah." His eyelids are at half-mast and never have I been so turned on. He helps me off the stage, careful to angle his body so I'm blocking the crowd's view of the bulge in his pants.

"I don't think you heard me." Before we make it back to the booth for our stuff, I stop and stare up at him until I have his full attention. "I said that we should go home. *Together*."

CHAPTER NINE

Tony

AFTER THAT PERFORMANCE and keeping her in front of me—which is just as much because I like her ass rubbing against my cock as it is to hide my hard-on—no one's asking questions when Inara orders our Uber. It was warm in this bar to begin with, but right now it's hotter than a damned sauna. There isn't a person in this place who doesn't understand our hurry to head somewhere more private.

But I'm nervous. Not because I'm new at this sleeping-with-people-I-hardly-know thing. Sex usually doesn't mean much and has never been a big deal for me. Just a couple of bodies taking care of business. Most of my partners have been hit and quits. But it's a new experience to go home with a woman, knowing she'll still be around the next day. There's a certain level of awkwardness attached I've never had to deal with, causing me to freeze up when we're alone outside of the bar as we wait for the car to show.

"You sure about this?" I'm not even sure who I'm talking to or that I've asked the question aloud until Inara glances at me over her shoulder.

Her hair is pushed back, and I enjoy the full view of every curve of her face. Her beauty steals my breath and she smirks as my gaze travels from her mouth and down the length of her throat to her rounded breasts.

"They say there's no such thing as a stupid question." The smirk on her face deepens and her brown eyes dance with amusement. "Not true."

Fuck nerves. I'd be an idiot to bow out now. Ever since we met, I've wanted to slide inside her. More so in the last few weeks, sleeping down the hall from her, hearing her throaty laughter, experiencing the rush of heat that accompanies every brush of her hand against mine. She's magic and perfection and . . . my wife. Somehow, though, the idea of Inara's approval is what leaves my palms sweaty and my stomach in sudden knots.

Fuck.

I'm screwed.

My mind is toying with my body. A mixture of desire and anxiety leaves me hot, then cold. My wife. The woman who's going to be my one and only for the next year. And if things aren't up to snuff this first time . . . Oh fuck. The pressure intensifies. And not the good kind of pressure. This is the weighty kind that makes it hard to breathe or think.

The Uber pulls up beside us and we climb into the back together.

My wife drops her hand to my thigh the moment the car pulls away from the curb, her fingers splayed across the wide expanse of denim. And I'm okay until she traces a nail across the inner seam of my pants. My world narrows into two warring factions: panic and desire. I stiffen in my seat. The urge to touch her in return sends blood rushing to my groin until my cock aches as it punches against my zipper. She reaches for me, chatting easily with the driver even as she grips my girth with one hand and gives an experimental squeeze.

The touch screams of ownership and a low, desperate growl rattles in my chest. I clutch the door handle tighter, hanging on for dear life. Once I start touching her, I won't be able to stop. Even as desire claws at me, I marvel at her boldness. She's talking restaurants and valet service while she strokes me through my jeans. There's an ease to the set of her shoulders and the rolling, confident way she's working my dick that speaks of familiarity. I'm not her first, and after this year is up, I know I won't be her last, but like a dumbass, I want to know what proverbial number I've pulled.

The Uber stops and we jump out, then stumble inside. I slam the front door shut, and as soon as the outside world is cut off, Inara pounces, seals our lips together, and plunges her tongue into my mouth. She makes quick work of my belt and before I can register what's going on, her slim fingers disappear beyond the waistband of my boxers.

Oh fuck.

I tear my mouth away from hers. "Bedroom."

Inara steps back, blinking up at me, and frowns slightly. Not as if she's unhappy, but more as if she's confused.

"Never pegged you as the shy type, but sure."

Me either, but somehow, Inara has that effect on me.

She grips my hand, tugging me toward the bedroom. She's single-minded and determined, and I miss her fingers wrapped around my dick, but also I'm reminded of a lamb on its way to the slaughter, and swallow hard past the lump in my throat. Overthinking is the quickest way to kill a boner, but it's too late. My dick is dying and the more I scramble to keep the poor guy blazing, the more gun-shy he becomes.

Great.

Awesome.

At this rate, I won't have to worry about whether or not Inara considers me a decent lover because I'll never manage to get that far. It's been a while since I've gotten laid, and just when I've managed to clear away one worry, another hits me.

What if I come too quick? What does she consider *too quick*? What's going to make it good for her? What's going to make me last long enough to find that out? Worrying is only making things worse and I'm one breath from hyperventilating because Inara isn't some fling, she's my wife. And deep down, I'm invested in how this all plays out. She's finally opening up to me, at least physically. If I disappoint her now, in the one way that she wants me . . .

We clear the bedroom door and Inara leans forward to capture my ear between her teeth. Her tongue delves across the sensitive skin and I shudder, my eyes rolling into the back of my head. I've always suspected Inara has more experience than me when it comes to sex, but I guess we're about to find out. And if her kiss is any indication, I'm doubly screwed. The woman can bring me to my knees with just a look and I can't even figure out where to put my hands.

Where the fuck do my hands go? Why do I even have hands? Have they always been this useless?

Her expert fingers move over the outline of my dick, stroking me through the thick material until the slightest brush of her nail across my length nearly sends me shooting out of my skin. Instinct regains control and my cock springs back to painful life. One problem down and a million more to go.

Inara doesn't touch me with hesitant fingers but jerks me close, the edges of her nails biting into skin and demanding more. She growls playfully against the side of my neck. "Why are you still wearing pants?"

"Sorry." I undo my jeans and shove them down in a rush to kick them away. Unfortunately, I am too close to Inara and our heads collide with a crack that reverberates through me. She draws back with a hiss and I clutch my forehead until the ringing goes away. I reach for Inara, who's crouched before me with her head in her hands. "You alright?"

"I'm fine." She stands and the look in her eyes is no longer sexy, so much as it is fiercely determined. I swallow hard, stumbling back as she stalks toward me. "Now let's get you naked, big guy."

A distinctly undignified yelp escapes my mouth as she starts pulling at my clothes. For a moment, my jeans are entangled with my shoes, and I have to sit bare-assed on the floor undoing my laces, so I can finish pulling my jeans and boxers off. Inara stands over me, staring like she can't quite believe what she's seeing. I have news for her. I don't quite believe it myself.

"For Christ's sake." Inara takes a deep breath, runs her hands over her face, and plops onto the bed. She regards me for a long, quiet moment. "Okay."

My eyes narrow as I shift nervously from sitting to standing. "Okay, what?"

She gets slowly to her feet and I stiffen, prepared for her disappointment. I should be better at this, so why do I feel like a teenager again? Awkward and unsure.

I jump when Inara's hand brushes mine and look up to meet her eyes. There's no disgust, no anger, no derision. Her gaze is unwavering but there's a hint of softness I've never seen before. She places her thumb on my chin to tilt my head forward the slightest bit. "Just breathe."

Without thinking, I do. Breathing deep so that our chests rise and fall in tandem. The noise in my head and the doubts in my gut slide away, and it's just me and Inara. The two of us. Alone. And before we go further, I take all of her in. I love her eyes, dark brown with hints of amber, pools I can get lost in. I want her so bad I can't speak, even when she cups my cheek with her cool hand.

"Get out of your own head." Gripping either side of my

face, she pulls me down until our lips are a breath apart. "You're here with me. Keep it that way."

Inara steps back and keeps her gaze locked on to mine as she crosses her hands and slowly—inch by slow inch—lifts the hem of her shirt.

"Holy. Shit."

She's perfect. Extraordinary. Exquisite.

She grins and chews one corner of her lip, ever the temptress. Her bra is frilly and lilac, flimsy in ways I never would have guessed she likes, but also one of the most perfect pieces of clothing I've ever seen. She unlatches the front closure and slips the straps down until it falls away. Her breasts are round and heavy with dark areolae, and glistening silver metal bars bisect the nipples.

Fuck. Me.

My fingers twitch, and I want to taste her, to roll my tongue around her nipples. My cock is heavy between my legs and I wrap my arm around her slim waist, lifting her off her feet. Lowering Inara down to the bed, I undo her jeans and begin to work them down her hips inch by inch. Her panties match her discarded bra and I take a moment to fully appreciate the contrast of delicate sexuality with the eroticism of her piercings. If I hadn't guessed it before, her nipple piercings would have been all the confirmation I needed. Sexually, she's in an entirely different league than yours truly, and it's a struggle to decide whether that's a bad thing.

On one hand, she's clearly more open-minded than I've ever been, both in the bedroom and outside of it. On the other, I have no fucking clue how to please a woman like her. And it's not like I can check the Yelp reviews for something like this. My fear of letting her down is a cold lump in my gut.

She pulls me down on top of her and presses her lips to mine and for a moment, the whispering doubts in my mind go quiet. I've never tasted anything as sweet as her mouth. She's warm honey and gingerbread, spice and sugar. My tongue delves deeper and for the first time, she moans, arching against me so that the hard points of her nipples slide across my chest. She trails eager fingers down the length of my body, across my hips, then down the sides of my thighs.

"What's this?" she whispers, toying with the scar on my left leg in a delicious way that makes me wish my entire body was made of scars.

"Bullet wound," I manage to say.

She pauses and then nips my lip. Her fingers move to the insides of my thighs and inch their way up until she can wrap her hands around my length. I shudder, bucking when she drags her thumb over the slit of my cock. Pre-cum soaks her skin and she rocks her thumb back and forth, bathing the rounded tip.

A low groan rips from my throat. I grip her hips as she kisses her way from my mouth to my chin. Her lips dance down the side of my neck, her teeth and tongue at war as she struggles to reach as much bare skin as possible. I lean in for another kiss and put my hand between her legs. God, she's soft. And wet. And still. So still I can't tell if she likes it or not, and I'm too embarrassed to admit that I have no idea what she likes. It's like I'm a virgin all over again. A virgin without a clue. So, I wiggle my fingers around, pressing my thumb against her clit and flicking until Inara mutters something that sounds suspiciously like, "*Dios mío,*" not quite under her breath.

Planting a hand against my shoulder, she shifts her weight and rolls me onto my back. Part of me is relieved to have her take the lead. Her weight is a delicious pressure against my aching cock and her breasts sway just out of reach of my mouth. Unable to help myself, I lean forward and capture one of her nipples gently between my teeth.

Inara gasps, her fists clenching in the sheets next to my head. I glance up the length of her body but can't quite read her expression. "Sorry, did I hurt you?"

With her piercing I should have considered the possibility before putting teeth on her, but I was acting purely out of instinct.

"No." She giggles and grabs the back of my head to hold me against her. I nuzzle her breasts with teeth and tongue, and she shudders helplessly above me. Oh, for the love of God, she's so hot. The faint taste of steel is overridden by the richness of her skin, and I growl against her flesh until goosebumps dance across her body.

She reaches across to the nightstand and pulls a condom from the drawer. After she tears the wrapper open, she grips my shaft and slides the condom on. My fingers grip the sheets of the bed as I fight to keep from coming. Inara holds my dick still while she slowly lowers herself down my length. I bury my face against her chest and grit my teeth as she lifts herself a few centimeters, only to come sliding back down.

A second time, and a third. I'm panting as I grip her by the waist and lift my ass off the bed as she lowers herself for the fourth time. One moment there's nothing but need and the next, my cock is working its way inside her. We gasp, breath mingling, as gravity pulls us both as close as we can get. She takes a moment to grow accustomed to my size and, with a flexing of my hips, I silently urge her to ride.

Straddling me, she grips my hips with her thighs, the muscles tensing as she works to meet my thrusts. The room is soon filled with the sound of flesh against flesh. Inara grabs my hand, pressing it against her breasts and I squeeze. She makes a noise that's half desperation, half frustration and presses closer. Chest to chest, our bodies still moving, still straining for relief, she kisses my throat and rakes nails down my shoulders, as if she needs something from me, craves it. But I don't have a clue what it is.

I hang on as long as I can, but there's only so much a man can take with a goddess riding his cock, especially when that man has been aching for this exact moment since I first laid eyes on her almost a year ago. My body clenches and then spasms with my release. "Oh, God!" Then there are no words as I ride the wave of my orgasm out.

When I come back to earth, I'm simultaneously exhausted and suffused in a warm, fuzzy sensation. "That was amazing. You're amazing. I didn't know it could be that wild."

Inara makes a strange noise in her throat as if she's choking back a laugh. Hard to know for sure because I can barely focus. I roll out of bed to make my way to the bathroom to clean up, intent on returning and satisfying my wife. But her voice chases me down the hall, the words causing both my stomach and my confidence to plummet to the ground.

"If you call that wild, we've got some work to do."

CHAPTER TEN

Inara

A S NICE AS it would be to play dumb, Taya won't allow me to get away without answering her question about my first sexual encounter with my husband. But this isn't a conversation I want to be having with anyone. I pick at the polish on my toes and grimace. Jesus. I must have been drunk when I painted them. "How was what?"

"Your one-way trip to pound town. That's what you called it the other day at work, right?" Taya lowers her voice on the other end of the call so it's barely a whisper. "Come on. I need 'dicktails.'"

I take a cotton swap and add some polish remover so I can fix the disaster that are my feet. "First off, don't ever say that. You lack the proper swag credentials to pull it off." I pick out a dark-purple polish and roll it between my hands. "Second, pound town is pretty apt because it was pretty much all pound and nothing else."

"That bad, huh?"

I consider the question. "Not so much bad as . . . super vanilla? Okay for the first time, except my husband seemed to be under the illusion that we'd done something wild and crazy, which is concerning." I swipe off the old nail polish. The bubblegum pink was cute at first, but I need something fiercer right now, especially since Taya's end of the line is silent. I sigh and pick up the plum-colored polish and begin painting each toe, trying to focus on the smooth swipes. But my night with Tony comes rushing back and my hands shake in response, ruining the polish. A color that is already hard enough to paint smoothly.

Taya's trying to be caring, making excuses on the other line, but I'm too focused on fixing these nails to care. I grab some Q-Tips and dip them in the nail polish remover. The sharp, acidic smell is enough to make my nose wrinkle, so I put the call on speaker and set the phone aside. This is serious business and I'm a multitasker. I scrub at the outline of my nails, growing more irritated by the second. "God, he has so much potential. That face, and those muscles. That smile. Perfect ingredients for some serious action. But nope. The only saving grace to the whole thing is that he's hung like a horse and he's so supersensitive, especially around the—"

"Oh my God," Taya interrupts, voice mildly desperate. "Please stop."

"You asked." I blow a curl from my face, examining each toe for any missed smeared paint. Although, doing the autopsy isn't so much fun since his is the only dick I'll be *enjoying* for some time. Maybe I should rethink my stance on making this work for longer than a year. Maybe Tony's right and our marriage should just be a short-term arrangement.

My chest tightens. I signed up specifically in hopes of gaining a real partner who would last and somehow ended up stuck with one who has a one-year limit. Sex was supposed to be a consolation prize, at the very least.

Taya huffs. "Maybe you just have to give the guy some pointers."

She's right, but I'm demoralized about the whole marriage again. "I'm not sure I'm cut out for teaching. Maybe in college, but we're in our thirties now. Shouldn't he have figured it out on his own by now?" My toes are basically dry and shimmer a luminescent dark purple. I admire them for a moment and continue getting dressed for work. No one will see my feet in my work shoes, but I like my toes and fingers to match, keeping that whole put-together vibe going.

"Tony's not the guy to slack on matters that are important. And the program isn't something to be taken lightly. I'm sure he wants it to work as much as you do."

I fall silent as my stomach churns. I haven't told her yet that he plans to bail after a year. My chest seizes again as hopelessness rises. I can't believe this is how things ended up. Stupid matching program. And I don't want to explain any of this to Taya. She wouldn't judge me for trying to make it work with Tony, even if it might be a lost cause. But my pride has taken beating after beating since I opened that IPP envelope, and I'm sick of it.

"Inara?"

"Hold on." After slipping my feet into a pair of flip-flops, I grab my keys and make sure to feed Simon before I head out. Once I'm in my car, I transfer Taya to the speaker system and start on the relatively short drive to Shaken & Stirred, but long enough for my toenails to dry. "If we can't get the sex right—the part that should come naturally—the rest of our marriage is doomed to die a slow and hideously painful death."

My heart twists because I hoped we could find something real together. I actually enjoy spending time with him. He's funny, warm, and far more caring and sharp than he likes to let on. But now, I'm almost as doubtful as the day I first opened the envelope.

"Inara, I'm not saying sex is the most important thing in the world," Taya says.

"But it's important for the intimacy to go hand in hand with the spiritual and mental connection." Oh great. I sound like some poet wannabe. Yet, I can't stop jabbering and my voice climbs in pitch. "Honestly, what's love without passion? Without lust? Without sensuality?"

And, what am I even saying? Tony and I don't have love. What we'd had was lust and now, based on his surprisingly bland, quick performance, even that's in severe jeopardy. Without that? We're two platonic roommates who barely know each other. Forced to shack up for a year for practicality's sake.

"Keep an open mind. Tony wouldn't be the first man to have performance anxiety. And remember, he's probably under the microscope with Redding, just like Jim was."

Maybe she's right. Back in high school, I'd always choked on tests. My vagina isn't AP Calculus, but I can understand why he might bomb under pressure. And, if I'm being honest, I'm partially responsible for that pressure. I chew the inside of my cheek while some of the tension drains from my shoulders. Plus, now that the shock is wearing off, it is kind of endearing to think he's not all the talk he pretends to be.

I spend the rest of the drive to Shaken & Stirred grilling Taya about her further adventures with her husband's interest in anal stimulation because, sadly enough, it's preferable than talking about my own life at the moment. By the time I stride through the front door of the seaside whiskey bar and restaurant, I'm in a much better mood. Plus, there's something peaceful about this place in the mornings. The empty farm tables stretch across the floor, their dark, wooden tops gleaming under splashes of sunlight. Mellow tunes pipe in through the scattered speakers instead of the late-afternoon battle of voices. Shaken & Stirred isn't super fancy, by any means, but it has a comfortable elegance that makes the bar a popular happy hour spot.

Taya walks in shortly after I do to begin her shift while I relieve Megan, one of the new servers. Business is slow this time of day, and when I'm not sitting, wiping down dirty menus—seriously, who splashes this much ketchup on a menu?—or seating the few people who wander inside for breakfast mimosas, I help Taya roll silverware in the back.

I'm standing at the booth contemplating whether this

plum shade was really the ideal nail color when a couple of familiar figures step through the door. *Mami* and Bennett have met for brunch once a month since before their divorce, and it's a tradition neither one seems too eager to break. I plaster a smile on my face and pick up two menus. I'm genuinely happy to see Bennett, and when he finally glances up at me, his eyes brighten with joy.

"Twice in two days. I'm a lucky, lucky man." He laughs as he wraps me up in a hug. "What did I do to earn such enchanting company?"

Bennett's always done everything he can for me. Like the way he started reading up on stepparenting the moment he asked my mother to marry him. He had these funny one-liners that always made me laugh, especially whenever I went through hard times while growing up. And he has to be the absolute king of picking up the check, a fact not lost on my mother.

"You two knew perfectly well I was working today." I shoot a tiny glare at my mom and she lifts her chin in defiance.

We head to one of the circular wooden booths in Taya's section, and when she spots Bennett and *Mami*, her expression undergoes a paroxysm of emotions—a wincing smile followed by one more genuine—that would have made me laugh if I hadn't done the exact same thing a moment ago. It's not that my mother is a horror show. She's just a lot to take on, especially when she's in the middle of a divorce. Between her painfully obvious attempts to get back with

Bennett as the threat of single life looms ever larger and the need she'd had to fix me up with a man since the day I turned twenty-nine—*literally anyone would do at this point, Inara*—I've been tempted to divorce her myself. I drop their menus onto the table, hoping to escape before they draw me into a conversation there's no getting out of. "Enjoy your meal."

Bennett slides into his seat, a second later wincing in pain as he reaches below the table to rub at his shin. We both stare at *Mami*, but she remains impassive. Bennett looks up at me, tries for nonchalance, and fails. "So, how are things going with your new husband?"

"Oh, we shouldn't pry." My mother straightens, pressing a hand against her chest as if surprised by the sudden line of questioning. But the three of us know damned well that's the reason they dropped by.

I stare up at the ceiling for a minute, hoping to find remnants of my lost patience there. Like Bennett, I fail miserably, wanting nothing more than to pour the mimosa she regularly orders on her head. "We're fine. Turns out married life suits one of us, after all."

I duck my head after saying it because that was a low blow. *Mami* might love to meddle, but she has no idea she's pouring salt on a wound. How could she when I haven't told her anything about how and why I married Tony? I love my mom, but she can be exhausting.

And honestly, I don't think the truth would be any kinder.

A breeze drifts over us as the front door opens and shuts. A respite. Salvation from my mother's version of the Spanish Inquisition. But as soon as my escape appears, my soon-to-be-former best friend snatches it from my grasp. Taya, coward and traitor that she is, rushes up to the hostess booth to greet the incoming customers, and takes them to a table belonging to the next server in the rotation.

Bennett pats the back of my hand. "I wanted to ask if you and Tony might be willing to come help out with the renovation of the house again soon. We've been a little shorthanded lately and could use you."

Last time, Tony and I had worked so well together, and he'd seemed to enjoy helping out as much as did. I suppose it couldn't hurt to give working together another go. Especially since I hate saying no to Bennett. "I'll talk to him and find out what his schedule is like."

Mami leans back in her seat and cocks her head to one side, considering me with those dark eyes that somehow always know all my wrongdoings before I do. When she crosses her arms, I step back and wave to both of them before she can utter a word. "I should get back to work. Your server will be right with you."

Once back at the hostess stand, I take a deep breath. I'll have some explaining to do to my mother at some point. Part of me wants to be an adult about it all, admit the truth of my relationship to Tony, and maybe even ask her for guidance on what to do. Then again, how beneficial would advice be coming from a woman with enough husbands to make up a bowling team?

CHAPTER ELEVEN

Tony

I SPENT HALF the night tossing and turning while attempting to grow enough balls to bring up the sex topic with Inara. And now with the morning sun lighting up the living room, I'm still unsure how to proceed. So, I lounge against the back of the couch and try to distract myself with a word search. Not that I'm having much success in the distraction department. Every few seconds, my eyes glaze over and I'm back to the night before, wondering if there's some kind of manual explaining the best way for a new husband to bring up how to better please his wife in the bedroom.

My hands tense, making the pen jerk across the paper, leaving behind a thick trail of blue ink. I sigh and readjust my reading glasses. I'm not getting anywhere, so I might as well finish this puzzle.

I look at the letters without actually seeing them.

I mean, it's not like the sex was awful for Inara, right? Just a little quicker than she might have hoped for. But that last thing she'd said . . . ouch. Part of me woke up hoping it was a dream, except the stilted silence between us tells me otherwise.

That whole night at karaoke, the tension built between us. Her hand on my arms sent shivers down my body all the way to the tip of my dick, and I still shudder remembering her ass pressed against it. Yeah, it was good, but I hate the idea all that tension fizzled away for her, or worse, that she left our night either unsatisfied or bored.

I hate the idea that I let her down.

I drop the word search onto the cushion and lean my head back, trying to remember the name of the last woman I slept with. Brenda or Brandie. Something with a B, I think. I don't know. For the life of me, I can't remember much beyond checking the clock to make sure I had enough time to get back to base. I'll be the first to admit my body count isn't nearly as high as I pretend it is. But to think there could be a tribe of women out there who think I'm a lousy lay isn't doing much for my mood.

I groan while slipping my fingertips under my glasses to rub my eyes. I'd always assumed I was good because no one until Inara acted otherwise. What was with that anyway? Did she find her comment funny? Because it wasn't. I mean if she cooked a roast and burned it dry, I would still chomp that thing down like it was five-star cuisine. But then again, even a burnt roast beef fills a hole, and the effort put into cooking one is probably a hell of a lot more than I put out. How long do roasts take to cook again? Two, maybe three hours? Meanwhile, I'd lasted all of four minutes. Maybe five. And that's being generous.

"I'm a moron." Gritting my teeth, I curl both hands around the top of my skull, wishing I had hair so I'd have something to yank out. I expel the bad air from my lungs in one giant whoosh. Okay, time to quit freaking the fuck out. Beating myself up sure as hell isn't going to solve this problem. And it's not like there's a crowd of dissatisfied customers lined up behind me.

No, I need to quit letting my fears run away with me. Inara didn't actually say she didn't like having sex with me. Although, that disgruntled noise she made, right at the end, and her parting zinger . . . *oof.* That right there pretty much guaranteed that I haven't hit her top-five list. Inara has no patience for niceties, so if she dislikes something, everyone and their mother is gonna know it.

My gut twists into knots.

Fuck.

What if she tells everyone?

She probably already told Taya. And Taya will tell Jim. Though Jim probably won't give me much shit about my in-the-sack skills given what his ex-wife put him through when it came to his sexual interests.

I sit up and straighten my shoulders. This kind of defeatist thinking isn't getting me anywhere. So maybe I hadn't hit the ball out of the park our first time. I also hadn't mastered every single element of basic training right away. Not that Inara is like basic training, but at the time, basic was brand-new to me—sort of like having a wife. Maybe I put too much pressure on myself to succeed right off the bat. And one thing everyone learns quickly in the military—there's always room for improvement.

I perk up. This situation is far from hopeless. I just need to fight harder to make things better. Practice makes perfect, right? I picture Inara's naked body and shiver. Damned if I'm not willing to practice as much as possible. Relaxing a little probably wouldn't hurt either. I'm a damn good cook. I could cook her something. I could please her in that way first and then she'll give me a chance to *really* please her in the way I want to, the way I know I can. Blood rushes to my dick just thinking about her moaning in satisfaction as I go down on her right on the kitchen table. I'm going to SEAL this shit, figure out what she likes, and give it to her . . . all night long. She just needs to give me the chance.

"Good morning!"

Oh shit.

Out of habit, I reach up and yank off my glasses, hoping I've successfully managed to tuck them between my leg and the side of the couch without her noticing. But I glance up and catch her staring at me with a smile tugging at her mouth.

"Are you trying to pretend like I didn't just see you shove those glasses into the couch?" she says.

Damn.

I widen my eyes and glance around the room. "Glasses? What glasses?"

Inara chuckles, placing a hand on her cocked hip. "You know, there's no need to be embarrassed. They look cute on you."

This weird heat flares across my cheeks. Almost like I'm blushing. It's an uncomfortable sensation, so I sit up straighter and puff out my chest. "Of course they do. Everything looks good on me."

I follow that audacious statement up with a wink, which prompts Inara to roll her eyes. But she's smiling too. At least that's something. Then the smile fades and her expression goes all serious. She perches herself on the edge of the sofa's arm. "I'm glad I caught you here because I need to tell you something." Her gaze drops from mine to study the way her fingers tangle in her lap.

My throat dries out. Oh shit. She can't even look me in the eye? This is bad. Real bad. My performance must have been way worse even than I believed it was. I suck in a deep breath, filling my lungs with air, and brace myself. Whatever she says, I'll do my best to take it like a man.

"I, uh, might have volunteered us to help out with Bennett again for a few hours over the next couple of weekends, if you're able. Sorry, he sort of sprung it on me while I was at work and my mom was harassing me, and at that point, I would have basically said anything to get her off my back. I can totally tell him that you can't make it if you're busy."

I'm so tense it takes me a second to process her words. Wait. Bennett? Her sudden change in demeanor isn't about my failure to satisfy her in the sack? She's worried that I'll be upset because she volunteered me to help her stepdad build some more houses for his community members affected by the hurricane?

Relief whooshes through me and I could not be happier right now that the only thing on the line is forfeiting a few weekend hours to a good cause. "Count me in whenever my schedule allows. I'd be happy to help out again."

The warm smile she flashes me lands a double punch, to my chest and my dick. "You sure?"

Like I could do anything else but agree when she's beaming at me like that, for probably the first time ever. "Positive. I like doing things with my hands in my spare time."

Our gazes connect. Some of that heat from the other night flares between us, and then Inara jumps to her feet. "Awesome. Great. Thank you so much, I'll let Bennett know."

She practically flees to the kitchen, leaving my head spinning once again and my groin aching. A situation not helped when she returns a few moments later, eating a peach and licking the juice off that's collecting at the corner of her mouth. If that isn't one of the most erotic things I've seen in a long time. She moves to pass me on the couch and hesitates, cocking a brow at me.

I blink and drag my attention away from her lips.

Now. I should bring up last night now.

Sweat prickles the back of my neck. I clear my throat and get ready to start again while she gazes at me with big, dark eyes. My phone rings while I'm still struggling to muster up the courage.

Without thinking I grab it from my pocket, not bothering to check the screen. One of my teammates—or a tele-marketer—had picked the right time to call.

"Tony? Long time, son."

The familiar masculine voice causes every muscle in my body to tense and my chest to constrict. Is it too late for a do-over? Because I'd rather have outed myself as a sexual failure than take this particular call. Guilt stabs me in the gut at the terrible thought. Even though it's true.

Honestly, I'd pick subjecting myself to just about any unpleasant task over suffering through a call from my father any day of the week, which is why I limit the calls to quick birthday messages or happy whatever-holiday-it-is. Our longer phone call is reserved for Father's Day when the guilt of not calling him more catches up with me. I suck in a deep breath. "What's up, *Apá*?"

When she hears my greeting, Inara quietly escapes down the hall. And just as quickly, I jump off the couch and start pacing, my heart rate steadily increasing.

"*Mijo*, I miss you. How's it going?"

"Been busy. How's work?" According to Yelp, my dad's a Zumba miracle instructor. People drive out over an hour sometimes to get to his class. I gotta say, I never expected a construction company owner to excel at something like Zumba. But we all have our things that keep us happy and this was what helped *Apá* keep my mother's memory alive.

"Got your text you were back from deployment. You should've called instead of texting." There was a long pause before he began again. "And work is going well. That's why

I'm calling, actually."

"What's up?" I fight to keep my tone pleasant, but it's tough. Any kind of conversation with my pops only stirs up a dark stew of disappointment. It's not that he was a bad father. In fact, he was a great father. At least, back when *Mamá* was still alive, when he was in a good enough mental place to parent at all. But after my mom's death, he had a hard time, for too long. It took him forever to recover. For years after we buried *Mamá*, my sisters and I had to both battle our own grief and at the same time support our father while he succumbed to his.

Nothing had prepared me for parenting my own parent. I was a kid who was suddenly responsible for taking care of my younger siblings too. So, while I love my dad, I also resent him for not being there when we needed him most. Plus, talking to him always brings back sad memories of my mother.

"Well, I'm planning on holding a fundraiser in honor of your mother for early November of this year raise money for cancer research and having the donation be in her name."

"Zumba's not exactly my thing." Both the hesitation in my own voice and my father's silence cause an image of his disappointed face to flash in my mind. I lean over, my thumb and middle finger massaging my temples. "Look, I can't make any promises, but I'll think it over. I mean I *would* like to see your famous moves."

My father chuckles. "It's mostly choreography, but I can still dance you right off the floor, choreographed or not."

The image brings a rush of memories. All of us—me, *Apá*, my sisters, and *Mamá*—diving into Zumba to help distract my mother from the diagnosis. I remember the pain on her face when she explained it to me and my sisters. I remember the fear racing through my veins when she uttered the words *lump* and *breast*, but mostly, I remember how her whole life changed after those stupid words. She loved being outdoors and used to spend hours gardening, but in the months before she told us, we'd seen her slow down, and grow pale and gray. Knowing *why* was only a small relief, and it did nothing to alleviate the terror that carved out a hole in my heart. It was hard to watch the woman I'd always looked up to, the one I had always seen as a rock, crumble bit by bit. That's when my youngest sister, Vanessa, suggested Zumba.

My stomach twists and there's a dull ache in my chest. I want to ignore him, to forget all the ways we failed her while she was alive and even after she passed. Her loss still weighs on me like a buried bullet that I'll never be able to cut out.

"It's for your mom, Tony." My father's voice, the pleading tone, shocks me back to the present. "There are a lot of details to work out still, but I'm hoping to host it in Virginia Beach, somewhere near the ocean."

I straighten, panic setting in. This all sounded okay in theory when it was happening miles away from me. "Why here?"

"Your mom always loved the ocean." There's an undercurrent of grief in his reply. "I figure we could host the actual

Zumba class on the beach and then head to a restaurant after for food and drinks. I don't know, I haven't worked out all the details, but I wanted to talk to you about it."

Except talking about it is the last thing I want to do. Not when the topic of *Mamá* always brings this tsunami of emotions with it. So I do what I learned to do years ago—I smash all the unpleasant feelings into a tiny ball and ignore them. "Sounds like you have some good ideas. What do you want from me, though? You need a poster boy? A hottie for all the soccer moms to come gawk at?" I joke because joking is way better than the alternative.

"*Mijo*, they'd probably leave thinking it was a Mr. Clean event instead!" *Apá* laughs, and a sense of ease flows through me. I'm sure the distance I've put between us hasn't been easy on him. But the loss of my mother carved out a piece of me I'll never get back, so, though I love my father and sisters, I avoid all the things and people she loved. Being around them hurts too much.

I roll my eyes. Clearly my lowbrow sense of humor is genetic. Then a sad sigh comes across the line. "Anyway, I know thinking about her is hard for you. But I don't want to do this without you, and your mother wouldn't have wanted me to. Maybe this will be good for you?"

I flinch. I would have been able to dismiss it no problem, but my resolve weakens when he mentions my mother and what she would have wanted. Mostly because I know he's right. Damn him.

Not one to ignore an opening, my father dives into the

silence, as if hoping to fill it before I come to my senses and hang up. "It'll be a memorial, but more than that, the proceeds will go to cancer research. Maybe talk to some of your friends on base, ask if they'd like to be a part of it? It would be a big help."

"Why not have it closer to home?" It's not that I don't care about cancer research, because of course I do. I'd do just about anything to keep other people from going through the same hell we went through. Anything but face the soul-shredding emotions that my involvement in this event will be sure to bring on. I drop back onto the couch, dig the fingers of my free hand into the cushion, and twist. "Why drag yourself all the way out here?"

"*Mi hijo*, you've pushed us away for long enough. I gave you time to grieve, and I know it won't erase what happened, but I think it's time we reconnect." He pauses, takes a deep breath that I hope means he's done, and then plunges on. "I wasn't there for you right after your mom's death, I know that." Even over the phone, the genuine remorse in his words hurts. "And I'm sorry I wasn't the best I could have been. But I want to try harder now. Your sisters and I want to see your home, your city. We want to do this there, around your new family and friends. We want to be part of your life."

"*Apá*, I appreciate that . . ." In a perfect world, having family around for support would be great. If things work out with Inara and me, I'm sure she'd want to meet my family. But life's rarely perfect and I've got a full boat of issues staring me in the face right now as it is. I mean, how do I explain my temporary marriage to a dad whose wife was his everything? "But I don't know if I'm ready."

I pause, take a deep breath, guilt settling with my decision. *Apá*'s grief may have made it so he hadn't been there for us right after her death, but I can't say the man didn't try. He'd kept his business going. He'd made sure to provide for us. I have to respect that. I can't cut him out forever. "I promise, I'll think it over." Which probably doesn't sound like much, but it's the biggest concession I've made to him since I moved away.

We wrap up the conversation, I tell him we'll talk again soon, then put the phone away. My father knows I might not call, and I know he won't push me on the fundraiser. But maybe doing the fundraiser will help a bit. Taking an active part in an event to honor *Mamá*'s memory would be a kind of closure.

"Tony?" Inara's voice cuts through the air.

My heart leaps into my throat. I didn't even notice her come back out of her bedroom and there's no telling how much she heard. Not that I need this to be some big secret, but I don't know that I'm ready to tell her all about my family.

She studies me with wide eyes that catch me right beneath my ribs and fill me with an urgent need to soothe her. Part of me wants to talk to her right here, to tell her everything, while the other part wants to evade. Why would I tell her my entire life sob story when in less than eleven months from now, we'll be going our separate ways? And I'm not ready to be so vulnerable, especially in front of the person I . . .

I freeze.

I . . . what?

My brain tries to shape the word, but I don't allow it. I can't.

"Is everything alright?" She steps toward me, reaching out, but pulls her hand back when I flinch.

I'm suddenly like a wild animal, except instead of a steel claw, I'm trapped by the confusing emotions she's arousing with her concern.

"Yeah, I'm fine." I don't think I'm convincing anyone, but thankfully she follows my lead and drops it.

"Okay. Just . . . if you need to talk, I'm here. You still good to volunteer with my stepdad?"

Bennett. Shit. Somehow in the span of thirty minutes, I'd managed to forget all about the community building project. "Yeah. I'll be there when my job offers me the opportunity to be. Not a nine-to-five, after all."

Now I'm just spitting out whatever comes to mind to push her away, to insert a little more space between us. I think it's working because her brown eyes go a little frosty. She straightens and steps back, folding her arms over her chest. "Got it."

And now I'm a total jackass. Okay. Slow down. It's not Inara's fault that my dad called and stirred up some emotions that I'd rather not acknowledge. I shove that part of my life back into its box and tuck it away. Best to keep the past in the past. Right now my wife is asking me to help underprivileged families have affordable places to live. This, I can do.

"Sorry, I'm just tired." After the emotional rollercoaster that was my dad's call, more like exhausted, but that's why my best course of action is not to think about it and focus on something else. "I promise, I'll make sure I get over there to help."

"Thank you," she says again as her rigid posture relaxes, and the renewed gratitude in her voice both warms my heart and makes me a little jittery.

But at the end of the day, I'm happy to help.

I just need to make sure I check caller ID from now on before I answer the phone.

CHAPTER TWELVE

Inara

I CHECK MY lipstick in the mirror. The plum color I bought at the boutique across the street settles perfectly on my cupid's bow. Taya snorts and shakes her head. Lucky for me, my shift is over. Unlucky for her, she still has five more hours to go.

"What a life. Work is over and now you get to go grocery shopping," she says.

"That's because I live with an eating machine with a never-ending stomach." I still can't wrap my head around how much food Tony consumes. At least we share a joint bank account due to military rules; otherwise, I'd be penniless.

"Speaking of Tony, how'd the marriage counseling go?" Taya says.

I release a heavy sigh as my shoulders slump forward.

Taya shakes her head and laughs. "That good, huh? Trust me, I've been there. My first session with Jim was about the most awkward thing ever." She pats me on the shoulder. "You, too, shall live through this."

I snort and groan at the same time. "I hope so. I think

ours was less awkward and more straight-up bizarre. Tony flipped the switch from mild-mannered goofball to tight-lipped SEAL mode at times, like he was suspicious that the therapist was trying to dig out some deep dark military intel or something." I pause and nibble my lip as I remember the way Tony's posture changed. The way he'd taken control. "Although, I can't lie, it was kind of hot, seeing that side of him."

"Bizarre yet hot, got it." Taya nods like what I've said makes sense, even though I'm still trying to decipher my feelings myself.

"Overall, he was pretty great, though. He had no problems talking about marriage-related stuff, or even joking about some of his insecurities. The only personal thing he clammed up about was his childhood." And his stonewalling on that front had come as something of a relief, because it made me feel better about not wanting to share my own childhood baggage. At one point, when the therapist was not so subtly nudging me to open up about any issues I'd had with my parents growing up, Tony and I had shared a commiserating look while the therapist was jotting notes in his notebook. Of course, next thing I knew, my screwball of a husband was pulling a hilarious face, and I'd had to bite my lip to keep from laughing out loud.

The session left me with questions, though. I know why I'm not eager to share my family life growing up, but what's Tony's baggage? I voice as much to Taya, but when I glance up, she coughs and turns her face away from me. "Sorry.

Must be my allergies acting up."

I narrow my eyes. Since when does Taya have allergies?

My phone vibrates, distracting me. I yank it out and read the text.

I'm on my way to the market. Need anything?

I show the screen to Taya. "Oh, how romantic, you two can go shopping together now."

I roll my eyes, but honestly, I'm not mad about sharing this chore with Tony. I shoot off a text telling him to wait on me there.

"Later, *chica*." With a wave, I spin around and head toward the exit of Shaken & Stirred while the conundrum of my new husband fills my mind. There's the easygoing, happy-go-lucky Tony, who jokes around at hospitals and therapy sessions. Then there's kindhearted, eager-to-help Tony, who readily agrees to give up his free time to build houses with my stepdad.

There's also guarded Tony, which I'd caught a glimpse of in therapy, and prickly, tight-lipped Tony, who won't talk about mysterious phone calls. I wish he trusted me enough to confide in me. Maybe I'd made a mistake in therapy not being upfront about how all of *Mami*'s failed marriages affected me. Maybe if I'd opened up, Tony would have followed suit and done the same. Next time will be different. For now, all I can do is try to help him sort out whatever he's dealing with. Maybe grocery shopping will put him at ease, and I could sneak in a few questions over thumping watermelons and inspecting cuts of beef.

Fifteen minutes later, I pull into the parking lot at the grocery store. Tony is waiting for me, leaning against his Durango, his brow furrowed as he frowns down at a word search puzzle book. I watch him for a few moments and smile. As far as addictions go, I can't complain.

When I open my door and climb out, his head pops up. He flashes me a sheepish grin. Dark shadows form semicircles beneath his eyes, reminding me that he'd gone straight from work to therapy and then back to work, and now here he is, waiting on me to go grocery shopping. The impact of my husband's grin combines with admiration over his work ethic and causes my heart to skip a beat.

He turns and tosses the puzzle book into the car, then shuts the door and faces me once again. "Are you trying to tell me something? Is purple lipstick meant to be some kinda aphrodisiac?"

I smack him softly. "Yeah, it's the color your balls are going to be after we spend the rest of our marriage sexless."

He winces. "That's cold."

He's right. We hadn't had a chance to talk yet about the other night, but given the way he'd been acting, he must've taken my flippant statement about his wildness or lack thereof in bed a little too personally. "Sorry, bad joke."

His smile returns. "So, you're saying that we aren't going to spend the rest of our time together sexless?"

His phone pings before I can reply. He tenses and shoves the device into his back pocket. Something is wrong. The last time Tony was this on edge was after Taya was attacked.

"Is everything okay?"

"Huh?" His forehead wrinkles as his brows pinch together, but the lines disappear as his eyes widen and brows lift. "Yeah, nothing to worry about."

Liar. But there's little I can do if he doesn't want to share. I rub small circles on his back, hoping to ease some of the tension as we head over to grab a shopping cart.

Tony swallows hard, his Adam's apple bobbing. "We both know you and I don't have these kinda conversations. Hell, I'm not asking you what your mother thinks of those little bars in your nipples."

"*Cabrón*, you can keep your secrets." I grip the shopping cart until my hands hurt and increase my pace, pushing the cart faster and leaving Tony behind.

"Where you going? Wait up."

My husband is a closed book. And I've learned from Taya he won't be able—and also might not want—to share what happens when he's sent on missions. But he's more than just his job, and I want to learn about those parts. I grind my molars and snarl. I'm not great at being the gentle, patient kinda gal who'll give him space to blossom and grow. I'm more of the "let's break down the walls with a sledgehammer" kinda gal, especially when time is sort of an issue here. Not the best quality for a caring wife to have.

As I'm about to enter, the door on the opposite side swings open and out walks a familiar face. I stop and wave just as my husband catches up to me. "Hi, Trevor."

Trevor rears back when he sees us. His eyes go wide and

his shoulders stiffen. He tries to hide a DVD under the Sara Lee frozen pie in his hand, but Tony grabs it. "*Jack Frost*? What are you, eight? Or is it some new porno version?"

I turn and lightly slap my husband's shoulder. "Not everyone's sitting at home watching porn all the time like you."

Trevor laughs and takes the opportunity to snatch back the DVD. "It's a bit of a birthday tradition."

I turn and pin my husband with the most serious glare I can muster. "You didn't tell me it was his birthday."

Trevor clears his throat and shifts his weight from one foot to the other. "None of them know. I usually just spend it alone, watching *Jack Frost*, eating key lime pie, and getting hammered on whiskey."

"Doesn't sound like fun. Let us throw you a little party at our place." Tony winks at me and looks entirely too smug.

I nearly choke on my saliva. Does Tony realize what he just said? I take measured breaths attempting to chase away the small bit of hope attempting to reside in my heart that my husband might be coming around to erasing the expiration date on our marriage.

I hike the straps of my bag higher onto my shoulder. My mission right now is to make sure Trevor isn't alone on his birthday. "We'll have everyone over, it'll be fun."

Trevor rubs the back of his neck and stares down at the floor. "Wouldn't wanna put y'all out."

The sliding doors swish open again, and we all step to the side to let a mom and her squealing toddler pass us by on their way out of the store. Once we're clear of the walkway, I smile at Trevor. "We'd love it. We'll have food and every-thing. You can bring *Jack Frost* if you want."

"You sure?" His blue eyes are so hopeful that I'm sud-denly extra glad that Tony asked.

"Come on over around eight. Tony will text you the ad-dress."

"Thanks, y'all. I really do appreciate it."

Tony claps his hand on Trevor's shoulder. "And happy birthday."

Trevor smiles and heads off toward the parking lot while we enter the market. My mind races as I begin creating a mental list of what I'll make, what we need, and whether or not we'll have time to get some balloons.

"Inara?" Tony tugs me back as I turn to head into the produce area. "Thanks for that."

I whip my head around and my brows furrow. "Thanks for what?"

"For supporting me with the whole party idea." Tony's unexpected gratitude warms me from the inside out. That, along with the sweet, caring side of himself that he just showcased by figuratively gathering Trevor under his wing like a mother hen.

Tony grabs the cart from me and trolls through a row of fruits. "Jim's still shutting him out when it comes to things other than work."

Jim can be so bullheaded. But I have no idea what it's like for any of them. I've never lost a close friend, especially one I work with. Nor can I imagine what it would be like to have someone new shoved into their tight-knit group. I shake my head. It must be so uncomfortable for everyone. "The team needs this celebration."

Tony takes his time inspecting the produce before placing each hand-chosen fruit and vegetable into a bag and gently setting them down in the cart. There's something about a big, brawny man delicately handling apples and carrots that makes me go all soft inside. Maybe because it seems so out of character with the macho front Tony often puts on.

While he continues to shop for our impromptu celebration, I pull out my phone and text Taya. Of course, she responds right away and offers to text the rest of the group so I can concentrate on shopping. I snort and look over at the cart. She has no idea. If Tony is left unchecked, we may be walking out of here with a three-hundred-dollar grocery bill, considering the cart is already half full and it's only been five minutes.

Tony and I blaze through the store and walk out, having spent two hundred dollars. By the time we get home, we have a few hours before everyone is supposed to arrive. The house isn't a mess, but Tony insists on running over everything and making sure it's all spotless. I knock on the door frame to the guest bathroom as Tony scrubs the sink. "So, I have some decorations stored in the garage from one of *Mami*'s old parties."

Tony interrupts me before I have a chance to finish. "You got one of those slow cookers, right? I make a mean salsa."

"Yeah, it's in the pantry," I say, gesturing to my left. "Right next to the sex toys."

Tony freezes at first, and then stutters. "S-sex toys, yeah, those are cool." His skin takes on a reddish hue and he fumbles around, knocking over the toothbrushes and hand soap. Yet another reminder he's not as much of an experienced player as he likes to let on. What's annoying about it, though? Imagining how much fun I could have teaching him new tricks.

I choke out a laugh and head to the garage to grab the decorations, glad for a few moments to chill out. When I get back, I plop the box down in the living room before I head into the kitchen to help Tony get the food ready. I start slivering onions and some jalapeño.

Tony reaches into one of the produce bowls, grabs a clove of garlic, and hands it to me. "You'll want to add this too."

"I know to add garlic. *Jesús*. I do it after I cut the other stuff up." I jerk my head toward the slow cooker where he's got food sautéing. "You better start breaking up that *chorizo* or else you'll have a sore shoulder trying to pry it to bits."

He nudges me with his shoulder. "Aye, you just keep your eyes on your stuff."

My body is extremely aware of his presence as we maneuver around each other. I'm genuinely impressed by how he moves while preparing food. There's no denying it—the way Tony handles himself in the kitchen is downright sexy.

The way he works the knife as he finely chops tomatoes. The motion and rhythm lead me to dangerous thoughts. Like how much raw potential is there, and how enjoyable it would be to lead him back to the bedroom right now and tap into that sensual energy. I shake myself when my sex starts to pulsate.

We have things to get done. Nonsexual things.

Once everything is prepped, I rush to my room and get ready. Taya's heading over early to help set up. Hopefully, Tony will have a talk with Jim about easing up on Trevor—at least for today. I mean, he doesn't have to love the guy, but it's so sad that Trevor was going to spend his birthday alone.

I shove clothes in my closet aside and try to find something that says homemaker, wife, and seductress all at once. A part of me wants to give sex with Tony another go tonight, but another part of me just wants him to hold me. If only he weren't so dead set on making our relationship temporary. Because all this party-planning business and cooking really shows Tony and I work well together. Which brings me right back to my outfit dilemma. Maybe I can make some headway into charming my new husband into changing his mind.

"Ah, yes." I grab a pair of high-waisted shorts and an orchid button-down crop top that ties just above the belly button. It's the perfect balance of cute and sexy once I add a pair of jeweled sandals.

The doorbell rings and I walk into the foyer just as Tony

shuts the door. I'm rewarded for the extra few minutes I dedicated to my outfit when his eyes move slowly, trailing from my wedge sandals up the span of my legs. He lingers on the exposed skin of my abs, which even I have to say are toned and tanned. His Adam's apple bobs and he turns his head away. A smile pulls at the corners of my mouth in response to his reaction. I can't deny that I enjoy having this effect on my husband.

Taya walks over and gives me a hug. "You look so cute."

"Thanks." I turn to Jim and Tony before they head off to God knows where. "Can you guys set up the decorations while Taya and I get the plates ready?"

The two men nod and grunt. Jim's not much for words, but this is the first time Tony's been so quiet. Cat must have gotten his tongue. I snort and grab Taya's hand, pulling her into the kitchen.

"I can't believe the guys didn't know it was Trevor's birthday?" Taya slams the forks down onto the countertop and huffs. "Though maybe they did."

I set the stack of plates next to her and place a hand on her shoulder. "From the shy way he was acting, I doubt they knew."

Taya laughs. "At least neither of our guys is Bear. God only knows what Marge did to the man after I texted her about the party."

Marge is a petite woman with the personality of an M-80 firecracker. The men are scared of her. Hell, at times, so am I. But I love her, just the same. And watching her with Bear always makes me believe love exists. The two are opposites in so many ways, yet were made for each other.

The doorbell rings and a moment later Lucas Craiger walks in, along with Bear and Marge. I hug Marge. "Where's Leslie?"

"Hayden's home. Nothing like a built-in babysitter," Marge says.

Bear grumbles a greeting just as Jim walks over, looking as if someone just inserted a stick up his ass. I scowl at him before catching Tony's eye and jerking my chin in Jim's direction. Someone better talk to the guy because I'm not looking for a fight to occur in my house.

Tony takes my hint. He claps his teammate on the shoulder and gives him a firm squeeze. "Better check the attitude at the door."

Jim presses his lips into a tight line but doesn't say a word.

Tony withdraws his hand and shoves it into the pocket of his jeans, but doesn't back down. "Look, the kid purchased a stupid frozen pie and movie that he planned on eating and watching *alone*. You know it's not how we do things. Not in our line of work. So, get your shit together."

Something flares in my chest as my husband scolds Jim and stands up for the newbie. Before I can examine the emotion, the storm door slams closed and everyone spins around. The guest of honor has arrived. We all rush into the foyer and scream, "Happy birthday!"

"Thanks again for doing this." Trevor is all bashful head

ducks and smiles. I never noticed before how white his teeth are.

Tony walks over and pulls him in as if he's about to wrestle him. "No worries."

Bear sidles in behind the duo and pulls something from his pocket. It looks like a twenty-dollar bill when he slaps it into Trevor's hand. "Here, kid, get yourself the latest Disney princess movie on me."

Trevor scoffs and shakes his head as laughter rings out around him. Some of my tension dissolves when even Jim laughs. Thankfully for Trevor, the spotlight moment is fleeting and we all dissipate soon after.

I move toward the side table by the door and stare at it for several long seconds before I realize what's wrong. My vase is missing. What the hell? My gaze jerks to Tony, who exchanges a wide-eyed glance with Lucas before looking back at me. He leans in and places his rough hand against the exposed skin of my back. "About that. I'll tell you later, and I'm sorry in advance." Then he winks and saunters off to get Trevor a beer.

I can't help but shake my head and laugh as he departs. God only knows what happened, and it wasn't even a real vase, just an old mayonnaise jar that I glued beads to. But Tony doesn't need to know that, or the fact that the typical husband-wife snapshot that just played out was oddly appealing.

After I make sure everyone has a plate of snacks, and Tony hands out drinks all around, I plop myself on the couch.

Now that the party is in full swing and appears to be going well, I can finally relax a little. Tony sits next to me and rests his hand on my knee. I must be buzzing off of everyone's happy energy. And I can't stop myself from leaning into my husband. He smells as good as his palm on my bare skin feels. My body is urging me to head into the ring for round two, while my wary heart reminds me to take care.

He leans closer, his breath hot against my cheek. "I think we did good here."

"Yeah, I think you're right. But I have to say, most of my meatballs are gone and your slow cooker of queso is still halfway full."

Tony throws his head back and laughs from deep in his belly, a sound that, despite my heart's cautious approach, still somehow manages to turn my insides to mush. "Well, I made a double batch, and you underestimated."

I give him a light slap on the thigh and laugh along with him, and I'm oddly content sitting here by his side. I take the next few minutes to enjoy the moment—the party, our friends, and simply sitting here without arguing—and then notice Tony's captivated expression and follow his gaze. Bear and Marge across the room, hands laced together, Bear leaning over her, Marge's face tipped up in adoration. Not a bad thing to aspire to. And I have to admit, the Issued Partner Program must be onto something because Tony and I do make a good team. Maybe science hasn't let me down yet.

I sneak a sideways glance at Tony. Now, if only I can get my husband to get on board.

CHAPTER THIRTEEN

Tony

WHILE HAMMERS BANG away, I tack on the final layer of sheetrock with the drywall nails and then grab my towel off the floor and swipe at the sweat that's trickling down my bare chest. Once I'm done drying off my face, I sling the towel around my neck and study my handiwork. Fourth wall I've completed at Bennett's site today. Not too shabby.

"Feeling proud of yourself?"

My gaze jerks over to where Inara's standing. Her sweat-dampened curls are pulled back into a messy bun and her tank top is so wet, it's clinging to her curvy form like a second skin. When she lifts her arms over her head to stretch, pulling the material taut over her breasts, I swallow hard. And then she turns to drop something in a toolbox, and it doesn't help at all. Her ass in those shorts is a work of art, and that damned butterfly tattoo on her left shoulder keeps taunting me. It's all I can do not to groan out loud. I've been kicking myself every time I skip out on speaking to her about our sexual encounter.

After the party a couple of days ago, she definitely appeared to be flirty and possibly open to trying again. But as is the nature of our jobs, the guys and I got the call we were needed, and any hope of either talking or having another shot with my wife went out the window. And after spending time with her, getting to know her more, my balls are constantly aching because she's sizzling—she's the whole damn package.

Inara stares at me, complete with a high-arched brow, and I shrug. "It's hard not to feel a sense of accomplishment when you build something and see the progress, but it's a team effort. We've all been working hard."

She gasps and presses a hand to her chest. "Will wonders never cease? Is that modesty I hear coming from Tony Martinez? I'd better mark this day on my calendar."

"Oh, you think you're pretty funny, don't you?"

She glances up at me from beneath her eyelashes and flashes me a sultry smile. "Oh, I don't *think* I'm funny—I know I am."

If I didn't know any better, I'd say that my wife was flirting with me again. To distract myself, I pull a cold bottle of water out of the cooler and flick icy droplets at her. She squeals.

"That's what you get for being so cocky. Remember, I might be built"—I flex a bicep at her—"but my ego is delicate. When I take the high road and act modest, that's the signal for you to shower me with accolades." I finish half the bottle in a few big gulps before offering it to her.

She downs the remaining half just as quickly. "Right. Sorry. I must have forgotten that part of the vows somehow." She turns to peruse the wall, rubbing her chin and prowling up and down the length like she's a paid inspector.

When she finally turns back to me, I waggle my eyebrows. "Well?"

She places a hand on her hip. "I was planning on giving you a hard time, but I've got nothing. You actually have done an amazing job. Even Bennett commented on how great it's been to have you here, taking charge and helping teach some of the younger guys the ropes."

Her heartfelt praise makes my pulse race. Heat rises to my cheeks. To hide my reaction, I toss my head and strike a pose, with one hand on my hip and the other behind my neck. "That's what I'm talking about. Keep it coming."

Inara snort laughs. "You're too much." She reaches out, grabs my hand, and tugs. "Come on. Let's go get some of that flan my mom sent."

"Don't have to ask me twice." Inara's mother makes the best flan. Before I moved here it had been months since I'd had a halfway decent one. In the neighborhood where I grew up in California, getting flan wasn't all that hard. And that was when I didn't have any at home freshly made.

We head to the folding table outside where a bunch of snacks are arranged, including my mother-in-law's flan. The hot sun feels good on my bare back. People scurry around, carrying more sheetrock and tools, while Inara and I help ourselves to bowls of the golden dessert.

Hammering and sawing provides the soundtrack while Inara and I sit on a tarp and shove forkful after forkful into our mouths. Nothing makes me hungrier than physical labor. Building this house is an energy outlet and distraction that I welcome, especially since I'm still trying to come to terms with my feelings for Inara.

Do I love waking up to her cute booty in those pajama shorts? Yes. Do I love the idea that each month that passes only brings us closer and closer to our eventual end? No. Not at all. In fact, the more time that ticks by, the more I question my plan to end this marriage before it's barely has a chance to begin. When we first got hitched, the idea of walking away was easy. Simple. Now I'm not sure if I'll even be able to crawl.

Of course, there's a part of me that wants to get the hell outta Dodge, the part that tells me Inara has no reason to want to remain a couple, even if I have a change of heart. Yeah, I've got some rock hard abs and yeah, I would die to protect her, but that's the problem—I could literally die at any point in this job. And there's no way I want to put someone through what my father and I went through when my mother passed away. Just like I don't want to risk getting so wrapped up in a woman that I end up like my dad.

I grind my teeth before exhaling. No reason to reminisce about things that can't be changed. Lifting the bowl and tilting it, I place my lips against the ceramic so I can slurp down the slight sheen of flan liquid left at the bottom. Just as the sweet syrup hits my tongue, I catch Inara's gaze on me.

I'm afraid she's going to lecture me, just like she did when she caught me drinking milk out of the carton. Instead, she tilts her head and nibbles on her lip.

Fuck it. Tossing the bowl aside, I place a finger under her chin and lift as I bend to meet her. Our lips are a breath away and I can't resist. Not with her sitting so close, surrounding me with her warmth and deliciously sweet scent. I press my mouth to hers, sealing my end of the deal. We kiss a few brief moments before someone whistles in the background, reminding us that we're not alone. She pulls away, giggling, but it's enough for now. I'm already planning the rest of the day out in my head. No more avoiding. Tonight, I'm going to seduce my wife and get her to show me everything she likes.

My body is already humming in anticipation when my phone buzzes. I glance down carelessly, but then go rigid. Quickly, I reread the message. Slower this time.

Son of a bitch. This is karma for the thoughts I had of running earlier.

"What is it? Is everything okay?"

Inara's worried voice breaks through my focus. I glance up from the text and force a smile, for her benefit. "It's Bear. Looks like we're getting shipped out."

"What? You guys have barely been back two months. And didn't someone on one of the teams just end up in the hospital, from a training exercise?"

I rub the back of my neck. If I didn't know any better, I'd think she didn't want me to go. "Yeah, but that's the way it goes. Welcome to SEAL life. Isn't it grand?"

Her hands clench into fists. "No, it's not. It sucks."

Then Inara shocks the hell out of me by stomping off toward the street, leaving me with my mouth gaping open. I know my half-hearted joke was pretty stupid, but still. I didn't mean to upset her. How had I managed to set her off so badly? Guess it's a good reminder that despite getting along better lately, our personalities just don't mesh.

I shoot Bear a return text and then take a quick look around. All my prior sense of accomplishment is gone. It disappeared with Inara. Now, all I notice is a shell of a house. Empty.

I shiver. This void is way too reminiscent of how I'd felt once my mom was gone. I stare off into the distance, already missing my wife's floral scent, and the sound of her throaty laugh.

Though, maybe I dodged a bullet. Karma had worked in my favor by calling me back to duty sooner rather than later. Spending so much time near Inara has been breaking down the walls I've built to keep me safe. A little time away with my men is exactly what I need to get my head back on straight.

The next ten months can't go quickly enough.

CHAPTER FOURTEEN

Inara

I PLOP FACEDOWN on my bed, my body beyond exhausted. Every muscle aches, even ones I didn't know existed. My skin is warm to the touch, thanks to the sun shining through the clouds, even though it's been overcast lately, leaving me with a slight sunburn.

The SAR callouts have been nonstop the past two weeks, on top of work and helping Bennett. My body needs a break. Not that I'm out of shape, because our trainings are no joke, but when it comes to saving someone, it gets a whole lot harder.

Half of me wishes Tony was here. It's a weird thing to admit, given the freak-out I had when I first discovered we'd been matched, but I miss having my husband around. Not only his sexy body and wisecracks, but the way he went out of his way to help me out. If he were home, I know he'd happily save me from dragging my exhausted body to the grocery store, have home-cooked meals waiting for me after extra-grueling days, and save me from the mountains of laundry I never quite conquer. All while making me smile.

The other half of me is happy he's gone. If he were back, I'd have to explain why I'd stormed off the day he left, and I'm not sure I'm ready to admit those reasons. Not even to myself. I'd gone for a drive while I wrestled with my unexpected feelings at his news, followed by a walk along the beach. By the time I returned home, Tony was gone.

Just as I'm about to knock out for a midday nap, my phone buzzes with a reminder. Shit. It's Taya's birthday. She didn't mention it, but with everything on her mind these days, *she* might have even forgotten.

Chingado! I close my eyes. I'm a terrible friend. But I can fix this. Hell, Tony and I threw Trevor's party together in a matter of hours. And of course my mind goes right back to Tony's goddamn sculpted and beautiful face, and the wounded look in his eyes when I'd rushed off the day he'd left for training. But I was scared. And I hate surprises. Especially bad ones. The two of us had been having a moment there, and then his phone buzzes and just like that, he's off on a new mission.

I lean back and sigh. And what a moment it was. Our lips had only met briefly, but I still remember the sweetness of the flan on his tongue, and the flames licking over my skin.

Stop.

What's the point right now of focusing on him or the sultry look in his eyes before he laid that last kiss on me? He's not here, so why torture myself? Besides, nothing has changed. If anything, the way he took off without a text or anything showed me all I need to know about how seriously he's taking this relationship.

I scroll through my contacts and text Marge, knowing if she can't find a babysitter, it'll be hard to get her out of the house. She calls me back almost immediately. "I'd love to celebrate Taya's thirtieth! Mason's mom should be able to keep Leslie a little longer since they're already on a playdate. Hell, she owes me one after Mason had the nastiest stomach virus while staying with us a few months ago. So, what do you have in mind?"

Shit, I don't have any ideas yet. Taya and Jim were going to fly out to San Diego for Comic-Con, but those plans changed. Nothing like Special Forces' schedules. I drum my nails against the countertop. Maybe there's another geeky kind of fun gals' day we can still pull off. "Marge, do you have a superhero costume?"

She chuckles. "Unfortunately, yes."

I speed through details of a possible plan with Marge as they pop into my head. Pretty much we're all going to be wild and silly, and all the things we often forget we are while our husbands are home. We'll wear our favorite costumes and go to the little tapas place that overlooks the beach. It'll be a nice distraction. Marge is on board with all of it and asks if Hayden could join since she's home for the summer.

"Of course," I say, and after a quick goodbye, I hang up and dial Taya.

She answers after what has to be about twenty rings. "Yeah?"

"Happy birthday!" I make sure to sound cheery and not at all as exhausted as I am.

Taya doesn't say a word, not even a thank-you. She just sighs.

"Yes, I know you'd much rather I had a sexy, deep voice and a nice big dick, but alas, you are stuck with my whiny voice. I have a fantastic idea. Get dressed in that digital-blue girl costume you were planning on wearing to SDCC. You know, the one from that video game you and your husband love so much."

"Um, why?"

"Because I've got a hell of a day planned for your birthday, so don't ask questions."

Taya grumbles but ends up agreeing. I hang up with her and start getting ready fast. I'm not great with comics, but I do have a Wonder Woman costume that still fits. I throw everything I can possibly need into a bag since I'll probably knock out on Marge's couch tonight. I text Taya to tell her to bring some comfy clothes as well and that I'll pick her up in twenty, and she agrees.

The blue spandex bottoms are riding up my ass and thick, scratchy material digs into my armpits. Part of me again wishes Tony were here so I can dole out the sass that comes with wearing this costume. What fun it would be to boss him around. The shit I do for my girl. Thankfully, the drive to Taya's is so easy I can do it from memory. By the time I get there, she is fully dressed and ready to go.

Taya climbs into my car and her eyes are a bit puffy with

a wet sheen. I shake my head and point a finger at her. "No tears on your birthday. I won't allow it."

She snorts but continues to stare out the window. "Last year was the first year my dad wasn't around. Plus, you remember what happened at dinner and how my birthday got ruined. This year Jim's not around, and it's my thirtieth. Not that I'm one for milestone celebrations, but for once, it would've been nice to have something that is all mine."

I reach over to give her shoulder a quick squeeze. "I know, honey."

"Not to mention, I just didn't know how much it would hurt each time Jim leaves."

When Taya says "each time" my heart speeds up. For some reason, the fact that being in Special Forces will have Tony gone for more than two hundred days a year didn't really compute until just now. It wasn't a fact I thought about when I signed up for the program, nor when Tony showed up. But now my chest aches from his absence. The more I see what Taya goes through, the more I question if signing up to marry someone in the military was such a great idea.

Given my reaction when Tony first got the news he was leaving? Yeah, I'm not so sure I'm cut out for this. God, I'm just like my mom. Jumping into marriage without thinking it through.

"I'm sorry your birthday last year sucked so bad." I put the car in park and turn to her. "But this one will be way different. Jim might not be here, but he'll make it up to you."

"You're right, he will. And I am kind of glad that you dragged me out of the house as I do have something to celebrate outside of my birthday." Taya fiddles with the strap of her purse as she takes a deep breath. "Lyons called earlier."

My brow quirks at the same time my eyes narrow. "To wish you a happy birthday?"

"And to let me know Santoro was not only convicted but sentenced to life in prison without parole."

She bursts into tears and I reach over and engulf my best friend in a hug. This is huge news. After a couple of minutes pass, I pull back and wipe the tears from Taya's face. "We do have a lot to celebrate. So, let's get started on enjoying our own ridiculous version of Comic-Con." My hand waves up and down our bodies, and we both explode into laughter, glancing down at our costumes.

We exit the car and meet at the back, already garnering glances from people in the lot. By the time I grab the door to the restaurant, Taya and I are not just comfortable in our garb but playing it up. Cue the blockbuster movie music in my head and slow motion entry—the superheroes have arrived.

"They beat us here." Taya points to a primo table with a killer view of the ocean where Marge and Hayden wave us over as inconspicuously as they can.

Marge stands to hug Taya. Damn, she looks sexy in her Catwoman getup. Fingers crossed I'll look that good after having children.

"You guys, thank you so much for doing this, for putting on these costumes and going out with me. And, Hayden, I know we don't know each other well, but I'm so glad you're here," Taya says.

"Any chance I have to put on my Harley Quinn costume is a surefire way to get me to go out," Hayden says.

We all laugh just as the server approaches, pulling out his pad and pencil. "I'd ask if you're having drinks tonight, but I can see that would be a stupid question."

"Ladies, a pitcher of margaritas to start?" When I get nods all around, I turn back to the server. "And can you start us with your best sampler?"

"The best? Ooh, that's a tough choice."

I wave my hand in the air. "Surprise us. We're wild women tonight."

He nods and sticks the pen back into his pocket. "You got it."

Taya catches my gaze and mouths a *thank you*, gratitude evident in her eyes, and my heart fills with warmth.

We spend the next few minutes *oohing* and *aahing* over our costumes, taking selfies, and laughing at the looks people are giving us. Then Taya fills the rest of our group in on the good news. Marge reaches across and grabs her hand. "Have you told Jim yet?"

"No."

I purse my lips. "He's going to pitch a fit you didn't call him right away with the news, which means we *all* are going to have to deal him being extra grumpy."

Taya rolls her eyes. "He'll get over it. And hopefully be relieved. Maybe even call off some of the team guys still here from being my *unofficial* bodyguards."

We all laugh having encountered her protection detail in one way or another. Like the one guy who insisted on coming to the movies with us. Or the newbie who followed us into the nail salon. We treated him to a pedicure.

When a runner brings our margaritas to the table, I hand him my phone and ask if he would take a group shot of us. After the photo is taken, I grab the pitcher and start pouring.

Marge lifts her glass in the air. Crap, a toast. Going from exhaustion to full-speed-ahead party planner was a whirlwind for my brain, so I appreciate the help. The rest of us follow her and clink. "Happy birthday, Taya."

I take one sip and set mine down—Marge seems to be at my pace—while Taya and Hayden keep theirs tipped back until they've got a nice buzz going. We chat and eat and have girl talk, and for a few precious moments, it's like we don't have a care in the world.

"This ceviche is to die for." I shove another loaded chip into my face and refuse to pull that *I'm going to the gym later* mindfuck.

"I like these melon-skewer thingies," Taya says.

Another pitcher comes our way as the once-bright sky now fades to a soft gray on this beautiful summer night. Taya pours this time and as she fills Hayden's glass, she says, "God, I love your hair, Hayden."

I was thinking the same, admiring how the pink at the

top blends into a gorgeous purple.

"Don't let Bear hear you say that," Marge warns.

"Who's Bear? We have no husbands tonight." I meant it to be funny, but an awkward silence passes over the table for a moment, and I want to kick myself.

Hayden clears her throat and waves over the server. "Shots! We haven't done a birthday shot yet."

Thirty minutes later, Marge and Taya head to the restroom and I get the pleasure of watching all the heads turn as they go.

"You went to Italy to study sculpting?" I say to Hayden.

"Yeah, it was a great experience. We studied under a master sculptor and then shared our work at the end of the class. I'm so glad I did it."

I'm genuinely shocked someone so young has had her artwork on display. When I was twenty-two, all I was doing was getting trashed and trying to keep up with my mom's relationships. "That's really cool. Did your family go out to see it?"

"No, Dad was either on a mission or training and Mom was with Leslie. I don't think they really know all the details or understand it fully."

"Well, I'd love to see your stuff someday."

Marge and Taya return arm in arm. When they sit down, Marge takes hold of Taya's hand. "I know this is still all new to you, and the other wives haven't been as comforting." Taya is smiling, but her eyes have a sheen on them.

I'm in awe of how put together Marge is. This has been

her life for most of her adulthood—having Bear leave over and over, never really being able to make plans together, never really knowing if he would be okay. And while our husbands are only gone at training right now, it's all a stark reminder of how often they do leave and what they're training for.

I raise my glass and salute Marge with it. "Bear's lucky to have you."

"Hell yes, he is, and you better bet I remind him every day." She pauses to wipe a small tear that runs down her cheek. "But I'm lucky too. He really cares about us." She looks over to Taya. "It doesn't ever go away, the missing and the fear, but you get more used to it. And you have us."

Taya leans in to hug Marge and it hits me that this is what it means to be a wife to these men. There's a strength most people don't realize. Through it all, these women have to be at home alone or act as single moms for months at a time. Even if things continued getting better with Tony, would I be able to handle a life like this?

Taya looks over at me and I try to hide the anxiety written across my face by taking a large gulp of my drink. But there's no use, since she knows me so well. She offers me a weak smile. "Is all of this getting to you?"

I set the glass back down and sigh. "No, I'm just thinking about Tony is all."

Marge's eyes go wide and she looks at me. "Honey, I'm sorry I haven't even checked in with you. This is your first time with Tony gone."

To my surprise and horror, my eyes start to well with soft tears. "No, it's okay, I'm fine." My voice catches in my throat. Christ, I'm far from fine.

"You probably miss him like crazy."

I don't need Taya's truth bombs at this moment. "Not in the slightest."

The three woman stare at me, eyes unblinking and with a slight tilt to their heads.

I quiver a little bit under their combined assault and throw my hands up. "Okay, I do miss him. I just don't know where we stand. Every time I think things are working, something happens to make us take two steps back."

Marge leans across the table and puts her hand on mine. "We've all let our husbands leave during some of the most inopportune moments. Their jobs don't stop for their home lives. And I think it's pretty evident Tony means a lot to you."

I don't want to be like my mother, divorce after divorce. But more than that, a big part of my heart wants things to work out with Tony for the long haul. Just for me. And I can't say his body doesn't light me up. We might have had a little bit of an awkward first time, but that can be worked through.

Let's be real. I would love to work through that part with him.

I wipe my eyes and tuck a loose curl behind my ear. "Hey now, we're not here to listen to me vent about Tony's being gone. We still got movie and wine time."

We eventually settle the check, and Marge and I make sure the other is okay to drive. We both tapered off our drinking earlier so that we wouldn't have to leave our cars here overnight. After Taya and I get into my car, I follow Marge back to her place and we all change into our comfy lounging clothes to finish the night gawking at a longhaired, buff, blond Asgardian god.

Although, deep in my heart, I'd do anything to be gawking at my husband right now.

CHAPTER FIFTEEN

Tony

GODDAMN TEXAS HEAT. And thank fuck for the AC in this hotel. Bear pushes me and I almost stumble as we head into the small dining area we've been monopolizing the past couple of nights. I turn and give the big behemoth the middle-finger salute, even though I'm not really mad. On tough days, Bear is the glue that holds us all together.

The training is long and exhausting, but there's something so satisfying about working my body to its limits. But I miss Inara. And her lips. And the way her tiny frame and curves fit right into me. The mere thought of her sends the blood pulsing to my dick, and I bite back a groan. Fuck, I can't be popping a boner right now.

"Inara say anything about the broken vase?" Craiger asks.

"Nope." I stop in front of the TV, shoulder to shoulder with Jim. A cable weather station is focused on the East Coast, and a blob containing a large amount of purple and red on the computer model is moving off the Atlantic, with the predicted path to take it right over Virginia. Exhaustion makes me a little slow on the uptake, but when I realize what

I'm looking at, my stomach dives into my boots.

"Shit." Jim steals the word right out of my mouth.

The weatherman starts talking and as soon I catch the words *storm* and *hurricane*, I whip out my cell and immediately call Inara. The phone rings and rings as I pace toward the back patio and with each passing second, the pain grows in my stomach. When the call goes to voice mail, I hang up and dial her again, standing at the door, unable to force myself out into the punishing heat.

"Tony?" Inara picks up at last, sounding out of breath. "Is everything okay? Are you hurt?"

Her familiar voice pours over me, and I close my eyes and picture her beautiful face while I hasten to calm her fears. "Everything's fine. I'm calling because I saw the weather report and wanted to make sure you were home safe. There's a storm heading your way and it's going to be a big one."

She releases a heavy sigh into the phone. "Oh, thank God. You scared the shit out of me. The storm's been all over the news here too."

I hold the phone away from my head and blink at it. Did she just admit that she'd been scared? On my behalf? That little detail shouldn't matter, but damned if I'm not all warm and tingly all of a sudden. I put the phone back up to my ear. "Can you repeat that?"

"I said, the storm's been all over the news here too."

"No, not that. The part before it. You know, where you said that you're worried about me. Like a real wife and all."

There's a pause where I can practically see her roll her dark eyes. "Seriously? You call from training to give me crap?"

I chuckle at the exasperation in her voice. Damn. I really do miss her and her spunky ways. "You're staying inside, right?"

There's another brief pause. "Not exactly. I'm needed on a callout to Shenandoah National Park."

Those are about the last words I'm expecting and my fingers tighten around the phone as if trying to crush it into pieces. The weatherman warned the storm would be one of the worst this year. "Inara, it's going to be too dangerous. If you get hurt, then you can't help anyone." I grip the cell tighter while my chest flutters, the lack of control causing my head to go light. "Please, stay home."

"Tony, you know how important this is to me. I promise, I can handle it."

I rub my hand over my smooth scalp to try to calm myself down and when that doesn't work, I hit my fist against the nearby wall. A woman pulling a suitcase behind her turns at the noise, then averts her eyes and picks up her speed toward the lobby. I try to keep my tone low and steady, but by the time I get to the end of my speech, it climbs again. "They're saying it's not even safe to drive. What do you think is gonna happen while you're hiking through the mountains?"

Her voice rises this time. "I'm doing an important job. I know it's dangerous, but what about your job? Yours is even more dangerous and I support you in all of it."

"You mean the way you did when I first got the news I was leaving?" I'd told myself that her reaction that day was no big deal, but I guess some subconscious part of me has been clinging to the hurt.

She sighs again, a soft sound that I barely catch. "You're right. I did react poorly, and I'm sorry. I was caught off guard. I'll do better next time."

"Well, okay. Good." While touched by her quiet admission, and also flustered, that is so not the point! Doesn't she understand I'm scared shitless for her? "But that still doesn't mean you should be out there."

"Why don't *you* explain to the missing girl how you deem my life more valuable than hers?"

I lean my head against the wall and exhale. "Shit. I'm sor—"

"And you might as well tell Jim to stop calling Taya because she's just going to say the exact same thing to him." She hangs up before I have a chance to respond, before I can mention that I respect what she's doing. I respect her strength, her courage, but I don't love the risk. I don't love that at any moment she could be called away and have to wade through dangerous settings to find someone. Aren't there limits, though, circumstances that determine whether or not she should go out? Surely a hurricane coming is grounds for sitting this one out.

I stomp back to Jim, passing the guys seated at a table, staring at their own phones. He's got the same irritated and worried face I must have. Jim rubs his eyes with his palms. "Let me guess, Inara's got the same idea as Taya."

"I don't know what the hell they're thinking." My stomach aches with a sourness I can't place. What if something happens to her and I'm not there? My mother's face flashes across my mind. This. This is exactly what I promised myself I'd avoid. I don't want to worry about someone else. To think about how devastated I would be if something bad happens to her. I've lived through that kind of pain once already. No way do I want to sign up for a second round.

Damn you, Inara.

Jim throws his hands up as he paces back and forth, his jaw ticking with each step. "I wish they would listen. And it's not like it's their job and they have to go."

Bear lets out a loud snort as his giant form rises, shakes his head as if we're too thick-headed to understand, and then walks over to the coffee station to pour a mugful. "You girls done crying into your hankies yet?"

Really? Here I'd been expecting Bear to share some kernel of wisdom, and instead, he shit-talks us? I shoot him a glare and Jim pretends to not have heard. Craiger looks up from his phone as if the show's about to start and Trevor fakes us out by getting up, walking toward the coffee station, and just continues on down the hall. Guess he didn't want to be a part of this discussion. I don't blame him.

Bear sips his coffee and steps closer, raking his gaze over both Jim and me. "Support goes both ways. Learned that the hard way with Marge when Splitsville came knocking."

Excuse me? My gaze jumps between Bear and Jim, and by Jim's wide unblinking eyes, I'm going to guess he didn't know this little tidbit of information either. But that can't be true. Bear and Marge? The perfect couple that all of us aspired to be? I just can't picture them as anything less than what they are now. They're so close that it's gross how close they are sometimes. I swallow and rub the back of my neck. "Had no clue."

Bear shrugs. "Was a long time ago. We had Hayden young and Marge was barely out of high school when we found out she was pregnant. She was a Valentine's Day baby." Bear smiles at the mention of Hayden, which times perfectly with the front-desk clerk coming over to check the coffeepot. She returns Bear's grin, and he gives her a polite nod that almost makes me chuckle.

"We didn't plan for her, and I wouldn't change that bit for anything, but we were so young. Didn't know what we were going to do, so I did what I had to do—enlisted. And I dragged Marge around, made her move with me." He pauses and his lips press into a thin line as he remembers.

"Must've been tough," Jim says, taking a seat on the couch.

"Tough?" Bear appears to roll the word around in his head in that unhurried way of his before snickering. "That's one way of putting it. Never once considered how a SEAL life would affect Marge. She's so smart, always did well in school, but I didn't even ask her how she felt about moving with me. About being at home alone with Hayden. Never asked what she had wanted to do after high school."

I join Jim on the couch, leaning my elbows on my knees as Bear scratches his head. By the looks of it, this story isn't something he's comfortable sharing. While we know more about one another than our wives do, some things we just keep to ourselves.

"So, what happened?" Craiger asks.

"After a few years, the trainings and deployments took a toll and one day she told me she was accepted to a college not far from her family. She moved back home, took Hayden with her, and I kept myself busy."

Craiger mouths a *shit* and I hang my head, seeing a flash of my possible future.

"Was angry for a long time. Until I missed her. Until I realized what a fool I was being, and all she had given up to be with me." He takes a seat across from Craiger at the table, setting down his cup and facing Jim and me with a fatherly expression.

Jim grunts and I just nod. There are no words. His story is not unusual. Happens to so many of us. Marriages to those of us in Special Forces fail about ninety percent of the time. Just never figured Bear and Marge had almost become part of that statistic.

"I've been blathering for too long already but let me just say this. I've been with Marge forever, but it also took me a long time to realize that relationships take a lot of work, and a lot of compromise. It's give-and-take."

Jim snorts. "Yeah, well, Tony wants to give it to her but

175

she ain't takin'."

I don't know whether to laugh or punch Jim's ugly mug, but thankfully, Bear's booming voice saves us both from either. "Look, you two are scared to death about what is going on back at home, but you can't take away the one thing those women really care about. It's not fair to them. Doesn't matter if it doesn't pay, it helps them in some weird way. Man, those four years Marge was gone were some of the worst years of my life." He shakes his head and then pins us both with a knowing glare. "I'm telling you this so you don't make the same mistakes I did."

Jim and I both nod. Then I pull out my phone and hit redial. I need to talk to Inara again and apologize. Instead of a ring, I get an automated message. *We're sorry, all circuits are busy. Please try your call again later.*

I try two more times only to get the same greeting. The storm must be causing problems already. I slow my breathing, work on calming myself down. She's with a group of people. She's not alone. And while that's what I need to keep telling myself, it's not enough. I need something to distract me and pushing my body to the limit seems like the perfect plan. "Hitting the gym. I need to train, and then I'm getting some fucking tacos."

Jim jumps up. "Going with you. Can't sit here thinking about Taya alone in this storm. Not with everything that happened."

I pin him with a semi-glare. "You know she isn't alone. My wife is with her. And let's face it, they aren't sitting at home either."

We head down the hall to the small hotel gym containing some dumbbells and a functional trainer cable machine, and I try to think of how strong Inara is, try to tell myself that she'll be safe. But all I see is her diamond-shaped face streaked with rain.

CHAPTER SIXTEEN

Inara

THE AIR WHIPS my face and stings my skin. We've been out here for hours and my muscles are starting to exhaust themselves. The weather has turned quicker than I anticipated. Though the rain is gentle, my clothes are already heavier from the water, and I'm having difficulty keeping myself warm now that the winds have picked up.

Every moment we don't find the missing girl means she's one step closer to being gone for good, especially since teams have been searching for a couple of days now with no success. But I can't think like that, I can't even consider it. So instead, I focus on my last conversation with Tony, which only makes my chest ache and doesn't push me any closer to having a positive mental attitude. Given his entire career path, I figured he would have been a hell of a lot more understanding than he was. But I haven't needed anyone to worry about me . . . ever. Well, maybe Bennett. But once *Mami* divorced him, I was back to taking care of myself since she was too busy dating. I jog to catch up to Taya ahead, but keep my eye on the ground as it's slippery as fuck.

Taya looks over her shoulder at me. "I swear it's as if I can hear Jim telling me I shouldn't be out here."

"Tony would literally swoop in, pick me up, and drag me back home if he could." The thought of him swinging me over his shoulder, though very caveman-ish, does cause some excitement to twinge between my legs. I'd give up a lot to see that side of him. However, given how upset he was on the phone, I'm not sure I'll ever get the chance.

"How are things going with him?"

The stubborn part of me refuses to admit my husband plans to bail in nine months when we go in for our one-year meeting with the IPP committee. Taya wouldn't judge me, but I just can't bring myself to say it. Like if I admit it aloud, I'm only a few steps away from being the same as my mom, first divorce in the making. I grab a low-hanging branch and pull myself up the small hill. "The man drives me nuts. If he was the Tony I met last year, I'd be able to definitively say things suck. But he has this whole other side to him I never would have guessed existed, and it puts us in this gray area. One where I'm not sure what to think and it's driving me crazy."

Taya waves a dismissive hand in the air as she trudges through thick brush. "I went through the same crap with Jim. Took him forever to open up. But in the end, it was worth it. It's like you told me, the whole experience is one big, ass-awkward date, except you knew who walked through your door."

I snort. "Tell me about it."

We finally get out of the thick brush and hike along a deer path. The rain is coming down harder, and the wind is whipping through the trees. In the distance, thunder rumbles, but we haven't seen any lightning, so we keep going. I pull out the radio and check in with command as Taya studies the topographic map of the area.

After I tuck the radio back into my chest harness, I sidle up to Taya and glance over the map. "We've pretty much covered the area. Let's double back and hang to the west a bit."

Taya nods.

I quirk an eyebrow at her. "You know Jim and Tony must be shitting bricks that we're out here."

She smiles and tucks away the map. "There will be hell to pay, especially since both of them have such an innate fear of losing people they love."

My mouth hangs open and I blink rapidly.

Taya catches my confused expression and huffs. "Let me guess, Tony hasn't shared with you that his mom died of cancer when he was in high school."

"What? No."

Taya grimaces. "Figured he would've told you by now. Jim mentioned it to me when I was recovering. Tony had been a bit overprotective, and I thought Jim told him to be. But turns out, it was all Tony."

I shake my head as we turn west in silence while I digest this shocking bit of information. "That sort of makes sense, because I caught him talking on the phone with his dad one day, and he was super-uncomfortable. Then he clammed up afterward."

I keep lingering on the idea Tony has this whole life I don't know about. I take a deep, centering breath. It's not like I expected him to tell me everything, but I wish he would have told me this. At the end of the day, if he isn't willing to open up to me, then I can't force him, no matter how much it makes me ache in a way I had long forgotten was possible.

The clouds above are swirling a deeper gray, and I curse under my breath. Shenandoah National Park is huge and the more time that passes, the more concerned I become the girl won't be found alive. My stomach twists and I clench my hands into fists. I still don't understand how a school could leave one of their students behind. But the girl has some basic survival knowledge, according to her parents, so I hope we can find her before the storm really hits.

Bennett is the one who introduced me to camping and who sparked my interest in search and rescue. The first time we went, I'd been super-excited to spend time in nature, hoping it would be some kind of cool, spiritual experience. It definitely wasn't. I returned home with probably a thousand mosquito bites, blisters on my toes, and very sore calves. But I fell in love with the outdoors to the point some days it is hard to convince myself not to run away and live off the grid in Alaska.

The sky lights up, and the woods vibrate with the loud crack that follows the lightning. Taya looks up and then back at me. "Shit, it's about to come down on us."

"We should return to the staging area. It's becoming too dangerous to be out here."

Taya nods and we turn to head back. After a few meters, my foot slips at one point on a too-smooth rock, but Taya catches my arm. Lightning continues to streak through the sky, and we quicken our pace. Instead of cutting back through the thick brush, we wander outside of our assigned area and hop on another deer path.

We're only twenty feet away from the falls when I hear it. A soft whimper. At first I stop and think it might be the wind, or a bird of some kind hiding from the storm. But then I hear it again, followed by sniffling.

I whip my head around and walk in a widening circle. "Julia? Is that you?"

"Yes! Yes, I'm over here."

At first I don't see anyone, but then the girl emerges from a forest-green tent a couple of meters to my left.

"Taya! Taya! Over here."

Taya runs over as thunder bursts overhead. Julia is a little sunburnt, badly bitten by mosquitos, and her lips are blistered. But she can walk, and more important than any other detail, she's alive. She hugs us, then pulls away and wipes her eyes. "I was so scared being out here. I tried to find my way back to a trail but couldn't. Everything looks the same. When the storm started, I thought I'd never see my family again."

"You're okay. We've got you." I hug her once more as

Taya radios in that we found Julia and that we are heading back down.

After grabbing some of Julia's belongings and making sure she is well enough to walk, we make our way back to the staging area. The poor girl finishes a granola bar Taya hands her in two bites. When we hit the edge of the tree line, the medical staff rushes over to Julia and takes over while Taya and I go to debrief.

To know that Julia will go home and be with her family after this experience because Taya and I and the rest of our team were willing to work hard means everything to me. When the girl gets into the ambulance and leaves, I turn to Taya and start bawling. Taya joins in immediately. With all the chaos in my life, everything with Tony and with my mom, it's just such a relief to know I can still do good in the world.

CHAPTER SEVENTEEN

Tony

THESE LAST SIX weeks have been grueling, but in an entirely new way. I hadn't expected to miss Inara so much. It's surprising how often I thought about things like holding her, lying next to her. I imagined her lips and her eyes, of course, but it was more than that. For the first time, I actually missed her being, like she'd somehow become a part of me, and I hadn't noticed until we were actually separated.

Bear was right about search and rescue. And thankfully, the storm passed and nothing happened to her. Though I still can't believe she was out there. I wish I could have been there to make sure she was okay, but she did it all without me—and they found the missing child. My girl is kind of a badass.

I shake my head.

I haven't been trying in this relationship as much as I should've been. Haven't told my wife anything about myself. Haven't asked her why she even signed up in the first place. Yeah, I have ideas. Mostly because she signed up right after

Taya's wedding, which is one of the only times I've ever caught Inara at a loss for words. I'll never forget the expression of absolute horror on her face when the screaming brunette woman in the parking lot mentioned she was Inara's date's wife.

I wince at the memory. It was obvious she'd had no idea the slick guy in the fancy suit by her side all night was already hitched. But ignorance wasn't enough to save you from the scorned partner's wrath. Been there, experienced that, years ago. Left with a black eye to show for it. So I'd ushered Inara to her car, quickly, while the woman was still fixated on her cheating husband.

Physically, Inara had been fine. Emotionally? I wasn't so sure. That night, I'd watched my now-wife shrink right before my eyes while her hands shook on the wheel.

So, yeah. I'm guessing the shock of discovering her boyfriend was married, combined with her mom's lousy track record, had a whole lot to do with her hasty decision to join the Issued Partner Program. Then again, when two people never have real conversations, all you have are ideas. And assumptions. And everyone knows what they say about those. So maybe, considering my lack of relationship experience, it's time I do more things that I've avoided. Things like actually *talking* to my wife.

This is the beginning of a new, motivated Tony, the kind of Tony that could actually make a marriage work. The kind of Tony that listens. I pull into the driveway and put the car in park faster than I should, given the sensitive gears. But I'm just happy to be home.

The key is like hot steel in my hands, and I fumble as I slip it into the lock. When I open the door, I'm so excited to see her that I'm practically bouncing, despite my exhausted legs.

"Inara?" I call out down the hallway. Silence greets me. Before checking the garage to find out if her car is gone, I head to the fridge to grab a glass of cold water. A note is taped to the door.

Painting the last of the new houses at the site with Bennett for a family with a little girl. Be back later. Welcome home! I cooked for you. Look in the fridge.

Disappointment that she's not home coils inside me, but I shake it off and check in the fridge to see what she's left me. After heating up a plate of her homemade enchiladas—which are literally the best thing I've had in my mouth since Inara's tongue, right before I left—I change clothes and shoot Trevor a quick text, asking if he wants to come with me to the construction site. During training, I made a unilateral decision to include the guy in more activities once we got back home. Jim's still working through some emotions, which is totally understandable. But that means someone else needs to step up to the plate and do what needs to be done. We're a team. A unit. Closer knit than a lot of families. Or at least, we should be. It's not right to hang Trevor out to dry just because he's the new guy and Jim's still haunted by ghosts of the past.

My phone buzzes. Trevor's a yes, so I head back out the door. I stop by his place on the way, and he hurries out to the car and climbs inside.

"Thanks for texting. I was still unpacking and already getting a little restless being home." He sounds so grateful that I'm doubly glad I invited him along. "Is that normal?"

"Everyone's different, but yeah, it can be hard to go right back to your regular life when you get home. Physical activity usually helps me a lot, so I figured might as well kill two birds and help out a local family while taking the edge off."

Less than twenty minutes later, we arrive at the construction site. Unlike the last time I'd helped Bennett out, this house is already built. We walk up the dirt road and enter the open door. Inside, the smell of paint is strong. A couple swipes rollers coated with a beige color on the walls. I don't recognize them, so after a brief wave, we continue on in search of someone we know. We run into Bennett in the kitchen, where he's helping another man install cabinets. He spots me and takes a break.

"Hey, Tony! I didn't know you were coming. Good to see you." He walks up to us and pats me on the arm. "And look, you brought a friend to help."

"Bennett, this is Trevor, one of my teammates. Trevor, Bennett. Inara's stepdad. He's going to put you right to work."

The two of them shake hands and then Bennett hands us

a couple of paintbrushes. "You ever painted a house before, Trevor?"

Trevor shakes his head. "No, sir."

"Well, today's your lucky day. Hey, Lucy," Bennett calls out of his shoulder. "Trevor here is new. You mind giving him a few pointers?"

A twenty-something-year-old woman with a blond ponytail rubs a hand on her paint-splattered denim overalls and turns to Trevor. "See this?" She wiggles a thick paintbrush at Trevor, and he nods. "This is a paintbrush. You dip this in the paint"—she proceeds to demonstrate—"and you put it on the wall."

I snicker. A smartass after my own heart. Meanwhile, poor Trevor's cheeks have turned fifty shades of red. Bennett gently nudges him forward. "Come on, Lucy, quit traumatizing the poor kid and show him how it's done."

I'm tempted to stay and watch as Trevor makes his way over toward her, but my teammate is right. I do miss my wife and now that she's nearby, I'm desperate to see her.

Bennett points to the staircase. "Inara's up there."

I toss one last look at Trevor, who's hovering a safe two feet away from Lucy, chuckle, and then bound up the stairs two at a time. It's quieter up here. I walk down a narrow hallway and the first room I peer into is empty. I finally find Inara alone in what I'm guessing is the master bedroom at the end of the hall. She's got earbuds in and is shaking her hips while she strokes paint onto the wall. Her back is to me, so I tiptoe up behind her and then, when I'm only a few inches away, I reach out and give her waist a quick squeeze.

Her shriek is so loud, I bet they can hear it the next town over. She spins and reflexively jabs out with the paintbrush, catching me smack dab in the chest as she pulls AirPods out of her ears. "Tony! You scared me half to death!"

We both look down at the giant blue streak on my old Metallica shirt. "I can see that."

Then our gazes lift and we stand there, just staring at each other like it's been years since we've been together. Mainly, I'm just drinking Inara in. Memories of how beautiful my wife is couldn't do the real thing justice. She's dressed in cut-offs that reveal her long, toned legs and a beat-up gray T-shirt that slides off one golden shoulder. Her hair is pulled back in a ponytail, and she has a streak of blue paint across one cheek. Adorable and sexy, all wrapped up into one package.

"Aw, come on, give your long-lost husband a hug." Before she can protest, I sweep her up into my arms and bury my face in her hair, inhaling that sweet, citrusy scent. "I missed you," I whisper, as her arms wrap around my waist and squeeze.

"Missed you too. Even if you can be an overprotective ass sometimes."

"Sorry. I'll do better next time." I hold her close for a few more seconds before finally stepping back. My gaze dips to her chest and I snicker. "Hey, look, twinsies."

She looks down at where the blue paint she'd splattered onto my shirt rubbed off on hers. Right across her left breast.

She swipes at the spot and somehow manages to streak it across the other boob, making me laugh even louder. "You think that's funny, huh?" She arches a dark brow at me and then, without any further warning, flicks her paintbrush at my arm. Sprinkles of blue land on my skin, from my wrist all the way up to my bicep. Then she starts to laugh. "You look like you have a case of Smurf measles."

Now she's gone and done it. "I'm way hotter than a Smurf."

While she's rolling her eyes, I dart for the paint can, prying the lid off and dipping my brush in before she catches on. When I whirl back around, her eyes go comically wide. "You wouldn't dare."

Before she can utter another word, I sweep my brush all the way down her left cheek to her chin and then paint a matching line on the other side. "Now who's the Smurf?"

My throat tightens up though when she closes the distance between us until her lips are just brushing mine. Her tongue sweeps across my lips, and a low groan emits from my mouth. The next moment, she grabs the back of my head in her hands and is rubbing her cheeks all over mine.

She steps back and admires her handiwork. "I'd say both of us."

My heart is still pounding away from that teasing almost-kiss. She should look ridiculous with blue paint streaked all over her, but instead, it only makes her look hotter. I'm tempted by an urge to take my brush and drag it all over her skin, from head to toe. Then, I'd drop her right there on the plastic floor covering and find out what kind of art we could create together.

Based on how she's staring at my lips—the way a starving man looks at a sandwich—her mind must be in the gutter too. She sways a little toward me.

Bennett's voice interrupts the moment. "Hey, is everything okay up there? I heard some loud noises!"

"We're fine! Just spilled a little paint!" Inara hollers back. She gives herself a shake and then nudges the paint can with her foot. "Come on. The sooner we get this room finished up . . ."

She doesn't finish the rest, but it's all the incentive I need. I scramble over to the paint and start slapping it on the wall in record time. Inara laughs softly to herself, but she's got a little extra spring in her step too. With the two of us on a mission, we make short work of the room. We finish the smaller guest bedroom just as quickly. When we're done, I follow her lead and head downstairs with our empty paint cans and brushes.

Inara places the empty cans on the floor in the kitchen and the paintbrushes in a bucket half full of water. She then turns to Bennett, who's already begun to clean up some of the supplies. "I think we're done for today. Tony just got back today from training, and I'm beat too."

I glance around the main living area. "Where's Trevor?"

"Paint ran out for the rooms down here, so I sent him on a paint run with Lucy," Bennett says.

Inara's eyes widen. "You paired sweet Trevor with Lucy?

Oh man. Poor Trevor. I bet today ends up being way more traumatizing for him than training must have been."

"It's good for him. Builds character." I wink and then pull out my phone. "Let me check in and ask if he needs a ride home."

"Oh, don't worry," Bennett says. "Either Lucy or I can take him, no problem. He's kind of quiet, but seems like a good man."

"He is. That's why I want to make sure that he doesn't get lost in all the upheaval that's been going on lately." I text him the plan and when he confirms he's good with it, I tuck my phone back into my pocket.

When Inara gazes at me, there's this warm, soft expression in her eyes. An expression I could get used to seeing. Oblivious to the moment we're having, Bennett finally takes a long look at us. "So, that's what all the shrieking upstairs was about—you both got attacked by the paint can."

I shake Bennett's hand, eager to get my wife home. "Thanks for letting me pitch in. Hopefully next time I can stick around for longer."

When Bennett releases and, after he hugs Inara goodbye, I grab my wife's hand and tug her toward the front door and to our respective cars. On our separate drives home, I caution myself not to get my hopes up. Just because we got a little hot and bothered for a minute there while painting doesn't necessarily mean that we're going to cap off my first night back with hot sex.

Then again, it doesn't mean we're not either.

I push down a little harder on the accelerator and hurry home.

Of course, Inara has already beaten me there. Wordlessly, we walk up the driveway to the front door. She unlocks it, steps inside, and I follow behind her. Once I'm in the entryway, I turn and close the door. The dead bolt slides home with an audible click. I barely turn back around before she's launching herself at my chest.

I pull her into my arms and lift her a couple of inches off the floor while I press my lips into hers like I'm in need of air. Her sweet tongue glides out and touches mine, all heat and confidence, with just the slightest tinge of curiosity. We kiss and it becomes everything I want all our other kisses to be. I lift her a little higher and then carry her the few steps to the couch, where I set her on the back edge and position myself between her legs. I grab her by the hips and pull her as close as I possibly can. I want every piece of this woman. I want her to have every piece of me.

I feel at home, with her, for the first time in a very long time.

"Missed you." My eyes widen and brows rise when the words slip out my mouth like gas in church.

"I guess I kinda missed your ass too."

I drop my head and chuckle. "And I guess I missed your smart little mouth."

I pop my head up when her hands reach around, slide into the sleeves of my shirt, and explore my skin. The soft sensation makes me want to pick her up, carry her to the bedroom, and show her all I've thought of doing with her this whole time.

"Yeah?" she says as her nails scratch against my back.

"Yeah…"

Inara leans in and nibbles my earlobe, tracing her tongue along the soft flesh. Even though I'm feeling good about my chances right now, her next words still floor me. "Well, why don't we both shower up super-quick and then you can take me to the bedroom like a real husband and show me just how much?"

CHAPTER EIGHTEEN

Inara

I'M PUTTING TONY'S shirts into one of the dresser drawers when he emerges from the bathroom. He's bare-chested and, holy hell, he's gained some muscle while being away. With water droplets glistening across his sculpted pecs and back, he looks positively scrumptious. But my stomach twists when my gaze lands on the shrapnel scar. He must've been lucky to walk away with just the one minor injury, and I'm not sure I really want to know what happened.

Tony pauses when he spots me. "What are you doing?"

I glance down at the last of his shirts in my hand. "Just putting your things away. If that's alright with you? I figured it was time for you to move into the bedroom."

Something flickers across his face and is gone the next moment. "That . . . that sounds nice, thanks." His gaze darts to mine and then drops to the floor. My big, brawny husband, going shy on me. It's adorable. Especially since I know he's not that insecure. Not with the way he'd turned painting into foreplay earlier.

My God, I can't stop thinking about his tongue, those

lips, and his arms just taking me and lifting me. I was so damn wet. I slam the drawer shut and hurry over to the bed, plopping down on it and waiting. I don't care if I look eager. I am eager. No shame in that.

I glance at the knotted towel around Tony's hips and lick my lips. Eager to get my hands all over my husband's naked body.

Tony is a little more hesitant as he climbs into bed. Into my bed. The scent of soap floats right under my nose and all I can picture is every place on his body he rubbed with that bar only moments ago. He smiles as if reading my mind.

"I'm happy you're home." I turn to him and my chest warms. After six weeks of missing him, it's nice to have him next to me. And now it's time to show him just how much.

I bite my lower lip and begin slowly undoing the top button of the romper I threw on over my sexy violet lacy bra while he was in the shower. "Really happy, actually."

Tony's eyes fixate on my hands and fingers undoing each button. I really want to rip the damn thing off, but I want to show him how nice a slow buildup can be. With each button I undo, the rate at which his chest rises and falls increases. And when I undo the last button, Tony groans.

I let the romper fall to the floor and stand in front of him wearing a violet-lace thong and matching push-up bra. I take a couple of steps closer to him and run my fingers along his exposed arm. "You like what you see?"

His Adam's apple bobs as he swallows but he doesn't respond.

I lift his hand and let his rough fingers run along the curve of my cleavage. "You can touch me, Tony."

I climb into bed and move the fluffy comforter aside so we're both exposed. I look over at Tony, still wrapped in a towel, as he gets harder and harder. His hand moves to his dick and he rubs it softly over the fabric.

"I was thinking we could do something a little different tonight." I reach over to my nightstand and pull out my favorite purple vibrator. Tony's eyes go wide. I'm not sure exactly how inexperienced he is in bed, but sex toys are one of my favorite things to incorporate, and I'm always thrilled to perform for my partners. The idea that they're there, watching me get off to them, always gives me some of the most intense orgasms.

And the idea I'll most likely be the one introducing Tony to this kind of play makes me downright wet.

"I'm not sure I know how to use that on you." His voice cracks the slightest bit as if he's embarrassed.

I reach over and run my hand across his bare chest. He is so defined, I want to stop and run my tongue along the lines of his muscles, down his stomach to the tip of his hard dick. I want to run the pre-cum along my lips and lick them so he can watch me taste him. But he also needs to learn what I like and, as Taya mentioned, I might as well teach him. "Well, maybe you can just watch instead?"

I lift the vibrator to my mouth and run it across my lips. I lick it from the bottom to the top, before pushing it into my mouth, showing him exactly what I can do. The action of prepping the vibrator for my body sends chills over my skin and causes my pussy to pulsate. I'm ready to show him exactly how I like to be touched and fucked. I turn the vibrator on, and Tony looks startled at first, but then like he just hit the jackpot. I wink at him and run the humming vibrator over his nipples. "It's only a gentle buzz."

Tony's eyes are glued to me as I lie back on the bed and lift my curls to spread across the pillow. I open my legs wide. I turn the vibrator off for a minute and let my hand slide from my neck down over my breasts. I lift one out of my bra and roll the nipple between my fingers and moan. Tony reaches over and I let him run his hand across the curve. He flicks my nipple, puts it between his fingers and pinches tight enough it stings a little, but in a good way. He's learning already.

"Mmm." I take his hand and run it down my belly and then off to my side, resting it gently on the bed. "Now, just watch," I say while shutting my eyes and licking my lips. As much as I want his hands all over me, I want to do this with him. I want us to explore each other in this kind of way.

I let my hand move back to the center of my stomach and then all the way to between my legs. Normally I would just slide my panties off, but there's something so hot about the idea of leaving them on. I spread my legs wider and use my other hand to push my panties over. I take my fingers and lick them before moving them to spread my lips and let my finger graze against my clit. The soft touch makes me shiver and whimper in pleasure. I inhale and plunge my fingers deep inside.

"Feels so good," I say, turning to Tony, moving my fingers in and out slowly while my other hand holds my panties aside.

"I'm so hard." His voice is raspy and his eyes are plastered to my body.

"Why don't you show me how hard you are?" I start running my thumb against my clit as he undoes the knot on the towel. My mouth drops open. He's hard and big, and the idea of having him inside me sends a shock of pleasure through me. I push my fingers in deeper and deeper, loving the image of him in my bed with his hand tight around his cock. We might be working our own bodies, but it's as if I'm closer to him in this moment than I ever have been. He starts moving his hand up and down the shaft, running his thumb over the tip.

"I like watching you stroke yourself like that." My eyes are half closed and my lip is between my teeth. I reach up and unclasp my bra, letting my breasts fall loose. Tony leans over and kisses my shoulders and my neck. Finally, when I can't stand it any longer, I reach for the vibrator. I sit up and push my back against the wall and turn my body slightly toward him. Tony follows my idea and sits up too.

I want him to watch how slowly I glide it in, how my pussy spreads for it the way it'll spread for him. He moans and his hand moves up and down quicker and quicker, but his eyes stay open the whole time. I take the vibrator and place it between my legs. I put the head right against my clit and I turn it on.

I can't help it when a deep, guttural moan escapes my lips. I love the idea Tony is sitting here, watching me get off like I've gotten off so many times when I've thought about his dick entering me over and over again. I let the vibrator slide into my pussy and I push my hips into it.

"God, you're sexy." Tony matches my rhythm and slows down. The deeper I go with the vibrator the lower he goes with his hand. He keeps his eyes on me as I pump it in and out. Finally, I get into a quicker rhythm and I can't contain myself. I lean over onto my knees and begin moving my hips, riding the vibrator over and over. Tony mimics my position and pumps his hand up and down fast, his other hand reaching behind for my ass, as if it's crucial we are touching through completion.

We lock eyes and my body builds in tension and electricity. I fuck the vibrator fast and hard until my pussy starts clenching. I grab Tony's face and I pull him in to kiss me. I want his mouth pressed against mine as I come. He moans against my mouth as I start coming and I can't stop mewls from slipping through my lips. He comes on my stomach and, moments later, his body softens and collapses into me. I fall back on the bed, the vibrator still in me and buzzing. I ride the sensation of the orgasm as it rises and falls in waves through my entire body. Tony leans over and licks my nipple before pulling it into his mouth and circling it with his tongue. This last bit of sensation is too much and when he sucks harder, I'm thrown into another orgasm that is just as long as the last one. I grab the back of his head, holding him there until I come back down.

"My God, that was amazing." I seriously haven't orgasmed like that by myself or with anyone else in a very long time.

After I remove the vibrator and wipe it off, Tony reaches over and pulls me to his side, his lips softly trailing over the back of my left shoulder. "I've been dying to do this for ages now," he whispers against my skin, before pulling me even closer.

It's so good to lean against his chest like this, spent and exhausted from touching ourselves. I did not expect for things to go like this when he got back, but I can't say I didn't think about him often while holding that vibrator while he was gone.

I pull the comforter over us and exhale a long breath. This is too comfortable, too real. Both what I hoped for and what I was afraid of. Every time we get closer to each other, I feel more and more for Tony. Which is perfect if we're trying to slow-burn our way into a lasting relationship. Not so perfect though, if all I'm doing is setting myself up for heartbreak.

Maybe I would have been better off ending this the second I opened the manila envelope containing the identity of the person I'd been matched with.

Even that would have been too late. We have to work as a couple for a year. The last thing I want is to be the reason he doesn't get into OCS. Especially now that I've seen more sides of him. Tony might clown around, but he's got a good heart. He's a good man. A caring, decent one. As an officer, he would make the navy proud. I won't be the one who costs him that chance.

Even at the expense of my own heart. Even if it means putting my own dreams on hold. The bed shifts beneath me, and Tony curls around my back, spooning me from behind. His strong arm wraps around my chest, and his chin rests on my head. "This okay? I want to sleep with you in my arms."

"It's perfect." The warmth from his body, from his words, seeps into me, winding its way to my heart. I melt against him as hope kindles at the way he's holding me like I'm something precious. Maybe the years of living through *Mami*'s failed relationships has made me too pessimistic. After all, tonight was a whole new level of intimacy and sensuality. I'm guessing that's true for Tony too. Maybe he started out with his own reasons for only wanting to remain together for the year, but that doesn't mean he can't have a change of heart.

We work well together. And physically, we fit together perfectly. I love being around him, having his strong male presence in my home, *our home*, feeling his touch, and yes, hearing his stupid jokes and his loud laugh. It's obvious that he enjoys having me around too.

This marriage might just stand a chance, after all.

CHAPTER NINETEEN

Tony

HOLY SHIT. THAT was amazing. I've never seen a woman use a vibrator on herself, outside of porn, of course. And the way she teased me, only allowing me to watch, made me rock hard. In retrospect, I'm kicking myself for being insecure and wasting all that time. Precious days where we could have been having sex like that. What difference does it make if I'm less experienced when I have a sensual goddess like Inara to show me the light? I never would have guessed in a million years that having a woman take full-on control could be so damn hot. Well, not any woman. Inara. My wife. Having her take the lead and tell me what makes her hot, and hearing her ask me to stroke myself, was the kind of experience I'll be thinking about way too often while I shower. Hell, my dick is already getting hard again.

I pull the covers up and over my waist as I recall how her mouth twists and brows furrow when she orgasms. The bathroom door clicks open, and a moment later Inara walks into the room. She climbs into bed and as she gets under the covers, I pull her in close to me once again, so close in fact that the heat of her body radiates against mine. She settles against my chest as I cover us both with the comforter.

"You sure you okay with me sleeping here?" While I absolutely would sleep on the floor of her bedroom or the couch for as long as she wanted, a part of me is asking just for her to tell me again that she wants me here, in bed, with her.

Inara laughs. "We touched ourselves in front of each other, so yes, I think we're okay to share a bed."

"Just checking." I kiss the top of her forehead.

Inara's fingers toy with the hair on my arm for a few moments, then stills. She makes a little noise in her throat. "So, there's something I wanted to ask you." Her voice is soft, almost shy. Very atypical for my brazen wife.

"Ask me anything," I say, charmed by this rarely seen side of her. At this precise moment, I don't think there's much in this world I'd deny her.

"When you were talking to your dad before you left, I heard you mention something."

I try not to groan. Except that. I really, really don't want to talk about my dad. But I did just tell her to ask me anything. "What's that?"

"Something about a fundraiser?" Inara's voice is soft. Hesitant. I get the sense that while she doesn't want to push me, it would mean a lot if I open up.

"It's something my dad dreamed up." I force myself to continue. "He wants to put together a fundraiser and he's actually thinking of doing it here." This seems like as good a point as any to start.

"That sounds nice. I'd love to get a chance to meet him. But what kind of fundraiser is it?" She angles her head closer to me.

"It's actually, uh"—I chuckle, slightly embarrassed—"a Zumba event to raise money for cancer awareness and research. He wants to donate it all in my mom's name."

She leans over and props herself up on her elbow. "Your dad does Zumba? That's awesome. And to do something in your mother's name is really special. Don't you think?"

She's wants more from me. No, strike that. She deserves more. I hadn't been planning on telling her much about my family, because, well, what was the point? Especially when I was sleeping on the couch. But it isn't right to keep her totally in the dark. I have to tell her about my mom, about my relationship with my family, all of it. But the visions I had of us connecting on a new level is harder than I expected. I look down at her hand rubbing my arm. And when my gaze returns to hers, I'm met with patience, and it's enough for me to move forward. "What I haven't shared with you . . . is something I don't talk about . . . because I don't even like thinking about it. But when I was in high school, my mom got cancer. It hit her hard and quick too."

Inara sucks in a quiet breath. "I'm so sorry, Tony."

I avoid her gaze so I can keep going. "We watched her fall apart, and it was one of the hardest times in my life."

The hand rubbing my arm slides to my fingers and laces

with mine. The connection gives me the resolve to continue. "During her illness, while she was still moving around okay, my youngest sister suggested we all do Zumba together to keep her moving, to do something fun and non-cancer related, and to get her out of the house." I stop and shake my head, smiling to myself at the memory. "She didn't want to at first. She thought it was a ridiculous idea. But then we all signed up. And we all took turns going to classes with her. Zumba was one of the few things that made her really smile and laugh, near the end."

"That must have been really hard for you, but what a great thing you did for her." Inara places her other hand on my chest and rubs it back and forth.

Now that I've started, the words flow more easily. "After my mom died, my dad kept going to Zumba. It was the only thing that helped him move through the grief. And he got so into it he decided to become an instructor. Now, he's apparently like one of the greatest instructors in the state, and people travel far to take classes with him."

"That's actually amazing. I mean not just finding a way to heal but turning it into a career." She smiles softly at me. "And you're going to do this fundraiser?"

I squirm. "Haven't decided yet. Thing is, when my mom died, my dad was kind of out of commission. He couldn't help it, but we needed him and he wasn't there for us. Now whenever I'm around him, all I think about is that and all I see is my family with a giant *Mamá*-shaped hole."

Her dark eyes are full of sympathy. "That's understandable. Of course it would hurt to be around them. But he's your dad, and maybe now is a good time to try to heal that."

"No." I don't like my tone, but I look her in the eyes and there's no irritation there.

She smiles. "I know it's something you really need to think about and decide for yourself. I support you either way. Thanks for telling me." She squeezes me tighter and gives me a soft kiss along my jawline.

"Thank you for saying that you'll support me either way."

"Yeah, I got this supportive-wife shit down. You taking notes?"

"Whatever." I pull her to my side and she leans into me. I've never had anyone to really talk to about this. The guys know my past, but nothing more than the basics. Telling Inara was a whole lot better than I expected.

I look down at her lying on me after really, truly, talking, and everything just feels so good. This year is going to break me in a whole new way. Has Inara thought about us beyond the year? I shake my head. That wasn't part of the deal. If anything, maybe we can stay close friends after the annulment.

I kiss the top of her head and breathe in the scent of her shampoo. "Now what about you? Is there anything you want to tell me that you haven't?"

She's making circles on my stomach with her finger. "I guess . . ."

"Whatever you want to tell me is good."

"Well, part of why I signed up for the program was because of how I grew up, like with all my stepdads. When I was younger, my mom went through a lot of relationships. She would meet someone, they'd be in love, and then a wedding would happen so fast. And then months later, the falling apart would start. My mom's never really been an open book. So I think, once she started feeling unhappy, she just shut down. She didn't talk, didn't try to fix things. She just broke it off."

All this must be part of why my wife's so willing to work hard at our marriage, even if it is only a year. She doesn't want to be the cause of us failing. The thought twists something in my chest. "That must have been rough. I'm sorry you went through that, Inara."

Her breathing quickens and her voice quivers. "It was. I mean, don't get me wrong, I love my mom. But she messed up a lot."

I move my hand to stroke her hair and wait for her to keep talking.

She starts again after taking a deep breath. "A lot of those relationships probably could have worked. Like, I think, one for sure could have. But she wasn't willing to try. She didn't open up. She didn't talk to them. She just let it fall apart. She's a failure at relationships, Tony."

Inara sits up suddenly and looks at me. Her eyes are wet with the possibility of tears. "I'm so worried I'll be like her. I'm so worried I'll be a failure at love. And I think that's a big reason why I applied to the program. If I haven't been able to figure out my own love life by now, then maybe someone else can match me up better than I can. I don't want to be like her." She reaches up to brush away a tear that has made its way down her soft cheek.

"Hey, hey, I'm sorry if I pushed you to talk about stuff you didn't want to talk about." I sit up, pull her into me close, and hold her as she trembles.

"No, I wanted you to know, I wanted to tell you all of this." She wipes her face and rolls her eyes at herself. "Sorry I'm so emotional."

"I'm glad you told me. And don't apologize, you're fine." I push a stray curl behind her ear. "And I don't think you will fail at love. Look at how much work you've put into us!" I motion to the blankets around us and to the room. "You mentioned your mom never communicated, never tried, but from the moment I met you, you've been pretty open and direct with me. Even now, you didn't have to tell me all of this, but you did."

"I guess you're right. It's just hard knowing none of my relationships have worked so far." Her mouth twists and she squeezes her eyes shut. "God, like that last guy. That was so awful."

"You mean, the married pendejo? From Jim and Taya's wedding?"

She shudders and wraps her arms around herself. "I can still hear that woman screaming they were married and how he'd lied. I couldn't move, couldn't breathe. I swear, it was like having an out-of-body experience. Thank God you were there to drag me away. I still feel guilty. I should have known, somehow. We barely dated, but he always had to meet me out somewhere, was always checking his phone."

I shake my head and cup her cheek. "Hey, don't do that. This is on him. He's the one who lied—to both of you."

For the sake of my career, I hope I never lay eyes on that guy again because I don't think there's enough willpower in the world to keep me from beating his ass. I don't want Inara blaming herself for anything. Not for what that pendejo did, and not for her mom's broken marriages either. If we don't stay together, will she think of herself as a failure like her mom? My heart twists as bile creeps up the back of my throat. I'm unsure how to soothe her, so I pull her in close and hug her. "You're with me now. I got you."

She giggles. "Well, now that I've orgasmed and cried, guess we should go to sleep." Inara turns toward me and lifts her hand to my face, pulling me in and planting a soft kiss on my lips. "Tony, I'm really happy you told me about your mom."

"Me too."

"Goodnight, Tony." She shifts positions and scoots back against me and fuck me if it isn't the best feeling in the world. One I can't imagine losing.

"Goodnight, Inara."

CHAPTER TWENTY

Inara

I WAKE UP pressed into Tony. God, it feels good and right. He's still asleep, so I lift his arm from me slowly then carefully get out of the bed trying to make as little noise as possible. After grabbing a sundress from the closet, I glance over my shoulder at Tony and smirk. The man can actually follow my lead pretty well.

Hell, practice makes perfect.

My heart sinks and a lump forms in my throat. Practice for what? For one final great bang at the end of this year?

Squeezing my eyes shut, I recall how much he opened up to me. And how I broke down in tears in front of him. I pull a sundress over my head then rub my palm against the center of my chest to chase away the ache forming. I hadn't meant to tell him so much, but everything just flowed out naturally. I showed him a part of me, the part of me I keep hidden, and he didn't judge.

I tiptoe out of the bedroom, careful not to wake Tony, and head into the kitchen to burn off some of that energy by making breakfast. After rummaging around in the refrigerator, I pull out onions, garlic, eggs, *chorizo*, jalapeños, and some sharp cheddar. I grab a pan from the cabinet, place it on the stove, add some oil, and wait for it to heat up. When enough time has passed, I slide the onions, garlic, and jalapeños into the hot oil and smile when they start sizzling but not crackling. The perfect temperature. My precise timing gives me a little twinge of pride. I slide the *chorizo* into the pan and start breaking it up with my spoon.

When the fragrant aroma of sausage and garlic fills the air, my husband stumbles in, rubbing his eyes.

"You're up," I say.

A wide smile spreads across my face as he makes his way over to me and pulls me into him. After pressing a quick kiss to my forehead, he pours himself a cup of coffee. "Need a refill?"

I shake my head. "I'm good, still got half a cup."

He fills his own mug, takes out the half-and-half from the fridge, and adds some before sitting at the table. There's an easiness between us now that wasn't there before he left. I smile. Look at us, the picture of domestication. I turn back to the pan and stir the contents. When he mentioned his family last night, I wanted to learn more about them. "So, you said sisters last night. How many do you have?"

He blows on his coffee. "Four. Nessa, who does moto-cross. Danni and Julianna run the family contracting business. And finally, Alexandra, who is a firefighter."

The *chorizo* is almost done so I take out the eggs and crack them into a bowl. I whip them with a fork and add a tiny bit of cream to making them smoother. Once the yolks and whites are all blended, I pour it into the pan and wait for the underneath to cook before I start breaking them up too much. Most people mix them right away, but waiting a little will allow the eggs to get fluffier.

He smiles. "You cook, you do search and rescue, and you're the damned sexiest woman I've ever known. Are you hiding anything embarrassing or are you just a superhero in disguise?"

I chuckle. I never thought of myself as a superhero, but I am definitely a catch. "In high school I was in choir. It was one of the few things that kept me sane in an all-girls Catholic school. Now I mostly belt it out at karaoke nights. Like the one night we went."

I pull out another pan to start heating tortillas and set the flame to low, so they don't burn. Tony grabs some plates, piles condiments, napkins, and utensils, and brings them over to the table before sitting back down. "Well, we can always go singing again. You were very good at it. And thank you for making breakfast. I love *chorizo* and *huevos*."

The corners of my mouth turn up into a wide smile as I shovel the eggs, tortillas, and *chorizo* onto serving plates and bring them to the table. I actually had a lot of fun seducing my husband that night and would gladly do it again.

Tony takes a quick bite before sipping at his coffee. A soft sigh escapes his lips when he returns the mug to the table and eats another bite. "Amazing."

I shrug, way more pleased than I should be. The next

couple of minutes we spend eating in companionable silence. When Tony finishes, he shakes his head. "Inara, that was so freaking good."

I push back my plate, my stomach full and satisfied. "Thanks, I'm glad you liked it. I like cooking for you."

"And I like when you cook for me. And when I cook for you. I especially like when we cook together."

Across the table, our eyes meet. The room grows warmer. I'm pretty sure neither of us is thinking about cooking anymore. At least, not the kind you do on a stove.

I'm seconds away from jumping up and dragging him to the bedroom so I can have my way with him when he beats me to the punch. He bounds from his chair, pulls me to my feet, and leads me through the back of the house to the sliding door. The next thing I know, he's turned me around so my back is pressed up against the glass. He doesn't say a word. He just starts sliding the strap of my sundress down. He kisses along the curve of my breast and suddenly yanks the top part down. A deep moan escapes me that probably carries across to all the nearby yards. I look around. Yeah, my yard is surrounded by a fence, but if any neighbors are watering their plants or hanging out on their balconies, they can see us, clear as day. The idea we could be caught is thrilling.

Tony drops down on his knees in front of me and slides his hands up my long legs until he gets to my panties. He hooks his fingers into each side and slips them down with ease. I lift my legs one at a time so he can take them completely off. As I go to put my left leg back down, he places his big, rough hand on my thigh and pushes it open and up.

"I'm going to need you wide open for this."

He starts trailing his tongue across my thigh, and my heart races. My breath speeds up. God, I'm so wet thinking about what we're doing, what he's about to do to me.

Before I know it, his mouth is against my pussy, and his tongue slips out to flick my clit. I let out another moan and push my hips into his face. He moves his hands to grab my ass and I keep grinding farther into him. As he moves his tongue, his nose brushes along my clit and the soft sensation causes an electrical storm within me, a bolt of sensation shooting up my spine as the hairs on my arms stand on end. He starts to hum softly while he tongues me and it's as if his face is a gentle vibrator.

"Tony. Oh my God." I reach down and place my hand on his smooth head and guide his rhythm. He starts to slow down, tracing circles around my clit, and the motion makes me shake. I'm so close to coming, but I don't want it to end yet.

His left hand moves from my ass and slides back down to my thigh. His tongue digs deeper into me, and I push into his face, moaning and whispering his name. I move my hand from his head to my nipple and twist and pinch it, making myself hotter. His left hand moves again and, before I can prepare myself, he pushes one finger into my pussy and I almost collapse onto his face.

"Oh my God!" My voice echoes through the room. I

can't believe he's going down on me in the middle of the day against the patio door. He slides in a second finger and I whimper in pleasure.

"That's it," he says against me and starts working both fingers in and out of me as he sucks my clit.

I keep grinding into him, mewling and gasping for air as I slide down the other dress strap. I lift my other breast from my bra and pinch both nipples at once. Tony continues alternating between sucking my clit and circling it. He pushes his fingers in and out of me, and I'm grateful for how big his hands are and how long his fingers are.

"Oh, God, Tony, yes, yes, yes!" I push into him and Tony sucks my clit quickly and pumps his fingers in and out as I ride his face into a sublime orgasm.

When I start to come back, my body slumping as it relaxes, Tony sets my leg down and stands, while keeping a hand on my hip to support my weight. He helps me pull my bra back up and lift my straps. I close my eyes as I lean my head back against the cool glass in ecstasy.

He leans in and kisses me, and I love that I can taste myself on his lips. "Hope this time I was able to satisfy my wife."

CHAPTER TWENTY-ONE

Tony

A COOL BREEZE rustles in, smelling of sand, salt, and the hint of seaweed. The sun is high in the sky and burns down into my skin. The heat courses through my body. I lift the beer bottle to my lips. The bubbles pour out into my mouth and fizzle. Nothing like an ice-cold one on a sunny day while we watch the waves roll in, a buzz moving through my body. I haven't had an afternoon off like this in a while to just hang out with the guys. Craiger and Bear sit next to me on the beach while Jim and Graves are in the water surfing. I can't stop chuckling every time Jim looks over at Graves and pushing ahead of him as they paddle toward a set of waves. Each time our newest teammate slips ahead, Jim rushes forward in competition. Those two have been getting along better, but it's clear Jim hasn't fully accepted the guy. After Lux's death, it's only natural to fight against his childhood friend's replacement, as it's a constant reminder Lux is gone.

I lift my beer can to my mouth again and look around. In front of us is a family. The toddler runs forward, stumbling on the sand. Her mother lifts her back up before making sure she's all right. I try to imagine myself being here with my own little family. A trio of tiny little kids running around, maybe eating *paletas* as the waves tumble and foam. Would it be Inara next to me, racing after the little ones to check if they're okay with each fall? We haven't even talked about having children, but it's only her face in the mirage in front of me. My mouth spreads into a grin and I purse my lips to try to hide it from Bear and Craiger. The daydream is getting to me and I don't want them to see the crushing giddy fool I'm becoming.

I go still a moment later. Hold up. Since when did the thought of having kids not prompt me to break out in psychological hives? Yeah, I might not have children of my own, but I'd already raised plenty in the form of my siblings and the idea of inflicting the kind of pain I'd experienced when *Mamá* died is still horrifying. Has a few months of being with Inara changed my outlook that much already? I gaze at the horizon, unsure what to make of this new daydream. Having fleeting thoughts of a family when I'm deployed and worried no one will be around to miss me is one thing. Actively thinking about the possibility of kids with Inara is in a whole different ballpark.

For the life of me, I can't tell if I should be happy or terrified.

My head tilts up and my gaze focuses on Craiger and Bear, who are both transfixed with the phones resting in their hands. I don't know that I'm ready to share with them how I really feel about Inara. They would probably be supportive, but I'm not ready to acknowledge I want this to become more. I don't even know if Inara and I are on the same page. Frankly, the idea that we aren't is scary. Way more terrifying than facing down an enemy in a country looking to kill us all.

Bear points his chin in the direction of the cooler that I have my elbow resting on. "Toss me another one."

I open the lid and the coolness that escapes coats my face. I reach in, my hand swimming in ice water, and pull out another beer. I throw it at Bear and he catches it with one hand.

"You too?" I ask, meeting eyes with Craiger. He nods and lifts his gaze from his phone in his hand. I throw one his way and he barely catches it.

Craiger unzips the tiny pocket in the front of his backpack and slides his phone into it. "Was talking to Lisa about scheduling a parent-teacher conference. It's impossible to get our schedules to line up."

"Can't believe Mason is finally in first grade. He's getting so big." Bear cracks open his beer and a noticeable *tsk* escapes the can just before he brings it to his lips to catch the overflow.

"And his school's getting pretty serious. He has homework. It's crazy," Craiger says.

I glance back over toward the water where the sun reflects off the breaking waves. Jim and Graves are walking slowly back in from surfing. When they make it over to us, they set their boards down on the sand next to the cooler before both reach in and pull out a beer.

"How was the water?" I ask.

Graves responds first. "Waves are coming in steady. Good day to be surfing."

Jim nods in agreement before taking a swig of his beer. I take my phone from my pocket and open up the web browser. The picture of the ring on the screen looks beautiful. I hope Inara will like it.

Of course, while I'm lost in thought, Jim pops his head over my shoulder and whistles. "Wow, I didn't know you'd gotten into sparkly jewelry. What's next, you gonna pierce your ears?"

"Very funny, smart-ass. It's not for me." The stupidity of my comment sinks in as there's no way in hell Jim thought I was looking at the ring for myself. Nosy bastard.

He peers at the image again, a white-gold band with a halo of tiny diamonds. It's a simple design, but the diamonds are all high quality. Jim lifts an eyebrow and takes a chug from his beer, a smile peeking out from around the can. "That's quite a wedding band."

The knowing tone of his voice makes blood rush to my face. I hit the button to turn my screen off. "Part of a deal from when I first moved in. She wanted to call it quits, so I agreed to get her a better ring." Jim doesn't need to know that she hadn't brought the ring up again since that first time. If he did, there'd be no end to the needling he'd give me.

I shove my phone back in my pocket.

A strong breeze comes and knocks a bit of sand into my face, which points out that even the universe doesn't believe the bullshit coming out of my mouth right now. Hell, my stomach does flips when I think of her and my hands tremble at the idea of touching her body. She makes me feel young again, like I'm in high school.

I'll be the first to admit it's scary as hell.

I take a few gulps from my beer and wait for the subject to pass, but the guys are all smiling at one another.

"Just need this to work for a year so that Redding doesn't fuck me over and ruin my chances at getting into OCS." I shake my head. I can't believe I put my career on the line. Not that it's turned out so bad. But if Redding even gets a hint that something is amiss, I might as well kiss my aspirations goodbye. Not to mention I'm ready to move on to the next stage. I am ready for more responsibility. I want to show everyone I'm capable of guiding others and being someone they can follow.

Bear rubs his beard while Jim sits up straighter. "Redding gave me shit too. Doesn't want to look bad. His ass is on the line just as much as yours."

Craiger looks at me. "Does Inara know about the threat?"

I nod and take a swig of my beer. "It's why she agreed not to run to the committee the first day I moved in."

I should be thanking my wife for putting up with my ass. From the beginning she's worked harder than me. She's done everything she could do to make sure it looks like we're both really trying.

Jim stands and picks up his surfboard. "Gonna try to catch a few more waves before I get too hungry."

"Yeah, I'm going to do the same." Graves grabs his board and runs after Jim, who grunts a bit too loud before he picks up his pace.

My stomach rumbles, so I dig in my backpack for some tortilla chips and a container of fish ceviche my mother-in-law made. There's nothing like eating fresh fish on the beach. The lime brings out the meatiness of the sole. She added huge chunks of avocado, which I love. I start dipping chips in and I don't offer any to the other guys because it's just too damn good. I get little bites of fresh garlic and red onion in each chip. There's so much flavor in this ceviche my mouth can't handle it.

As I'm shoveling chip after chip into my mouth, my gaze falls to a group of women walking with surfboards. Bear puts his hand over his eyes to block the light and glances over in the same direction before looking over at the food in my hand and his lips part just barely.

"Don't think about asking. This is mine. I'm sure Marge made something for you."

Bear snarls and starts digging around in his bag. He whips out a PB&J sandwich from its stained the plastic bag. I pick up another chip and bite into it slowly, adding a moan for good measure.

Craiger laughs, then turns his attention back to the

group of women. While I'm admiring the surfers' skills as they ride the waves, I spot Bear's big hand reach over out of the corner of my eye. Before I can react he grabs a chunk of fish and tosses it into his mouth. Once he swallows he smiles wide. "You were right. Totally delicious."

I grunt and move away from him so he doesn't have another chance to steal any more. He scowls at his pathetic mashed sandwich while I eat like a king. Yes, in that moment, with a ring looming on my phone and a lunch made especially for me, I feel like a fucking king. Like anything's possible.

CHAPTER TWENTY-TWO

Inara

MY TORTOISE TRUDGES along on the hardwood floor and makes his way over to his bowl by the dining room table, where I've just placed a bunch of chopped lettuce and shredded carrots. My cheeks lift as my mouth spreads into a grin. Simon is so adorable when tries to hurry over to his food. I scooch closer to him and give his shell a pat while he eats. My own stomach rumbles, so I get up and head over to the kitchen. I open the pantry and move around some boxes of snacks until I find the old pickle jar I keep pistachio nuts in. I love buying bulk when I can. On all the shelves are rows and rows of old pickle jars and mayo jars I have used for storing rice, beans, tea, and other things.

Tony's in the shower and I'm crunching away on pistachios when a loud ringing shocks me. I jump and almost drop the jar of pistachios. Tony and I have had many arguments about how loud his ringtone is. I rush over to the living room to silence the evil jingle that's threatening to live in my brain for the next three days when my gaze lands on the bright light of the screen. A picture of Tony and a man that looks like an older version of my husband illuminates. The caller ID displays *Apá*. My heart jumps and I hold the phone closer to my face. If his dad is calling, it could be an emergency, so I quickly answer the call. "Hello?"

"Hello." The man on the other end sounds about the same way that I do. "This is Tony's dad. Who's this?"

"Hi, this is Inara." I search my brain for more to say, but if he's calling, I should probably just listen to him.

"Hi, I'm Felix." His voice rises in pitch and I sigh, releasing the tension in my shoulders.

"Hi, Felix." My voice squeaks and I start pacing around the living room, regretting taking this call. I don't know how much he knows about Tony and my marriage, and also, I sound like a total dork. I pull a piece of hair from behind my ear and twist it around my finger. "Tony's in the shower right now. He was dirty from helping me and my stepdad build houses. I was worried something was wrong, so I answered his phone." I must be nervous because I'm blurting out more information than needed.

"Good. Put that man to work. He's got the construction degree, so he might as well be useful while he's there." He laughs and the sound echoes. It's the same kind of belly-deep laugh that Tony has, and I smile widely.

His laugh causes me to chuckle as well. "Oh yes, I am definitely putting him to good use." In more ways than one. Not that I plan on sharing that info with his dad. "Did you need me to tell him something?"

There's a silence on the other end of the phone. Then he

sighs. "No, no message. I was just hoping to reach him. I haven't talked to him in a while and there are some things I would like to discuss with him."

I move back and forth in the living room. The sound of his voice causes my heart to sink. He doesn't sound as cheery as he did a minute ago. "Oh, okay, well I will definitely tell him you called." I don't know what else to say. My chest aches hearing the man sound so upset and knowing he and Tony haven't been close. I turn toward the bookshelf in the living room and start rearranging some of the books. I have so many nature guides for the local area that I've been meaning to organize. My body relaxes as I move them around, now that I've found something to keep my hands occupied while we speak. "He's said some really nice things about you. How dedicated you are to Zumba."

"Did he say that, really?" His voice sounds almost musical, soothing and almost familiar. "He's a good man. So, I take it you and my son are dating?"

A book slips from my hand and thuds to the floor. "Uh, dating?"

I give a fake little laugh while I turn to glare daggers in the direction of my bathroom. What the hell? Tony hasn't told his family he got married? Sure, my mom found out by accident, but that was a day after we'd officially gotten married. Not months. What am I supposed to say now? One thing's for sure. I'm not going to lie. "What exactly has Tony told you about me?"

This time Felix is the one who hesitates. "Oh, well . . ."

He clears his throat. "You know . . . we don't talk much. Hardly ever."

So, nothing. Tony and I have been married all this time, and yet until this moment, his dad didn't even know I existed. My lips press together into a tight line as my nostrils flare. And while I try hard to contain the frustration boiling in me, it's too late. "I'm Tony's wife."

Silence greets me from the other end of the line.

"Hello? You still there?" I slap my palm to my forehead. Not the best tone to use to have blurted out my husband's relationship status. And I wouldn't blame the poor man for hanging up either.

"I'm sorry. Yes, I'm here. Just, wow. Tony married, how about that? Congratulations to you both. I'm very happy for you." Despite the shock he'd just received, his voice is warm and welcoming.

"Thank you, and sorry. I shouldn't have yelled the information at you and probably should've let Tony fill you in." I pick up the book and place it back on the shelf.

"No, no, I'm glad you told me. Like I said, Tony and I aren't as close as we used to be. It's been a while since we've had a nice long talk."

"Tony can get pretty busy with his job and, well, our marriage, it all happened so fast." If my husband didn't tell his father he got married, sure enough Tony didn't fill the man in on the program either. Not to mention, *Mami* doesn't know all the details either so it wouldn't be fair for me to spill all the beans.

"Ah, love at first sight, eh? I know how that is."

I suppress a slightly hysterical giggle when I think back to the hospital, where Tony tried to pick both me and the nurse up with the same terrible line. More like irritation at first sight. We'd come a long way since then. Or at least, I thought we had.

"I'm glad Tony finally found someone to settle down with. I just wish he would have been comfortable enough to tell me. My only son got married. You know, it's not something that happens every day. I would have liked to have been there."

I move over to the couch and sink into it. My stomach knots at the thought of our parents being robbed of a wedding day. For our parents not to be there must have really hurt them. I lean back into the couch and stare at the ceiling. Balancing the phone between my ear and shoulder, I reach back and bunch up my hair into a bun. "I know it's no consolation, but no one knew ahead of time. Not even my mother."

"Things happen, no need to be sorry. And just between you and me, I think he still hasn't dealt with his mother's death and I'm too much of a reminder. He's told me many times how it pains him to talk to me, to us." Tony's dad pauses before continuing. "I tried to get him to help me with a fundraiser I have planned, but he isn't giving me a clear answer."

I think about our night in bed when Tony told me all about the fundraiser. It could be a great way for him to reconnect with his family. "Tony mentioned the fundraiser, the Zumba one, right?"

"Yes, that one. I'd like to do it in your area so I can ensure Tony will be there, but I don't have a place yet." His voice has a hint of hope, but it also sounds like he's building to something. Like he's looking for help.

I push back my hesitation and take a chance for the sake of Tony and his dad. "I work at a place called Shaken & Stirred. Our restaurant is great at hosting all kinds of events. Our kitchen can accommodate most sizes and they make great party foods."

"That sounds perfect. I hate to be a bother, but could you give me contact info? Maybe the name of someone who will help me set it up?" The crinkle of shuffling paper comes through the phone as if he's looking for a piece to take some notes down.

"Please let me help. Give me the date and some details and I'll book it for you. It's a wonderful thing you are doing in honor of your wife. She'd be very proud." A warmth blossoms in my chest and spreads through my body. If only I could share a love like that one day. Find a man whose love for me never wavers, even after I leave this earth.

Tony's dad relays some necessary details and, as I take them down, I don't know if I'm more excited or nervous about stepping in. I just hope that my assisting doesn't cause me to lose any ground I've gained in my relationship with Tony. "I'll have my manager call you to firm up all the details."

"Thank you, Inara." He pauses for a moment, then continues. "And if I could just ask one more thing?"

"What is it?"

"Could you please tell Tony what we talked about? I think he will take it better coming from you."

I'm not sure I totally agree, but there's no turning back now. I just have to find the perfect time to broach the subject. "I'll take care of it. It sounds like a great event, and I'm sure Tony will come around and be supportive."

"I really appreciate that. And of course, I can't wait to meet my new daughter-in-law."

The corners of my mouth lift into a stupid grin at the term *daughter-in-law*. There's something about belonging to another family that makes me giddy. A part of being married I hadn't thought of. Come to think of it, I have four new sisters I haven't met. "Well, I can't wait to meet you and the rest of the family."

"I will let you get back to your day now. It has been very nice talking to you. I hope to meet you soon." Every word is clear with a hint of sweetness behind it. Then the line disconnects.

But now that the room is quiet once again, my stomach drops as if I'm on the largest rollercoaster ride. What have I done? I swallow hard and hope Tony will forgive me and that he comes to understand I was just trying to help, even if it stings a little at first.

My potential freak-out turns to sadness. I can't fully understand what it's like losing a parent because of death, but from what I've gathered, I don't think my husband has had closure on the subject, which means he's still suffering and will continue to do so until he takes that step. If he doesn't learn to process it and work through the loss, that cloud will haunt him for a long time.

I check in on Simon and then settle back on the couch. Tomorrow is Little Creek's annual barbecue and is my first time going. With everyone there, Tony will be in a great mood, and probably more receptive to me filling him in on the fundraiser. I catch my gaze in the mirror by the front door and try to convince myself it's not a move right out of *I Love Lucy*, and that I haven't overstepped. I mean his dad was going to have the fundraiser here anyway, so I was only being polite by helping him out. Still, I did agree to help convince my husband to go. I just believe that if he doesn't, he'll regret he missed out on an important family event. There are some moments you can never get back, like not having our parents witnessing us getting married.

I stand and head to the kitchen, picturing myself telling Tony tomorrow. But my mind can't seem to conjure him up with a smile, dammit. If he gets mad, then I'll put on my big-girl panties and deal with it.

I open the fridge and my cheeks inflate. *That's it.* Tony mentioned in passing once how much he loved his mother's empanadas. How he used to make them but stopped a long time ago. He told me that before he opened up about how his mom died, which leads me to believe that he stopped making them after she passed away. If I could convince him to make them again, wouldn't that be a step toward healing?

I lean down and check all the drawers before moving on to the freezer. I grab my phone and start a list. I'm going to convince Tony to do an empanada cook-off. I'll make some, he'll make some. We'll share them with everyone at the barbecue. I know mine are supreme, but I can hold back and even tell everyone to vote for his. I'll need to pull this together fast and get Tony on board. I bet my mom will even chime in at dinner. She loves that he cooks.

I've got a shopping trip to make between now and the barbecue, but at least my mind is at ease. Between good times with his friends and a little ego stroke for his cooking, Tony will be primed for me, and I have the best chance to pull this off.

CHAPTER TWENTY-THREE

Tony

I HAVEN'T COOKED an empanada in years, but when Inara suggested making them, a warmth spread over me. And when she said we should turn it into a competition, a fire lit in me and I became excited. Especially if it means I'll show my wife once and for all who the kick-ass cook is in this relationship. Plus, I can cook my mom's recipe in my sleep, even if I have been out of practice.

Inara pops her head into the kitchen like a spy as I grab a fistful of garlic. My hand pauses above the bowl and my eyes narrow. "Hey, ya cheater, what do you want?"

The guilty smile on her face is so sexy I'm almost tempted to throw her down on the table, right here on top of all these ingredients. She flicks her hand casually in the air. "Just seeing how you're doing. I can give you a hand if you need it."

I'd been asleep when she cooked her batch. She'd agreed to be the one to get up early and use the kitchen first since this whole thing was her idea. I glance down at my crotch, my hands out to the side, one holding garlic, the other still sticky from onion. "Actually, I could use your hand right about now. You look hot in that sundress." I have yet to recover from the last time she wore a sundress, a fantasy fodder for years to come.

"I don't think so. I don't need any excuses from you when I win." She waves and heads down the hall to change clothes.

"Keep dreaming, wifey!" With a smile on my face, I continue working. As nervous as I am about making empanadas again, this is nice. Maybe next time, Inara and I can make them together. When we're in the kitchen together, we move around in a way that's exciting. Every soft touch is a turn-on. Every snarky comment is like foreplay. We make a great team, and more than that, I just have fun with her. That, combined with the fact that sex together is explosive, makes me incredibly lucky to have been matched with her.

I glance over at my phone to check the time. My brows pinch together when I think about the ring order saved in the browser history. Inara hasn't mentioned anything about the piece of jewelry since the first time she made the request. Has she forgotten about it?

Shaking my head to clear out the distractions, I finish cooking, then clean up. The doorbell rings as I'm wiping down the counter, so I toss the dishtowel aside and head over to send whatever salesman is on our porch on his merry way. But when I open the door, it's not a salesman standing there. Or if it is one, he's definitely decided to dress down. He's a fifty-something guy wearing a pair of faded jeans with holes in the knees and a T-shirt that reads *Nope*.

I fold my arms across my chest and broaden my stance. "Can I help you?"

"Is Inara here?" The man leans over and tries to peer beyond my shoulder into the house.

My hackles rise. I step outside onto the porch and close the door firmly behind me, forcing him to take a step back. "I'm sorry, she can't come to the door. If you leave your name, I can tell her you stopped by."

The guy snorts as he eyes me up and down. "How about you give me your name? You been staying over a lot?"

Now I'm getting pissed. My eyes narrow on his ratlike face while I draw myself up to my full height. "Seeing as how I'm her husband and all, yeah. I've been staying over a lot. So, kindly tell me who the fuck you are and what business it is of yours, or please get off my porch."

He takes another hasty step back while his eyebrows shoot up. "Whoa now. This is just a misunderstanding. I'm Leiland Rivers, Inara's landlord. I was in the neighborhood and thought I'd stop by. After all her arguing and whining, she's been making her increased rent no problem these past few months. Guess now I know why."

Something resembling a growl rumbles up my throat, but I swallow it. This is Inara's landlord and while, granted, he's clearly a giant prick, we still have to deal with him. I tap my chin. "Huh, and here I was under the impression that landlords had to give notice for any visits or inspections, except in cases of emergencies." Then I smile and stick out my hand. "Oh, and excuse my manners. I'm Anthony Martinez, United States Navy. Nice to meet you."

Inara's landlord's Adam's apple bobs in his scrawny throat. He gives me the world's quickest handshake, yanking his hand away like he thinks I might crush it. "Sorry to bother you, hope you have a nice day. Tell Inara to add you to the lease at her earliest convenience. Oh, and congratulations."

I wait on the porch, arms crossed, as he gets into his car. What a gross little man. I hate the idea of Inara having to deal with him. But at least the guy had the sense not to cause an issue today. Most landlords don't cause problems where service members are concerned, grateful both Oceana and Little Creek bring them tenants. And now that Inara's landlord knows who she's married to, hopefully he will back off.

When his taillights disappear, I step inside and close the door, making sure to lock it behind me, then return to cleaning the kitchen. I don't bother mentioning his visit to my wife when I go to take a shower and change because nothing is going to ruin today.

Two hours later, we pull into Little Creek, skirt the edge of Lake Bradford, and park at the edge of SEAL Park. All the familiar faces are here. Jim's leaning on a tree near the water, talking to Craiger. Marge and Taya have commandeered one of the picnic tables under the wooden pavilion and are snacking on some chips. This is my family.

Inara and I each grab our pans and head toward the table

where Bear has joined Taya and Marge. The sweet and spicy aroma of beef wafts over from one of the park's nearby grills, making my stomach growl. We set our food on the warmers Marge had agreed to bring—mine on one table and Inara's on the other—and then head back to the car for more stuff.

Once we're done unloading, Taya comes over and starts undoing the foil covers. "Everyone is starving. I wouldn't let them eat, so hurry your asses up."

Inara smacks her friend's hand away. "Don't worry. *I* will satisfy everyone's hunger soon."

My brow cocks in her direction. "Think again. I'm the one who's going to kill it."

Inara holds a hand up at me. "Don't get too cocky. I made a mean chicken empanada."

Behind her a soft *ooohhh* comes from Taya, and I can't help but laugh. This is going to be a lot of fun. When my wife is finished setting up, she turns to face me. "Should we make it a blind taste test?"

Taya snorts. "With this opinionated crowd? Not necessary. Besides, you're more likely to win if people know whose is whose. Tony's annoyed more than his fair share of folks."

I pretend to sputter. "Hey, now. I heard that."

Taya winks at me before addressing the crowd. She stands between Inara and me as she talks to everyone around us. "Okay, so the rules are simple. We get to chow down and then we vote for a winner. The person with the most votes wins. Am I clear?"

"Perfectly clear," Inara responds.

"One hundred percent," I say.

"Then let's eat!" Taya shouts.

As everyone starts grabbing empanadas and piling other food on their plates, I stand off to the side and study peoples' reactions as they take their first bites. No one balks, but I can't really decipher who is enjoying which batch more. Of course, Bear is standing with a plate full of food, but he's still talking, so I head off toward him. Of course, he's droning on about Leslie's costume plans for Halloween and what they'll be dressing up as, and all I want to do is pick up and empanada and shove it into that big hole he calls a mouth.

The smell of perfectly seasoned meat combined with soft fresh corn dough is enough to distract me, so I grab a plate and start piling on food, starting with my own empanadas because I need the taste of home right now. The first bite is simply delicious, and pride fills my chest. Another one and I'm hit with a flood of memories and emotions, equal parts wonderful and heartbreaking. I remember laughter at the dinner table. My sisters giggling and sneaking bites of empanadas before they're ready. *Mamá* shooing them away from the oven with an exasperated grin. My dad coming up behind her and wrapping his arms around her waist.

"Your *mamá* makes the best empanadas in the world, don't you ever forget it," my dad would say every time, like clockwork, and we'd all chime in with our agreement.

What would she think of all this if she were here? No doubt in my mind she'd love Inara. But what about *Apá*? Would my mother be okay with the way I'd cut him out?

The way I've included my teammates on important decisions in my life, yet I hadn't even returned his phone call from earlier today?

Grief and shame mix below the surface for an instant. Then more memories flood my brain, and the remorse turns to resentment. Because after the good times, came the times when my mother grew too weak to make empanadas by herself, so I would assemble them while she directed me from a chair, her bony frame looking frail. Her once-boisterous voice thin and her cheeks pale. Then one day she was no longer there at all. Her vivid, beautiful presence, just gone, leaving the once-warm kitchen cold and empty. And when she disappeared, my dad did too. I didn't lose one parent the day *Mamá* died. I lost two. My dad abandoned us emotionally, right when I needed him most.

The familiar anger is a comfort as it chases away my regret. In this moment, reliving all the trauma of the past, I'm grateful I never committed to my dad's harebrained idea when he first called about the fundraiser. I'm still not ready to deal with his desertion. Not now. Not today. Maybe never. Only time will tell.

I scan the area until my gaze falls on Inara and, the second she turns and smiles at me, something in my chest loosens. I bathe in the relief that washes over me for several long moments before the reality of my actions hits me, causing my lungs to compress again. When did I become so reliant on her? Start looking to her for reassurance? Because getting too comfortable in this relationship is dangerous.

PARIS WYNTERS

Good things never last.

I shake off the unsettling feeling, telling myself I'm making a mountain out of a molehill. Yeah, I felt a boost in my mood when Inara smiled at me, so what? That doesn't mean I'm getting too attached. My wife is hotter than hell, and I'd challenge any red-blooded man to stand in my shoes and not feel the same way. We're talking empanadas here. Not a lifelong commitment. But enough of that. Today, with my friends around me, with my chosen family who have never abandoned me in my time of need, with my wife, I choose to focus on this—my mom would be so damn proud of these empanadas.

I push away the uncomfortable idea she might not be proud of other things and instead focus on a squirrel that scurries down a nearby tree trunk, his nose twitching. Even the wildlife knows these empanadas are something special.

I catch Inara's gaze on me and smile a "thank you" I hope she can read in my expression. Then I wink at her as I lift my plate because it's time for sentiment to be over and ass-kicking to start. "You ready to find out what a real empanada tastes like?"

"You ready to taste defeat?" Inara gestures to her own plate.

Marge and Taya are breaking into my ground-beef ones and I smile as the steam rises when they crack them open, the dough crumbling a tiny bit. Taya closes her eyes as she swallows and practically moans. "These are so good."

Bear just picks up his empanada and shoves the whole

240

thing into his mouth. So much for savoring his food. When I turn to Inara, she grabs one of my empanadas from the tray and bites into it. Her eyes close as she chews slowly, as if she's savoring every last ingredient, and a small sigh escapes her mouth.

Hell fuckin' yeah. I won for sure.

My focus returns to the judges as Marge bites into one of Inara's empanadas, then reaches for her water and takes a big gulp. "This is a bit spicy but also so good."

Jim breaks into a coughing fit, his face turning red as he reaches for his own water. "Fucking Christ, Inara. What the hell did you put in this?"

Inara snorts. "Not my fault you can't handle spicy."

I grab one of her empanadas and bite into it. The chicken is juicy and soft. The salsa is cooked down into a chunky sauce with bites of habanero. The heat is rounded out by the *masa*. I shove the rest into my mouth. "Damn, Inara. This is good."

Everyone continues to pile food into their mouths as they chat among themselves, discussing who to vote for. Some, like Taya and Craiger, are more adventurous and are eating Inara's empanadas, while others like Jim are playing it safe and sticking to mine. Once the votes are tallied, Taya stands. "And the winner is . . . Tony!"

Inara rushes over and gives me a tight squeeze and kisses me on the cheek. "Congrats. They were really good."

Inara and I head up to the designated food table by the grills and grab some ice cream and a bottled water before settling down on an empty bench. She shovels a big spoonful of chocolate into her mouth, leaving a smudge on her upper lip. Just one more reason to keep her. After a moment of fidgeting with her treat, she straightens and turns to me. "I have to talk to you."

"Uh-oh, sounds serious. Did I leave the toilet seat up again?" I'm in such a good mood right now. The sun is shining, and I'm outdoors, eating great food with my best friends. If Inara has a little gripe she needs to get off her chest, now is the perfect time. There's nothing she can say right now that will bring me down.

She avoids my gaze and bites the corner of her lower lip. "Your dad called while you were in the shower the other day and I answered because I thought it might be an emergency. It wasn't, don't worry."

My shoulders tense and I swallow hard. "And?"

"I, uh, kind of let the cat out of the bag. About the two of us being married."

Air rushes from my lungs. "Did you ever stop to think there might be a reason I hadn't told him yet?"

I run my palms down my face trying to process the information. *Apá* is undoubtedly hurt I haven't told him about my wife. And God himself only knows the wrath I will incur from my sisters. I probably should have told my family, but ultimately, that's my choice. My life. Not hers. A big part of the reason I didn't tell them about Inara was because I knew they'd jump on the excuse to ramp up their calls. Or worse, try to enlist Inara to help reconnect the family. Hopefully, my wife would never do something like that behind my back.

An image of Inara laughing in the kitchen surrounded by my dad and sisters fills my head, causing my pulse to sky-rocket as my teeth to grind together. It's maddening the way she's pushed past my boundaries like this.

She wraps her arms around her waist and drops her gaze to the ground. "He caught me off guard."

"I don't talk to him much. Haven't for a long time. But whatever, it's not that big of a deal. I was going to have to tell him sometime. Now, my sisters on the other hand . . . I may just leave you to fend them off yourself." With effort, I reach out and tweak the tip of her nose, attempting to let my frustration go.

She giggles, then turns and places a hand against my chest. "That's not all. He told me you haven't been returning his calls about the fundraiser. I agreed that we'd help him host it here, at Shaken & Stirred."

I stare at her, uncomprehending at first. "I'm sorry, could you repeat that? You did what exactly?"

She sets her ice cream cup aside and moves her hand on my arm. "I agreed to help your dad set up his Zumba fundraiser."

My throat constricts, making it difficult to swallow or breathe. *What would* Mamá *think of you now?* a sneaky little voice in my head asks. *When your new wife, the one you didn't even tell your dad about, talks to your dad more than you do?*

That's just it. I don't want Inara talking to my dad. Not

a little, not at all. She needs to worry about her own family and leave mine alone. The anger that I'd just managed to push away comes roaring back. It's one thing to answer my phone, and another to tell my dad we're married, but what the hell is with this conspiracy crap? "You guys are planning shit behind my back?"

"I was only trying to help. He sounded so excited and proud. He really wants you to be a part of it. And I think it would be good for you, a way to help heal. I'll support you however you need me to."

Her voice is so careful, so sympathetic. Like the way my teachers used to speak to me when I'd act out in class after my mother died. Like she thinks I'm a little kid. What. The. Fuck. I don't need her pity, and I sure as hell don't need her interfering with my family. "Heal? I'm not a patient in a hospital. I don't need to heal. And support, really? That's what you call blindsiding me with this?"

My body goes cold, yet at the same time, a fire burns in my chest. She said heal. HEAL. Like there's something wrong with me. Something broken that needs fixing. Which is bullshit. I don't need to heal. What I need is for her to quit inserting herself into my life, like she's here to stay. Because she's not.

I want to howl. Scream. Instead, I swallow and clench my jaw so tight my molars might crack from the pressure. This is my fault. From the start, I knew better than to put my hopes into a long-term relationship. I grab the water bottle and take a long swig in an effort to keep my anger under control, but it's in vain. "This whole thing was a mistake."

She winces and places a hand on my forearm as I stand up. "I'm so sorry, you're right. I should have talked to you first. Your dad seemed so nice though, and I got caught up in the moment. I made a mistake."

I jerk my arm away from her, hating the feel of her skin on mine right now. "No, not just this time, this whole thing. It was a mistake to ever talk to my dad in the first place. A mistake for you to answer my phone and stick your nose in my personal business, to try to worm your way into my life permanently. A mistake to think this could ever work between us. But the biggest mistake in my life? That was the day I signed up to join this stupid program."

Tears gather in the corners of Inara's eyes. "Tony, please. I know you're upset, but we can work through this. I want to be with you. And not just for a year, but after that as well. I want to grow old with you."

"You only want me because you can't afford your god-damn rent anymore. Which is fine. Hell, it's better than the reasons I signed up for IPP, which by the way was because I had a momentary lapse of sanity when I was lonely and feeling sorry for myself. Not because I lost a card game. And at least be honest about how you're using me—the same way I'm using you to get into OCS."

She rears back as if I'd slapped her. Her face drains of color and her lower lip trembles. Tears streak down her face. Somewhere, beneath the ugly storm of emotions assaulting me, regret twists in my heart. But then she wipes her face quickly and looks at something over my shoulder. Someone clears their throat, and I spin around.

Fuck me.

Of course, Redding just had to show up at that very moment. And next to him is one of the IPP program committee members from my original interview. And just like that, my chances at getting into OCS are shot straight to hell, along with the rest of my career.

Biggest fucking mistake ever.

CHAPTER TWENTY-FOUR

Inara

I REACH INTO my purse and fumble around as I hurry toward the parking lot, trying not to let any more tears fall. Finally, my hand brushes against my phone's protective case and I pull it out to open the Uber app. When Tony had been pulled away by his commanding officer, I jumped up and left. No need to stick around for the sympathetic glances from our friends. Thankfully, there's an Uber driver close by and I track their route, only having to wait two minutes for them to arrive.

The driver isn't one of the more social ones and I'm grateful for the silence. Everything passes by in a blur outside the window, my heart heavy with Tony's admission. Leaning my head back, I close my eyes. I try to force back the tears threatening to fall and inhale the salty breeze rolling in through the open window, forcing myself to swallow past the giant lump in my throat.

The driver arrives at my house and I get out, standing on the sidewalk as if Medusa turned me into a stone statue. How I wish I were like the sun in the sky, hiding behind clouds so no one can see me. Every nerve in my body begins firing off. Normally, anxiety isn't a problem for me, but after seeing Redding's face, after the meeting he demanded Tony attend, I'm not sure what to expect when my *husband* gets home. Even before Redding showed up, the security of my marriage was in jeopardy. So, I do what any person in my circumstances would do . . . walk the handful of blocks to my mother's house.

My sanity has definitely left the building, but I don't know what else to do.

Mami opens the door immediately. "Inara, what's wrong."

"Something bad happened with Tony. Something that might end our marriage." Then I can't say anything else because I'm bawling.

Mami pulls me into her arms and rubs my back as she embraces me. "There, there, *mi hija*. It can't be as bad as all that."

When I calm down a little, she ushers me inside, and into the kitchen. As I sit at the kitchen table, she heads to the stove, turning it on and placing a teakettle on the burner. She hands me a box of Kleenex and I blow my nose. My fingers drum against the plastic tablecloth as she scoops tea leaves into a strainer. God, how did this all go so wrong? And what am I going to do? Tony could lose his chance at Officer Candidate School, all because I stupidly stuck my nose where it didn't belong. And I'd lost my chance at a lasting marriage.

Who am I kidding? Based on what Tony said, we never had a chance to work. No matter what his actions had led me to believe, he'd never had any intentions of taking us seriously. He was only in it for his job.

But where did he get off telling me that I was only in it for the money? That's not why I signed up. I didn't even find out about the increase in rent until after I joined the program. Having someone else to be able to split the rent with me was a last-minute perk. But it's not the reason I want to stay with Tony.

I want to be with him because of the way he cares for others. Because of the way he makes me scream in ecstasy. And because I've fallen in love with him.

I love my husband. I love Tony.

But the revelation doesn't offer comfort. Or joy. I'm not jumping on *Mami*'s couch. Not after what just happened. Instead, my heart only aches more because by overstepping I've not only thrown a lit match on our relationship, but dumped a gallon of gasoline. All unintentionally. *Mami* joins me at the table as the water for tea heats and places her hand on top of mine. "Do you want to talk to me about it?"

"The short version—I interfered with his family and Tony blew up about it in front of his boss."

Mami pats my hand. "I'm sorry, *mi hija*. Marriage is hell sometimes. Why do you think I had to start over so much?"

Great. Not exactly the pep talk I'd been hoping for. Then again, what did I expect? Maybe my mom was right all along. Maybe some people just weren't made for the long haul.

I sigh and place my elbows on the table, resting my face in my palms. More like hiding behind my hands. My body aches and the hollowness in my chest keeps growing. So wild how quickly things can change in a matter of seconds.

The kettle whistles and *Mami* stands, a moment later returning with two cups of tea. The jasmine aroma floats up from the steaming liquid, filling my nose as I wrap my hands around the fine china, enjoying the warmth seeping through the cup.

Mami sits and sips at her tea. When she returns her cup to its small saucer, she meets my gaze. "I think Tony is a great man. But I just don't know if he is the one for you."

My head jerks up, my mouth hanging open. What the hell did she just say? The woman has been looking to marry me off for years and now she's backpedaling. After the shock of her words dissipates, I sit straight and cross my arms. "Care to elaborate?"

She looks down and spins her teacup. But a second later, she glances around the room and waves her hand toward a shelf full of pictures from her numerous weddings. "Then again, what do I know?"

She's been through four marriages. None of them lasted long because she always found some problem. My mother worked full time, made dinner most nights, and took me to all my after-school activities and church. But anytime someone would step in to help—like one of my stepdads— she would always start a fight, needing to prove she could handle everything on her own.

Of course, sometimes the problems were more valid, like with the man she married around the time I was in the fourth grade. She met him at church. He was so devoted to religion and family life, but she wasn't as driven by religion as he was, so she ended up closing herself off. That marriage ended in less than a year.

And then there was Bennett, the longest relationship my mother was in. He was the only one she dated for a good two years before they actually got engaged. They met when I was entering junior high, a rough time for me. Bennett was the perfect father figure, helping me discover ways to express my passions. Like when I lacked self-confidence, he signed us up for a family karate workshop. Anytime I had friend troubles at school, he was willing to listen, even if it was petty drama. Bennett was the only real father I'd had in my life. And for a while, things between him and my mom were great. Until they were over as well.

And now, here I am. Apparently doomed to follow in my mom's footsteps. I'd be seriously depressed right now if I weren't still reeling from the pain of Tony's harsh words at the park.

We stand and I hand her the mug. "Thank you for the tea."

She offers a weak smile as she takes it. "I have faith in you, Inara. You're much stronger than me."

Though I can't agree with her in this moment, I appreciate her words, and just knowing I have my mom behind me gives me a little hope. Even if we disagree on so much, at least I have her in my life. I'm sad for Tony, sad for the burning ash of our relationship, and if I'm being honest, more than a little pissed. How could he let a misunderstanding come between us like that? Wasn't I worth more to him than that? Yes, I messed up, but I apologized and wanted to work it out. Why didn't he care enough to try? I could take all the blame, but one thing I learned over the years with *Mami* is that marriages take two committed partners to work. Me wanting this marriage to work on my own? It's not enough. And that kills me because we have something special.

As I walk the mile back to my house, my throat tightens as questions continue to bombard my brain. Especially because I don't know how to answer any of them. With a huff, I open the door to my place, walk in, and head to the bedroom, where I collapse on the bed. Immediately, the sound of a soft scuffle against the wooden floor fills the space, as Simon's little feet shuffle down the hallway. What an easy life he must have.

I groan and cover my face with a pillow as the ache in my chest ratchets up a notch. I don't know where we stand. Tony claims signing up for the program—and being matched to me—was the biggest mistake he ever made. No matter what, I don't feel the same way. I haven't for a long time now. I can only hope that was just his anger talking.

There's so much good to Tony. He's kind, and he's hilarious and snarky in a way that makes talking to him fun and playful. He's so helpful, supportive, and willing to learn and grow, both in the bedroom and outside of it.

There's also a lot that makes being with him so hard—the exact things that just reared their ugly heads at the park. He's blocked off his family because he is unwilling to work through his pain. And he even shuts me out. But I've fallen hard for him, regardless. Even with all the difficult parts, there's still a list of things we can work through.

But no matter how much I'm willing to try, this relationship could fail, just like all the marriages that failed for my mom. That's why I try to be open, try to communicate. I try to do things that I know will make Tony happy.

I plop my hands on my face while I lie in bed, staring at the ceiling. Truth is, I've been working so hard to avoid becoming my mother that I haven't stopped to think about what I want. I've only focused on the things I don't want. I don't want a failed marriage. I don't want to be closed off. I don't want a husband who is like a roommate. But I've gotten it all backward.

I need to focus on what I do want, on what makes me happy. I have been so fixated on not being broken that I haven't focused on doing what makes me whole. If I spend my life doing things because I'm afraid of failing, then I am not actually living my life at all. I'm just living entirely in fear. And that isn't okay.

Everything that happened today was because I ignored what my husband needed and focused on what I believed he needed. How can we have a real relationship if I keep thinking about what I *should* do dictated by a set of rules that has nothing to do with me and Tony as a couple? We are in this together and have to figure it out together. I can show Tony that I can be the wife he wants and, more importantly, I want to be that person to him. But between how hurt he is and his commanding officer witnessing the blowup, I'm not sure if we'll ever get the chance to make it up to each other.

All I know is that my heart demands I at least try.

CHAPTER TWENTY-FIVE

Tony

I TURN THE steering wheel and guide the car into the long driveway that leads to what is now no longer my home. I shift into park and cut the engine, my chin dipping and my hands reaching to cradle my face. My heart races and my hands start shaking.

The whole day had been building to something great. I really did want a life together. Now there's no way that could ever happen. Not when this stupid program has cost me my dream. I open the driver's-side door and my feet find the asphalt. I walk up to the house without thinking about where I'm going. The keys are still in my hands and I slide them into the front door lock. I can't make myself move any faster. I open the door and walk inside.

Inara greets me right away. "Tony, I'm glad you're home. Look, I just need to say—"

I hold up a hand. "I don't think I can talk about this. It's been a shit day."

"I just want to say that I'm really sorry." She keeps going and it takes everything in me not to just turn around and leave through the door I just walked in from. "I should have waited until we got home to talk about the fundraiser. And though I was only trying to help, I understand I overstepped and caused you pain."

After the meeting with my commanding officer, mentioning the fundraiser is like another defeat slapping me in the face. The empanada-off was such a great experience. I hadn't cooked those since my mom was around. My chest had ached to share the experience with Inara as soon as she'd mentioned it because I thought it would bring us closer, and it did. After winning and sharing our empanadas with everyone, I was so happy.

We were happy. And then Inara had to go and ruin it all.

My legs are heavy, and I have to drag myself down the hallway to the bedroom. Once inside, I bend down and angle my head to see where my duffel bag is beneath the bed. Of course, it's shoved all the way in the back by the wall, and I have to get on my chest and stretch to reach it.

Inara's feet are almost silent as she steps into the room. "Look, I am sorry, Tony. What more do you need?"

After pulling my bag out, I stand and turn toward my wife. Her arms are crossed in front of her. A part of me regrets the pain this is clearly causing her, too, and the pain that is yet to come. But my mouth is dry and I don't even know what to say. Instead, I walk over to the closet and start shoving hangers apart, digging around for the clothes I have to take with me to training.

Inara sits on the bed, just above where my duffel bag is.

Instead of acknowledging her, or speaking, I keep focused on packing. I find one of my boots in the bottom of the closet behind all Inara's bright tennis shoes and high heels. I chuck it over my shoulder toward the bag. I reach for the other one and do the same.

"You're not going to even look at me, Tony?"

"I'm leaving for training."

"So, you're going to leave and not say anything else?"

I grab shirts and throw them into the duffel, not even bothering to fold them, which will cause wrinkles, but at this point I don't care. I move over to the dresser and start pulling out briefs, socks, shorts, while Inara just stares at me, her lips barely parted.

"I don't know what to say." I bend down to add the socks to the bag, then stand up and sigh. I have to tell her about the meeting, but on top of everything else and having to leave, it's like the weight of giant tires stacked up on my back, like any second they will just topple over.

"Look, I'm out of options. Our fake-turned-real relationship is over." Not exactly the truth, but she doesn't need to know they gave the choice to me. Especially since it was a shit choice. I mean, go to counseling and talk about my feelings on the off chance that they'd let me stay in the IPP, while I kiss OCS goodbye? What would be the point? No, better to pack up this charade before anyone gets even more badly hurt.

My heart twists, but I ignore the pain. I bend down and lift the duffel to toss it on the bed next to Inara. The zipper is tiny in my hand and I pull it with as much force as I can without ripping it off. I swing the bag over my shoulder and move toward the living room, my shoes squeaking as I turn out the bedroom door.

Inara follows me and when I get near the couch, darts between me and the door, blocking my path. "Sit down," she says with so much force, my spine automatically stiffens. "Please," she adds in a softer tone. "I want to know what happened."

One glance at her glassy eyes makes me comply. She sits on her knees in front of me and places her hands on my legs, and I can't look anywhere but at her big brown eyes. Will this be the last time I gaze into them?

"So, what does this mean?" Her lips are tight, and the words come out slow.

"My application to Officer Candidate School has been rejected." I barely manage to spit out the words. OCS is what I have wanted for years, the big dream I had for myself. I chose to be a SEAL because that's what seemed right at the time, like something that would pull me out of the pit of depression I'd slipped into. But now I'm ready for more, to be more than just a supporting member of the team. I want to lead and train my fellow SEALS. I've been preparing for OCS for years and it was all taken away from me in one afternoon.

"I'm sorry." Inara rubs my leg with her hand, her lip quivering as she says the words. She didn't want things to go like this today, but there's nothing that can be done now.

Not for OCS, or this sham of a marriage.

I grip her hands and lift them off my legs. Her eyes turn downward, and a single tear falls down her cheek. She pulls her hands into her lap and stands, moving away from me. My legs are tense, and I fight the urge to shake them by standing instead. I throw the duffel bag over my shoulder again and walk to the front door. I turn and face Inara one last time before leaving. I take in a deep breath. "You know, I thought we were good, Inara. I really thought we could work as a couple, keep things light and fun. But you had to keep pushing. Put yourself into parts of my life where I didn't ask you to go."

Her lip trembles again. "I don't even understand what that means, Tony, or why you're acting this way. This is just a misunderstanding. We can work through it." Simon crawls on the floor near her feet, and she bends down to pick him up.

I choke out a harsh laugh. "Work through it? My entire career just went down the drain, the career that was the only thing making me stick to this marriage in the first place. What is there to work through?"

As I talk, the helpless flood of anger resurfaces, pulsing up through my body and out my mouth. "Look, I tried, Inara. I really did. But you didn't respect my choices. If I'd wanted you to meet my dad, or make plans with him, or have you anywhere near that part of my life, I would have told you. You have no idea what it's like to lose a parent, what it does to you. You treated me like a pity case, not a husband—which is exactly why I didn't want to tell you about my past in the first place."

"That's not true!" Her voice wobbles, but she lifts her chin.

"It is true. You said so yourself, you want to help heal me. And your landlord let me know that you were in it for the rent." That isn't fair, but I'm beyond caring. I'm drained. I just want this torment to end. "I should have known better than to let you get close. It hurts too much when people let you down. I'm sorry, but I can't do this anymore."

Inara's dark eyes flash dangerously and her nostrils flare. "That's bullshit, and you know it! Do I seem like the kind of person who'd get married just to be able to afford the rent? No, don't answer that," she says, holding up a hand. "I can't be held responsible for the state of your balls if you do."

No problem there. I'm too stunned by the vehemence of her sudden outburst to utter a single word as she launches into a full-blown rant. "And I didn't sign up for this program because I wanted to heal anyone, you jackass. I signed up because I wanted a life partner. Someone I could raise kids and grow old with. You want to know exactly why I signed up? Because I didn't trust my taste in men after all my mom's failures, so I figured I'd be better off letting an impartial algorithm pick." She pauses to blow a curl out of her face and laughs, but it's a caricature of her usual laugh. A bitter sound that almost makes me flinch. "And yeah, sure, at first, I thought there must have been a massive screwup, matching me to you. But I vowed not to give up, and then I got to know you, the real you, and we had the makings of something real. Something good. Except you're running away. You might be brave when it comes to missions and gunfire, but when it's relationships on the line? You, Anthony Martinez, are a damned coward."

While I'm reeling from that blow, she throws one last punch. "And for the record, I've lost a parent. Multiple, in fact. First my biological dad, then a parade of stepdads over the years. So yeah, I know how much it sucks. But that's not a good enough reason to close yourself off from everyone."

On top of everything else that's happened, losing my mom is about the last thing I want to think about. I can't. I can't do this right now. I'm still so mad. About what my wife did, about my dad, about my career. I need to get the fuck out of here. Every muscle in my body is coiled tight as I walk to the front door and open it. I pause for a second, my hand gripping the doorknob. "I've already filled out the annulment paperwork. All you need to do is sign."

A choked sob escapes Inara's lips, and it's like a surprise kick to my soul. "Don't do this. Talk to me. Don't you think we're worth it?"

I squeeze my eyes shut. For a second, I'm torn. A voice in my head urges me to turn around, gather her in my arms, and tell her hell yes, we're worth it, and that everything is going to be alright.

Except, I can't say those things because it would be a lie. Everything isn't going to be alright. Not when I've already lost my chance at OCS. Not when there's this aching hole burrowing itself into my chest. Caring about someone doesn't protect you from the harsh realities of life. In my experience, the exact opposite is true. Caring for someone makes you even more vulnerable to pain.

My grip on the cold metal doorknob tightens. I'm not a coward, damn her. I'm just being logical. This is all for the best. For me. For Inara. For everyone involved.

I straighten my shoulders, lift my chin and, without a single look back, walk out of the open door and out of Inara's life.

CHAPTER TWENTY-SIX

Inara

I CAN'T BELIEVE he left me. Just like *Mami* did to her husbands. Just like so many stepdads over the years. Tony walked out two weeks ago and I'm barely holding myself together. My mind is no longer my own. My thoughts float by like clouds that drift along in the sky above a beach. I am numb to everything. I held on to a sliver of hope for a short time until the annulment paperwork arrived a few days after he left, reality finally hitting me.

It's a Wednesday afternoon. I've only been at work for three hours, and already I've been here way too long. I am supposed to be focusing on the new menu we are implementing at Shaken & Stirred, but every time I sit down to study it, my brain fogs up. I even tried to go back to kickboxing. It helped for the one hour I was there, but then as soon as I left. I was back to wandering around aimlessly.

Taya walks up to me and puts her arm around me. She whips her phone out of her pocket and shows me the new paint job she's added to her motorcycle. She talks quick and her smile is wide. Her eyes light up. I can't bring myself to be excited for her even though I know she wants me to be. Taya pulls me in closer. "Hey, you doing okay?"

"I don't really know how I'm doing right now. I'm just so out of it." I look down at my hostess stand and I start wiping down the same menus I cleaned an hour ago.

"I know it's been a rough couple of weeks for you. Why don't we go out tonight? You and I are off at the same time, and I know how much you love Karaoke Wednesday. What do you say?" Taya's eyebrows are raised and her eyes look hopeful.

I want to say *No thanks, I'd rather be at home.* But she is my best friend and is only trying to help. Every time we work the same shift since Tony left, she is up here at the hostess stand as much as possible. She brings me little snacks to make sure I'm eating, and she shows me videos of motor-cycle riders and cute Comic-Con outfits. She is doing everything she can to distract me, and I've been a terrible friend by being barely responsive.

"I'm not up to it . . ." I start to say.

Her face droops and her smile fades. "That's okay, I get it—"

"But I'll put on my big-girl panties and do it. Because we haven't had a duet in too long, and we could use a girls' night." I snort at the idea of us standing up on stage singing and dancing, enjoying the night without any guy drama.

Taya starts jumping up and down while she claps her hands together. "Yes! I am so looking forward to it."

We are interrupted by a couple who come in and need to

be seated. I take them to a table in the back with an ocean view, then spend the rest of my shift rolling utensils in linens and wiping the same menus over and over again between seating guests. There haven't been too many to distract me and I find myself, for once, wishing it was a Saturday night so it would be busy. At least then my mind would be distracted. By the time Taya and I are ready to clock out, I start regretting agreeing to karaoke. Singing is the one thing that brings me joy and peace, but my heart isn't in it.

"Ready?" Taya asks, her grin so wide all her teeth are showing.

I can't bear to let her down. Not to mention, she's probably lonely with Jim gone too. I owe it to her to go out. And focusing on her might help bring me out of my own head. "Let's go, *chica*."

We walk out the restaurant door and I fumble in my bag, looking for my favorite plum lipstick because, whenever I wear it, I feel like I'm glowing. Once I'm in the car, I slide the lipstick over my lips and double-check how I look in the mirror. My eyes look swollen from days of tears and lack of sleep. I pat them with my finger and try to bring myself back to the moment. My hands clench the steering wheel and it's as if my body wants to pull me back home, so I move one step at a time. Put the car in drive. Steer my way to the bar. Get out of the car. Walk inside. Soon enough I can go back to the depths of my despair.

The bar is packed for a Wednesday night since it's one of the best karaoke nights around. I haven't gone to this place in a while. The neon lights shine on my body like a welcome home. Marge already saved a bar table for us all. She holds up a glass of red wine as if it's an offering to convince me to walk all the way over there.

"Thank you, I'd love some red right now." I take a sip and let the full-bodied oak flavor overwhelm my tongue. Red wine has always made me feel seductive.

"No problem." She leans over to give me a side hug, which I return. Marge's hugs are warm and soft and everything a mom's hug should be. "It's good to see you, Inara."

"It's good to see you too. How is Leslie doing?"

Marge shakes her phone back and forth at me in response. "She was giving the babysitter a bit of a heart attack by hiding under the bathroom sink. But it's resolved. She knows all the good hiding spots now."

Taya and I laugh. Leslie is a handful, such a smart and sweet girl.

"But we're not here to talk about the hiding habits of my baby. How are you doing? How's everything been, you know, since the picnic?" Marge always gets right to the point and I'm sure my emotions are plainly written on my face.

"Things are rough. I'm guessing you heard Tony's application to OCS was rejected and he's out of the IPP program? And if that wasn't enough, he made it pretty clear where he stood on the whole marriage thing." I lift my wineglass and take a small sip. Taya reaches over and rubs my back. I want to hold my emotions in, but they just spill out. "He just said, 'gotta go to training' and left." I look down at my own hands and play with the chipping polish on my pinky nail.

"Well," Taya begins, "I know he's hurting, too, but that was a dick move."

"Yeah, but he was devastated about OCS, and I did hurt him. I'm to blame too."

"You really care about him," Taya says. "I mean, it's written all over your face, not just now, but every time you talk about him."

"Yeah, honey, even I gotta say it. You have a bad case for Tony. And I can't deny it, you two were, or are, a good match. Truly." Marge reaches over and puts her hand on mine. "We all mess up in any relationship, it's a given. It's how we make amends that determines the outcome."

"Well, even if I did love Tony, it's clear he doesn't love me back the same way. And now that we are out of the program, there's nothing keeping us together." I grab the cocktail menu on the table and browse the appetizers to take my mind off this fact. *I do love Tony.* And right now, he wants nothing to do with me.

Marge pushes down the menu I'm attempting to hide behind. "It doesn't seem like he *doesn't* love you. And the matching program doesn't matter anymore. This is about you and Tony. These things take time, you know?"

"Yeah, I mean, look at what Jim and I went through." Taya shoves a breadstick in her mouth and rolls her eyes.

Part of the reason I signed up for the Issued Partner Program to begin with was because of those two. After the fiasco at their wedding, I'd pretty much given up on dating. Then one day while I was at Taya's house, she was video chatting with Jim. At the beginning of the call, his eyes were droopy, and a deep frown marred his face. Then after five minutes of talking to his wife, he became all toothy grin and big dimples. It was adorable. So, I figured maybe science and the committee were the way to go. The proof was in front of me.

But it wasn't always that way for Jim and Taya. There was a lot of heartache there too.

"I know things were rough for you guys to begin with." I raise my voice so she can hear me over the sudden "I Want It That Way" flashback playing over the loudspeakers, with a tipsy woman on stage, swaying and belting out the song.

Taya picks up another breadstick and starts breaking it into pieces. "Things were seriously rough. There were so many nights we wouldn't talk, even as we lived under the same roof. The first months were hard, and for a minute, I thought it was over too. We had our own big fights, but then we started clicking. We got each other. Now look at us. It all takes time."

"And look, honey, don't even get me started on all the fights Bear and I have had. The road we traveled to get to the marriage we have now was a bumpy one for sure. You gotta give it some time. And be kind to yourself. This is new. You guys jumped straight in. You might have had an idea what being with a SEAL was like, but it's different once it starts." Marge lifts her glass and doesn't just take a sip of her wine, but a big damn gulp.

Both of them were right. If things were going to get better, it was not going to happen overnight, but at this point, Tony doesn't seem interesting in trying. I twist my glass in circles by the stem. "It's just hard to know we left things how we did."

"Yeah, well, trust me, I'm sure there will be more moments like that. I mean, have you seen them? Aside from Bear"—Taya looks over at Marge—"they're like a bunch of feral dogs. They're easily jumpy and just as feisty." At Taya's comment, all three of us start busting up laughing, and we have to quiet ourselves down because the person now singing "Ironic" from *Jagged Little Pill* seems to think we are laughing at her.

"Thanks, you two. This night is actually making me feel a lot better, like I'm finally out of my head. Hearing someone belt out nineties flashbacks is really refreshing," I say just as someone gets on stage to sing Nickelback.

Taya flings a small piece of breadstick at me. "Good. I'm happy you got out a bit. And when Tony comes back, maybe just try to talk to him. He'll be fresh out of training, and some time away might have given him space to think."

I smirk in response and lift my wineglass to my lips. There's only a small bit left but I swing the glass back and let the red coat my throat. "Well, at this point, by the time he gets home, he's going to have to come looking for me. You know he has not texted, or called, or anything since the moment he walked out that door?"

Marge and Taya look at each other with wide eyes.

I set the glass down on the table a little too hard and

huff. "He's angry and I get it. But he's been gone two weeks. And every day that passes makes the stabbing feeling in my chest worse." I try not to think about how many times I check my phone each hour when I'm home alone. "You know I spent so much time avoiding turning into my mother, but maybe I should have embraced it."

"Don't say that. You and she have very different lives to lead." Marge pats my hand and leans in when she speaks.

"I am tired of relationships. I am done with love." As the words fall out of my mouth, my heart plummets into my stomach. I always thought of myself as someone who knows what she wants in a relationship. But lately I am beginning to have doubts. As much as I care about Tony, how can I be with someone who can so easily leave me and not look back? I have talked about my mother as someone who made all the wrong choices, but at least she avoided all the heartache coursing through me. She did not have to waste time trying to teach a man how to love her the way she wanted to be loved, or how to open up to her.

"I understand, but don't limit your future because you're hurting right now." Taya leans over and gives me a big hug.

Her words ring true. Of course pain is influencing what I say and do. And I'm a bit tired of it. So, I jump off the stool. "Okay, look, I think we have had enough of this absolutely god-awful relationship talking. We came here to sing and I want to sing."

I rush over to where the list is and immediately find a song I want to sing—Marina and the Diamonds' "How to

Be a Heartbreaker." I don't know what things will look like when Tony gets back, but I don't want to keep sitting around waiting for a love who isn't sure if he wants me. Yes, I love Tony, but I deserve better than that. And if he can't see it? Well, then there's truly nothing I can do to salvage our marriage.

CHAPTER TWENTY-SEVEN

Tony

CORONADO, BEING SO close to San Diego, has been amazing. I haven't had *carne asada* fries in so long and they have the best ones. This is one of my first off days, and I'm heading toward my old stomping grounds, but instead of looking forward to some delicious food, my hands are clammy and my heart is racing.

I'd spent most of last night running through my big blowup with Inara for the millionth time. How had I let things get so far off track that I'd panicked and walked away? Had I made the biggest mistake of my life? The angry texts I kept getting from Taya and Marge, saying exactly that, didn't help. So, when my dad texted during an especially dark moment, I caved and told him I was in town. Of course he asked if I'd meet him for a meal, and I agreed.

And just like the time I signed up for the marriage-matching program, when the dust settled, I once again regret my actions. But it's too late. Even I'm not a big enough of an asshole to cancel on my dad this late in the game. Although, Inara might disagree.

I wince. It's unbelievably pathetic, my inability to go more than fifteen minutes without thinking of her. When I spot my dad waiting for me outside his car in the Coronado Visitor Center parking lot, I'm almost happy for the distraction.

He spots me and his eyes shrink to near nothing because of how wide his smile is. I don't contain my grin either, as complicated as it is to see him. A warmth spreads over my chest. He has not changed one bit, except for maybe leaned out from all the Zumba, but his eyes are still his eyes and his smile is still his smile.

"It's been too long." He pulls me in for a hug and I let myself fall into him, or onto him, given how much bigger I am.

"It's good to see you." I give him three strong pats on the back causing short breaths to leave his lungs. I didn't intend for them to be that hard.

He steps back and looks me up and down. "You look different. Good, but different."

"Thank you." My voice sounds so formal and I wish it wouldn't. But I can't shake the nervousness nor the anxiety I have pushed aside for a few years too many.

"Why don't we head over to Roberto's?"

I nod and step around him to get into the car. I haven't had their surf-and-turf burrito in years, but the idea of going there makes me salivate. "Let's go."

We cross the bridge, the city coming into view about forty minutes later, and I can't help but feel nostalgic having my dad drive me somewhere. It's both pleasant and painful, if that's even possible. We drive over to the tiny taco shop with the mosaic-tile tables and gaudy umbrellas. We can only sit outside, but I don't mind, even with the chill in the air. And the noise of the passing traffic drowns out other customers. We order our food and sit and wait for them to call out our names. This is an unrecognized gem in Oceanside, but the food is five-star.

"How long has it been since you've been here?"

I groan. "Too long."

There is a moment of silence between us before *mi apá* clears his throat. "So, I think it's time we talked about the fundraiser."

I recoil, every muscle in my body going rigid. The fundraiser is an extra-loaded subject now, since it's a big part of the reason Inara and I broke up. "Do we have to do this now?"

He takes in a slow, deep breath while momentarily closing his eyes. "Yes, I think we do. Talk to me, *mi hijo*. Just tell me what you're thinking."

Like it's just that easy. Talking, and about this subject.

He glances over at me. "Come on. Give it a try. Good or bad, tell me what you're thinking."

I try one of those breathing things Inara always does. Count my inhales. Count my exhales. To my surprise, the vise gripping my throat loosens up a little and words start to pour out. "I want to help you. I want to be a part of it. But I don't know if I can relive all of that. Talking about *Mamá* is hard enough. Putting on a fundraiser in her honor will bring it all back and make it all so much more . . . unfair." I am staring at my hands to avoid looking my father in the eyes. I feel like a failure somehow, and I hate it.

"I know, and it was unfair, it really was." He exhales after a few seconds and continues. "But I want you to know, as much as I understand, I only push you because I think it will be good for you. Raising money, it has been a highlight for me. And it has helped me connect more with your mother." He taps his chest over where his heart lies.

I have not felt my mother, or her memories, in years. I clear my throat and meet my father's gaze. "But doesn't it hurt to carry that all, every day?"

"Some days more than others, but mostly, it feels healing," he says.

The men at the counter call our names and we stand and walk over to pick up our burritos and chips. We bring them back to the table and start opening the tiny half-ounce containers of salsa.

"It's your decision, son, but one thing I know for sure. You can't avoid the pain that life comes with." He lets the words hang in the air a beat before he spares me from having to respond. "Now, tell me what I really want to know. How is Inara? How are you two?"

Damn. I didn't even think about this. I was so worried about one difficult conversation, I didn't prepare for the other topic that was likely to come up—my fake wife-turned-lover-turned-not-wife.

"Things aren't good, *Apá*. Not at all. I wasn't very honest with you about that relationship." I pour green salsa all over my burrito and take a big bite before I continue. "What exactly did Inara tell you?"

"Not much. Just that you kind of rushed into things," he says. "Like you got married pretty quickly after meeting. From what she said, I've been imagining love at first sight."

I chew slowly and contemplate how much I want to tell him. As I swallow, then stuff a chip into my mouth to buy more time, I know I am tired of secrets and avoidance. I just want to be honest. "Well, the rushing into things is true enough. But we didn't exactly fall in love spontaneously. We were assigned to each other. The military has a spouse-matching program they created." His eyebrows furrow together at that, but I go on explaining. "Basically, it was like a blind date. We both took personality tests, had numerous interviews with a committee, and were eventually paired up."

His eyes open wider and he takes a bite of his burrito, just like I did to buy time. "Well, then, you two must be a good match."

"I thought we were, but our relationship is over. We got into a fight and I said some harsh things. The program director overheard. He cut me out of the program." I take a few more bites and savor the shrimp and beef combining in my mouth.

"That's rough. And now you're all the way out here."

Part of being away has been good. But the past few days, I find myself wishing I was home, trying to work through this with Inara. Coming to training, even if it's required of me, was running away. My shoulders slump forward and I wince when once again, I relive the words I'd flung at her in the heat of the moment. Things that, even in the midst of my anger and pain, were grossly unfair. "Yeah, it was very sudden. But fight or not, it's part of my life. They also rejected my Officer Candidate School application because of it all. Everything I have worked for, gone."

My dad sets his burrito down and reaches across the table to squeeze my shoulder. "I am so sorry that so much went wrong so fast. What happened, if you don't mind an old man asking? What did you fight about?"

I clear my throat and look down at my plate. "You, actually. The way she talked to you on the phone and helped organize the fundraiser, behind my back."

My dad's eyebrows lift. "Really?"

My neck heats up. I want to escape this terrible conversation, but we're here now, and I'm trying to be honest about my feelings. Might as well see this through. "Yes, really. When she told me about your conversation, I don't know, I just saw red."

My dad takes a sip of water, the knowing quirk of his lips that used to drive me nuts when I was younger setting in as he returns his glass to the table. "And why do you think that is?"

I stifle a groan. "Because I was mad she'd pushed past my boundaries and tried to worm her way into my extended family against my wishes?"

He reaches down to pick up his burrito. "Or maybe you were scared."

I scoff. "Scared? Why would I be scared?"

Apá swallows a bite and pats his mouth with a napkin, before shrugging. "Maybe you're worried to take a chance again? After your *mamá* died. You might have been away from home for some time, but I know you. I know your heart and your eyes." He goes back to his burrito. "What I see in your eyes is love, *mi hijo*. And if you love her, you would want her to be part of your family. Unless you're afraid of something. Like maybe, afraid that she won't always be there."

I stare at my food, tearing bits of tortilla away with my fingers. That's so stupid. He is right about one thing. I have been away for a long time. But he doesn't know me. Not anymore.

And yet, the gaping hole that took up residence in my chest after I moved away from my family has grown a thousand times larger since I left my home with Inara. There's also all the times throughout a given day that I light up when I think of something funny to tell her, only to deflate that we're no longer together. I miss everything about her, so much that it's a physical pain. Her scent. The silky texture of her skin. The husky sound of her voice when she comes undone in my arms.

Guess my dad is right about two things, because I do love Inara. Which means, maybe he's right about the other part too. I bite into my cheek as I recall our fight and how earlier that day, I'd sought her out for reassurance and taken comfort in her smile, only to become uneasy immediately afterward. Was my underlying worry about growing dependent on Inara because I couldn't rely on her to stick around, making me all the more vulnerable to falling apart if she left?

Guess the joke is on me. Turns out, I pulled that switch way too late to save my world from imploding. "You're right, I do love her. And I don't know what to do. I'm thirty-five and this is practically the first real relationship I've been in. Not to mention how right it feels. That's not scary, it's downright terrifying." I take a few gulps of my horchata since I've mangled my tortilla to the point it's beyond repair.

"That is how I felt with your mother too, Tony. An overwhelming sense of rightness, but also fear, because it was new in so many ways. If you love Inara, you need to fight for her, and be honest with her. And whatever you did, you make it right."

"But, *Apá*"—I pause and my heartbeat speeds up—"what if I do all that and then . . . something happens to her? Like what happened to *Mamá*. I don't know if I can go through that again with someone else in my life." I fidget with a chip, breaking it into tiny bits.

All this time I've been afraid of what it would mean to really love someone. I was afraid of giving someone the opportunity to break my heart again by leaving. That's why I got so overprotective on the phone about search and rescue. It brought up the very real possibility that someone I loved could be taken from me again.

"Tony, I know losing your mother so young was difficult for you. You suffered and it changed your entire life. But you cannot live in fear. You cannot make choices with the idea that terrible things can happen at any time." My father leans in and puts his arm on my shoulder again, giving me a tight squeeze. "What I had with your mother, it was the most magical thing I had ever experienced. It was a love that I will cherish for the rest of my days. I do not regret any part of that relationship."

I look into his eyes and ask the one question I need my father to answer wholeheartedly. "What about now, knowing all that you know? Would you do it all over again?"

"Absolutely," he says without a moment's hesitation. "She was a beautiful person, inside and out. And she brought me so much joy, including my five magnificent children. She was a wonderful wife and mother. I don't regret any of it. I would do every single day again, even knowing the hard days were coming."

My eyes start to sting and I'm overcome with a longing to have my mother here. To see her again. And even as my chest aches in this longing, it's the closest I have been to her. And when my gaze connects with *Apá*'s again, all the same emotions are reflecting back at me. How could I have been this selfish for so long? I closed up, turned my back on Inara because of my pain and anger. The same thing he had done to me. So how could I not forgive him if I expect Inara to forgive me? "Thanks, *Apá*, for saying all that. I know it was so hard for you then, and must still be hard for you now."

"Losing her was hard, but the risk was well worth the rewards." He takes a bite from his burrito and turns his head to the side to hide the tear rolling down his cheek. When he recollects himself, he turns to face me again. "Our entire lives are risky. Look at you, here on training. When you signed up for the SEALs, you knew you would live a life of risk. All the time you are gone, both in training and in very real dangerous situations. Yet, Inara still chose to be with you. She knew the risk and she chose it anyway."

Being married to a SEAL brings a level of uncertainty to life every single day. Marge and Taya experience it, but I never stopped to think, or ask, how my job affected Inara. She never had a father or stepfather remain in her life for a long period of time, yet she still chose to try to make things work with me, even with the very real possibility I could return in a pine box. My stomach drops. Yet I did leave her in a different way when I walked out to come to training, cutting her off completely.

Hell, I made her live through my own fears. Because while my dad hadn't walked out physically, he'd checked out emotionally. For so long. And yes, that still hurt, but I understand him a little better now. He'd been dealing with his own demons, and he'd done the best he could. Young Tony hadn't understood that at the time, but adult Tony could.

I toss a chip onto the table. "God, I'm such an asshole. How could I leave Inara without saying anything?"

"We all make mistakes. I have my own regrets, about

how I should have taken better care of my mental health, back after your mom passed, instead of just going through the motions. I blame your marriage problems on myself." My father reaches across the table and grips my hand before I can speak, his eyes blazing with a fierce light. "But now is the time for you to turn that around. Yes, pain is the risk that you accept when you put yourself out there, when you put your trust and heart in someone else. But without that risk, there is no reward. Do you think, in a million years, I would trade all those wonderful days with your mom if I'd known that she would get sick? Would *you*?"

I swallow the knot in my throat and shake my head. No. Never.

He nods. "Then if you love this girl, you will find a way to make it work."

I had forgotten how comforting my dad's advice was, especially when it came to love troubles. My mind wanders to the ring, to the fact that before the picnic, I had already made up my mind about making it work with Inara, but my stupid fucking pride got in the way. That, and my own poor way of dealing with grief. All these years I'd been upset with my dad for the way he'd handled *Mamá*'s loss and, yet, look at me. Here I am, blowing up my life, all because I'd locked away so much of my pain and refused to process it. No, it wasn't Inara's fault that one day the tight lid I kept on my past exploded off, unleashing a decade of pent-up reaction that cost me everything. I need to fix this. If it isn't too late.

After we finish eating and pay the bill, my dad and I

MATCHED

head back out to the parking lot. It's nearing sunset by the time we leave. He drops me off at the ferry for the last trip back to Coronado. He isn't a fan of driving that long-ass bridge, so I appreciate he was there to pick me up. Plus, I like the idea that I'll have the ride back to the island to process everything we spoke about. And I'm grateful he didn't pressure me about the fundraiser, even though he wants me there. He was a huge support to me today, and I have to return the favor.

The sun is on the horizon line by the time we arrive at the drop-off point for the ferry. I am ready to leave the car when my dad stops me. He grips my knee and looks right into my eyes. "Son, I need you to know that I am really sorry I was not there for you when your mother passed. I really am."

"I know, *Apá*. I know it was hard on you."

He nods and his eyes gloss with tears that threaten to slip out. "But it wasn't fair to you and your sisters. I promise you I will be there for you in whatever ways you want me to be there from now on." He pulls me in tight for a hug and even though the gear stick is poking my thigh, I lean into it. I have spent so long feeling like I had to protect others, protect myself, and sitting here with my dad reminds me how much I was afraid of, how much those fears influenced my life. And how much I wanted someone to protect me.

We part ways and I board the ferry, willing myself not to look back. Instead, I focus on the horizon and how the golden rays escaping the line remind me of Inara and her

283

warmth. I close my eyes and let the heat wash over me.

I told Inara that signing up for the program was the biggest mistake of my life, but that isn't true. Not even close. No, the biggest mistake of my life was not bending down on one knee and proposing to the best thing that has ever happened to me.

Now, all I can do is hope that I'm not too late to make things right.

CHAPTER TWENTY-EIGHT

Inara

I'M NOT THRILLED about the fact that I have to come into work on my day off, all because the restaurant booked a last-minute, private party. As I pull into Shaken & Stirred, the parking lot is overwhelmed with cars. Lovely. Another hectic Friday night. I was comfortable at home, relaxing and pretending things were better than they have been, until Taya called and asked me to come in. She made it sound like an emergency, and by the looks of it, it clearly is. Thankfully, I had a nice black-lace cocktail dress, and my jacket had just been dry cleaned. Of course, when I pull into the lot, I have to park all the way in the back because of how packed the place is. After cutting the engine, I smack the steering wheel and just sit in the car for a few minutes, trying to quell the storm of emotions brewing in my chest. After applying some coral lipstick, I click my phone on to check for text messages or missed phone calls, but all I find is my background image—a picture of Tony, with a party hat on, placing a tiny party hat on Simon. Of course, it could be worse. I could have put a background picture of Tony shirtless. Then each time I looked, I would have to be reminded of both the love and dick I lost.

I turn on the radio and am overwhelmed by Amy Winehouse. Her vocals wash over me like a cool mist. As much as I want to pretend that I have been okay, I haven't been. The last couple of weeks have been spent hiding out in my home, watching television, drinking wine, and reading all the romance novels I could get my hands on. I tried to pretend I wasn't as heartbroken about Tony as I really am, but there is no denying it. There is a hole in my heart that only a buff and bald-headed man could fill. Unfortunately, he made it clear that was not at all what he wanted. I love Tony, completely, but he has wounds that run too deep for me to try to heal. And if he doesn't want to make things work, I can't force him.

Granted, maybe I shouldn't have taken liberties by helping to schedule the fundraiser, but shit, any decent person would have done the same. And yeah, I could have waited to tell him until we got home, but it's not my fault he overreacted, and in front of his CO. I hope in time he'll understand that a relationship is going to have ups and downs, but when two people care about each other, they work through that stuff.

Together.

But he won't be figuring out all those problems with me. Some new woman will get that luxury.

My chest constricts and before more negativity consumes me, I turn off the radio, step out of my car, and start the long walk to the restaurant. My low heels click with each step, and I kick every pebble that stands in my way. By the time I make it to the door, my fingers are curled into tight fists, my nails biting into the skin of my palms. I want to back out and head home, but Taya needs me.

As I open the doors, Taya rushes toward me, almost slipping. She grabs my arms with both her hands and shakes me softly. "I'm so glad you are here. The private party is driving me crazy. I need you to head back there and talk to them. They have all of these demands and I don't know how to—"

"Say no more. I will handle them." I lift my chin and shake my hair back over my shoulders. I pull my small jacket down and smooth my dress. I am in no mood to deal with irritating customers, but I know exactly how to keep people in line with a kind, yet no-nonsense voice, and I am not afraid to whip that voice out right now. Hell, I need to whip it out.

I head to the back of the restaurant and am smacked with the balloons, streamers, colorful flowers, and two giant posters of Simon. *Simon? What the hell?* But that isn't the most shocking bit.

As I step farther into the room, a song starts playing, and on a makeshift stage with a small amp next to it, Tony stands in his Navy dress whites. My God, he looks amazing. My head spins, from both the pain and wanting. What kind of fresh hell is this? The soft intro to a song by Foreigner starts playing, and I never, in all my wildest fantasies, imagined this scenario—Tony is singing!

Air rushes from my lungs and I gasp. Then things venture even further into the Twilight Zone. Tony steps off the stage and begins serenading me. By the time he gets to the chorus, I am almost positive I have caught at least a few flies because of how wide open my mouth is hanging.

I'm in a daze when he starts belting out about knowing what love is. His voice cracks and he is entirely off-key. Like "I had no idea he was so bad at singing" off-key. He gets on his knees and grabs my hand. Maybe it's the confusion and shock, and two seconds later I'll be crying, but right now, I start laughing.

Correction, cackling.

He has made me furious and sad and irritable in the span of only a few weeks. But as confused as I am, I love it. I love it because it's a very Tony thing to do. This is not some random encounter. He planned this. Tony did all this because he knows me, he knows what I love, and he wanted to show me that. My heart is racing like a freight train, the emotions overwhelming. I'm scared and hopeful and mad and touched and . . . ugh, I'm about to climb out of my own skin.

The song ends sooner than I'd like it to, and Tony is back on his feet. He pulls me in and presses his lips against mine and, after everything we have been through, all I can think about is how much I have missed him, how much I have craved his lips, and how I pray this is not a dream.

"I know this must be a surprise," he says as he pulls away from me.

I can't do anything but nod in response, especially as I look around and take in all the familiar faces. Holy crap. Taya, Jim, Craiger, Bear, Marge, my mom, and even Bennett. Everyone is here.

"Can we talk outside for a minute?"

I nod again and take his hand as he leads me to the deck out back. When we open the doors, we are met with a view of the waters and a fresh breeze of sea air mixed with jasmine.

"I don't know what to say," I tell him.

"You don't have to say anything, just listen." Tony holds my hands and takes a deep breath. "I met with Redding and told him about my past, my issues with my mother and how she died. Of course, the military was aware she died from cancer, but they had no idea about the rest of it."

I reach out and stroke his arm. "I'm so proud of you. That's a big move to tell them."

He grins and leans on the rail of the deck. "I told him that the day he caught us arguing, it was really my fault. That we were talking about my mother. I told him I never really dealt with her death, and that was a moment where my grief was escaping."

His lips tremble and he looks out to the waters. I can't believe he really opened himself up like that. Especially to his superiors.

I reach down and squeeze his hand.

He turns to face me again and pulls me in closer to him. "I told them that I signed up to meet with a grief counselor too. And I really did make the appointment. Redding was surprisingly very understanding."

"I can't believe you did all of that. I think going to a grief counselor will really help you, and it'll help keep your mother's memories alive. She would be very proud of you." My voice cracks and my eyes start to tear. This whole time I wanted him to be this open, to share these emotions with me and others, and now that he is finally talking about it, I'm overwhelmed.

"The thing is, Inara, I could not have done this without you."

He reaches up to place his hand against my cheek. I put my hand over his and hold it there. I have missed his touch so much.

"While I was at training, I met with my dad."

I suck in a sharp breath. I just can't believe it. That is such a huge step for him.

"We reconnected finally, in person. And it was really good to see him. We talked for a while and patched things up."

I step into his space and wrap my arms around him, gripping him with all my strength. He really does seem happier. Each of these changes is going to be so good for him, and they will really help him heal.

"It was all because of you," he whispers in my ear. "I made that appointment with the counselor because you helped me understand that I needed assistance in processing my grief. And I am also rebuilding the relationship with my dad. I am a better son, and SEAL, because of you. I am a better lover"—he pauses momentarily to waggle his eyebrows at me—"because of you. You have made my life more meaningful and greater in more ways than I can count."

My lips part and I let out the breath I had been holding. I relax into his body as tears stream down my face. "Tony, all I wanted to do was be a good wife and show you how much you deserve love, even if I was a little annoyed to be matched with you at first." I lean away for a second to glare at him. "And I definitely did not let you into my bedroom just because you helped pay the rent."

He ducks his head in shame and then meets my eyes. "I know. That was just a convenient excuse to help convince myself that running was the best plan."

"Just don't let it happen again."

"Deal."

I soften as I search his contrite face. "I am so happy you finally understand how good things can be with your family, with work, within yourself. I love you, Tony."

"I love you too." He reaches into his pocket and takes out a blue velvet box and gets down on one knee. "Will you marry me, Inara? I want you to be my wife not because some program paired us up, but because I cannot imagine my life without you in it."

"Yes! Of course!" I kneel to meet him and plant my coral lips on his, as I press my body into him as much as I possibly can in this position. I want every piece of me to be touching him right now. I am overwhelmed with happiness, like a champagne bottle about to burst. But then he pushes me away gently and I glance at him, confused.

"Wait. I jumped the gun." He pulls us to our feet and then reaches into his pocket and pulls out folded pieces of paper. "Read this."

Biting my lip, I take the papers from his hands, open them up, and start to skim. I get to the end with my heart pounding. Words like *transfer of ownership* and my address and my landlord's name and a startling sum of money. "I don't understand. Is this a deed? To my duplex?"

He reaches into his pocket, withdraws his reading glasses, and wiggles them in front of my face with a grin. "Looks like maybe you need a pair of these too. But yes. Your deed. I bought the building for you. No strings attached. No matter what decision you make about our relationship, the place is yours. I figured that was the least I could do for acting like such a jackass. Plus, even if we don't work out, I don't want you to worry about rent anymore."

My eyes flood with tears. "Tony, you didn't have to—"

He cuts me off by pressing his lips to mine. "I love you so much, Inara. Please let me show it."

My heart is so full, it's in danger of bubbling over. But before I can jump back into his arms, Tony takes my hand and slides the ring onto my finger. It's white gold with a halo of tiny, yet perfect, diamonds. Then he kisses me and, while still holding my hand, leads us back into the restaurant where everyone greets us with confetti and shouts of congratulations. I look around at all my friends, the people I care about. This is more than I could have ever dreamed of.

Guess the Issued Partner Program committee really did know what they were doing.

EPILOGUE

Tony

I'M STANDING INSIDE the public restroom, checking my outfit, checking my moves, and trying not to psych myself out. Who in the hell would have ever thought I would be doing Zumba for a fundraiser? After my visit with my father, I realized that pushing away the painful parts of my life also meant pushing away the memories of my mom. And since my visit, I've begun to reconnect with my family, and it's as if I can hear *Mamá's* laugh again. See her dimples in Vanessa's face when we virtual chat. All the time spent pushing my father away because I didn't want to face losing my mom ended up with me losing him too. I never want things to go back to that.

I make one final adjustment to my attire and exit the restroom.

The Zumba class is a small part of the bigger fundraiser and is being held on a swath of golden sand overlooking the ocean. Luckily, this November day turned out to be pleasantly brisk. The breeze fluttering through the guests' hair holds the promise of winter, and the sand cocooning my bare feet is chilly rather than summer hot. Perfect for not sweating my ass off. *Apá* is waiting for me at the head of the class and he has a microphone in his hand. Speakers are set up on each side of the block of people who are currently half stretching, half mingling.

"Who is ready to shake their boo-tay?" My father cups his ear and leans toward the crowd as they yell back in response.

My cheeks are already heating and sweat lines my brow. I jump up and down, shaking my hands, hoping to chase away the nervous energy. Then the music starts, and I cannot believe he chose "Despacito" as the first song. The nerve of this man. I shake my head and laugh. There's not much I can do at this point but roll with it. We start moving and he guides everyone in with easy-to-do, warm-up moves.

"Okay, everybody, let's go side to side, and side to side," he shouts enthusiastically. There's a whole new side to my dad I'm learning about as he bounces from left to right. His stage presence commands such attention that even I jump alongside him without thinking twice.

I look out into the group and spot Bennett and Inara dancing near each other. Damn, my wife is adorable. Her mother is nearby and, if I'm not mistaken, she's taking a few glances at Bennett as my dad switches to the "around-the-world" movement. Inara does a double take at her mother, then rolls her eyes. I wink at her when she turns to face me.

Inara mirrors the moves, but from the waist down, which is different than most people around her, and I'm already captivated by her swirling. I look away from her, not wanting to get too *distracted* right now in my athletic shorts, and fall back into the crowd.

I am surprised by how many people are here. Jim, Taya, Craiger and Mason, Bear, Marge, Graves, and little Leslie all came out to support me. Even Hayden is in the crowd. She must've flown home from college for the weekend. When I finally opened up to the guys about how difficult things had been after losing my mom, they were more than understanding. And when they found out about the fundraiser, they all immediately signed up.

Mason catches my gaze and starts jumping up and down, waving at me. He's not exactly doing the moves anyway, and his smile is infectious. I wave back and then give him a thumbs-up.

Next, I sidle over to Jim, hoping *Apá* doesn't notice my half-ass participation. Jim is only barely moving, though. Before he can utter a word, I shoot the biggest, toothy grin at him. "Jim, boy, gotta start swirling those hips. Gimme some pelvic action!"

His face turns crimson, and I'm not sure if he's going to hide or kill me, but he's such an easy target, I really can't help myself most days. He picks up his pace and glances at Taya, who is clutching her stomach, unable to control her laughter or maintain her dance moves.

My father really has got this crowd moving. "Now grapevine, everybody. To the left. And to the right." They'll be starving by the time we get back to Shaken & Stirred to join the others who couldn't do Zumba for the main part of the fundraiser.

I look over and Bear seems to be doing some version of terrible line dancing, kicking up sand with his giant feet as he goes. Marge is actually pretty good, and she keeps stopping her husband then moving his hips with her hands. But he just pulls her in for a twirl and a kiss. This isn't exactly the ideal, most true-to-style Zumba class, but it is a fundraiser that everyone wanted to be a part of and, hell, they're having fun.

I move once again and spot Graves in the very back. Damn, he's pretty good too. He should probably be helping lead this class instead of me. And the way Hayden's ogling him isn't lost on me either. At least her father is too busy paying attention to her mother to notice.

I go back to stand next to my father as the songs continue to blend, one into the next, and I'm sweating, despite my plan to keep cool. My father is, too, and unfortunately, he's wearing Spanx-style shorts. Inara has made her way to the front toward us, and she winks at me with each shuffle and merengue march.

Warmth radiates from my chest to my limbs. To think I almost ruined our relationship by not dealing with my baggage because now, I can't imagine any part of my life working without her.

When the class finally ends, my dad gets back on the mic. "Just a reminder, everyone, to head over to Shaken & Stirred for food and festivities. We also have a raffle going on and all proceeds will be donated. You can win a year's worth of Zumba lessons at a local venue, an iPod for all your workout needs, and a gift card to the restaurant."

Everyone cheers and shouts before rushing to grab their things. It's a short distance to the restaurant, so many of the people walk over. *Apá*, Inara, and I head over to our car after we pack up. We step inside and my chest expands, as I'm overwhelmed by how many people are here. I'm not sure how I could ever repay everyone's support or show my appreciation to my wife who helped make it all happen. She even went the extra mile and rented one of those mobile stages, which is parked facing the restaurant, right along the sand.

Taya bounds up onto the stage, grabs a mic, and asks for everyone's attention. "Hey, everyone, you are all basically like family to me, and I could not imagine telling you all any other way. Jim and I are having a baby." She unleashes a spray of confetti from a popper she brought up with her.

Everyone cheers and my wife rushes to the stage and gives her best friend a bear hug, being careful not to squeeze too hard. Jim is so pale, I'm concerned he might pass out. The public announcement for a guy who is overly private leaves him wide-eyed and still. If any of us had done that, there'd be hell to pay and a couple of black eyes. But his wife can get away with just about anything.

I find myself beaming as I head over to my teammate and give him a strong hug and pat on the back. "Congrats, man. You'll make a great father."

He looks around for a moment and doesn't respond as he takes in everyone's excitement. Then he takes in a deep breath. "I think so."

"I know so." We shake hands and I head to the side of the stage and grab a water bottle.

Inara wanders over to me, leans in after wrapping her arms around my waist, and whispers in my ear, "Nice moves, by the way. Maybe you could give me a private lesson later." She bites my earlobe as I chug my water, trying to keep dirty thoughts from entering my mind. But my wife just giggles, then reaches down and takes my hand into hers. "Do you think we should tell them?"

After meeting with the grief counselor and talking with my commanding officer multiple times, my application to Officer Candidate School was finally approved. I was ecstatic when I found out. The only downside to this endeavor is that we will have to move temporarily.

I kiss my wife on the cheek and squeeze her hand, ready to step into a new adventure with her. "We probably should."

Inara trots back up the two steps leading to the makeshift stage and takes the mic from Taya. "One more announcement, please? We are so happy you all could be here for the fundraiser. I know how much this means to Tony's family, and Tony and I also want to thank you for your support. Plus, we also wanted to let you know that Tony has been accepted into Officer Candidate School!"

She shouts the last part and some feedback causes a

screech in the amp. Everyone claps as I make my way to her side. Inara and Taya turn and embrace one another, holding on for a while. They are bound to remain close friends, since the two have been through so much together. We might be moving away for a while, but that will not break the bonds we've formed with these people we call family.

And the move will strengthen the bond between Inara and me. We are in this for the long haul. Together. And nothing will ever come between us again.

THE END

Want more? Check out Taya and Jim's story in *Issued*!

Join Tule Publishing's newsletter for more great reads and weekly deals!

If you enjoyed *Matched,* you'll love the next book in….

THE NAVY SEALS OF LITTLE CREEK SERIES

Book 1: *Issued*

Book 2: *Matched*

Book 3: *Coming soon!*

Available now at your favorite online retailer!

ABOUT THE AUTHOR

Paris Wynters is an adult romance author repped by Tricia Skinner at Fuse Literary. She lives on Long Island (in New York) with her family, which includes two psychotic working dogs. Paris is a graduate of Loyola University Chicago.

Paris and her son are nationally certified Search and Rescue personnel (she is a canine handler). She is a huge supporter of the military/veteran community. When not writing, Paris enjoys playing XBOX (she is a huge HALO fanatic and enjoys FORTNITE), watching hockey (Go Islanders), and trying new things like flying planes and taking trapeze classes.

Thank you for reading

MATCHED

If you enjoyed this book, you can find more from all our great authors at TulePublishing.com, or from your favorite online retailer.

TULE
PUBLISHING

Made in the USA
Coppell, TX
28 January 2023

11876919R00171